S0-ADG-108

JAMES

ALSO BY PERCIVAL EVERETT

Dr. No

The Trees

Telephone

The Book of Training by Colonel Hap Thompson of Roanoke, VA, 1843: Annotated from the Library of John C. Calhoun

So Much Blue

Half an Inch of Water

Percival Everett by Virgil Russell

Assumption

I Am Not Sidney Poitier

The Water Cure

Wounded

American Desert

A History of the African-American People [Proposed] by Strom Thurmond as Told to Percival Everett & James Kincaid

Damned If I Do

Grand Canyon, Inc.

Erasure

Glyph

Frenzy

Watershed

Big Picture

The Body of Martin Aguilera

God's Country

For Her Dark Skin

Zulus

The Weather and Women Treat Me Fair

Cutting Lisa

Walk Me to the Distance

Suder

The One That Got Away

Re:f (gesture)

Abstraktion und Einfühlung

Swimming Swimmers Swimming

Trout's Lie

JAMES

A NOVEL

Percival Everett

DOUBLEDAY NEW YORK

 Published in the United States by Doubleday, a division of Penguin Random House LLC, New York, and distributed in Canada by Penguin Random House Canada Limited, Toronto.

www.doubleday.com

DOUBLEDAY and the portrayal of an anchor with a dolphin are registered trademarks of Penguin Random House LLC.

Book design by Anna B. Knighton
Jacket illustration © Smith Collection / Gado / Getty Images
Jacket design by Emily Mahon

Library of Congress Control Number 2023012817
ISBN: 978-0-385-55036-9 (hardcover)
ISBN: 978-0-385-55037-6 (ebook)
ISBN: 978-0-385-55088-8 (export edition)

MANUFACTURED IN THE UNITED STATES OF AMERICA

7 9 10 8

First Edition

For Danzy

JAMES

THE NOTEBOOK OF DANIEL DECATUR EMMETT

I come to town de udder night,
I hear de noise, den saw de sight,
De watchmen dey be runnin' roun'
Cryin' Ole Dan Tucker come to town.
Git outen de way, Git outen de way,
Git outen de way, Ole Dan Tucker,
You's too late to come yo supper.

Sheep an' hog a walkin' in de pasture,
Sheep says, "Hog can't you go no faster?"
Hush! Hush! Honey de wolf growlin',
Ah, ah, de Lawd, bull dog growlin',
Git outen de way, Git outen de way,
Git outen de way, Ole Dan Tucker,
You's too late to come yo supper.

Here's my razor in good order,
Magnum bonum–jis hab bought 'er,
Sheep shell oats, an' Tucker shell de corn,
I'll shabe ye soon as de water gits warm.
Git outen de way, Git outen de way,

Git outen de way, Ole Dan Tucker,
You's too late to come yo supper.

Jay bird in de martin's nest,
To sabe his soul, he got no rest,
Ole Tucker in de fox's den,
Out come de young ones nine or ten.
Git outen de way, Git outen de way,
Git outen de way, Ole Dan Tucker,
You's too late to come yo supper.

I went to de meetin' de udder day,
To hear Ole Tucker preach and pray;
Dey all got drunk, but me alone,
Make Ole Tucker walk jaw bone.
Git outen de way, Git outen de way,
Git outen de way, Ole Dan Tucker,
You's too late to come yo supper.

Old Zip Coon

I went down to Sandy Hook to-der af-ter noon;
I went down to Sandy Hook to-der af-ter noon;
I went down to Sandy Hook to-der af-ter noon;
And de fust man I met dere was old Zip Koon.
Old Zip Koon is a very larned scholar,
Old Zip Koon is a very larned scholar,
He plays on the Banjo Konney in de hollar.

Did you ever see de wild goose sail upon de ocean;
Did you ever see de wild goose sail upon de ocean;

Did you ever see de wild goose sail upon de ocean;
O de wild goose motion is a very pretty notion,
For when de wild goose winks de beckon to de swallor,
And den de wild goose hollor, google, google, gollor.

If I was president of dese United States;
If I was president of dese United States;
If I was president of dese United States,
I'd suck 'lasses candy and swing open de gates;
And dose I didn't like I'd block 'em off de docket,
And de way I'd block um wou'd be a sin to Crockett.

Turkey in the Straw

As I was goin' down the road,
A tired team an' a heavy load,
I crack'd my whip and the leader sprung
And says day-day to the wagon tongue.

(Chorus)
Turkey in the straw, turkey in the hay;
Dance all nighty and work all day;
Roll 'em up and twist 'em up a-high tuck-a-haw,
And hit 'em up a tune call'd Turkey in de Straw.

Oh I went out to milk and I didn't know how,
I milked a goat instead of a cow,
A monkey sittin' on a pile of straw,
A wink in his eye at his mother-in-law.

(Chorus)
Turkey in de hay, turkey in de straw;
The old gray mare won't gee nor haw;
Roll 'em up and twist 'em up a-high tuck-a-haw,
And hit 'em up a tune call'd Turkey in de Straw.

The Blue-Tail Fly

When I was young I used to wait
On my massa and give him his plate,
And pass de bottle when he got dry,
And brush away the blue-tail fly.

(Chorus)
Jimmie crack corn and I don't care,
Jimmie crack corn and I don't care,
Jimmie crack corn and I don't care,
My massa's gone away.

And when he'd ride in de afternoon,
I'd follow after with a hickory broom,
The pony being rather shy,
When bitten by a blue-tail fly.

(Chorus)

One day he ride around de farm,
De flies so num'rous they did swarm,
One chanc'd to bite him in de thigh,
De devil take de blue-tail fly.

(Chorus)

De pony run, he jump, he pitch,
He threw my massa in de ditch;
He died and de jury wonder'd why,
De verdict was de blue-tail fly.

(Chorus)

Dey lay him under a 'simmon tree;
His epitaph is dere fo to see;
"Beneath this stone I'm forced to lie,
A victim of the blue-tail fly."

PART ONE

CHAPTER 1

THOSE LITTLE BASTARDS were hiding out there in the tall grass. The moon was not quite full, but bright, and it was behind them, so I could see them as plain as day, though it was deep night. Lightning bugs flashed against the black canvas. I waited at Miss Watson's kitchen door, rocked a loose step board with my foot, knew she was going to tell me to fix it tomorrow. I was waiting there for her to give me a pan of corn bread that she had made with my Sadie's recipe. Waiting is a big part of a slave's life, waiting and waiting to wait some more. Waiting for demands. Waiting for food. Waiting for the ends of days. Waiting for the just and deserved Christian reward at the end of it all.

Those white boys, Huck and Tom, watched me. They were always playing some kind of pretending game where I was either a villain or prey, but certainly their toy. They hopped about out there with the chiggers, mosquitoes and other biting bugs, but never made any progress toward me. It always pays to give white folks what they want, so I stepped into the yard and called out into the night,

"Who dat dere in da dark lak dat?"

They rustled clumsily about, giggled. Those boys couldn't sneak up on a blind and deaf man while a band was playing. I would rather have been wasting time counting lightning bugs than bothering with them.

"I guess I jest gwyne set dese old bones down on dis heah porch and watch out for dat noise 'gin. Maybe dere be sum ol' demon or witch out dere. I'm gwyne stay right heah where it be safe." I sat on the top step and leaned back against the post. I was tired, so I closed my eyes.

The boys whispered excitedly to each other, and I could hear them, clear as a church bell.

"Is he 'sleep already?" Huck asked.

"I reckon so. I heard niggers can fall asleep jest like that," Tom said and snapped his fingers.

"Shhhh," Huck said.

"I say we ties him up," Tom said. "Tie him up to dat porch post what he's leaning 'ginst."

"No," said Huck. "What if'n he wakes up and makes a ruckus? Then I gets found out for being outside and not in bed like I'm supposed to be."

"Okay. But you know what? I need me some candles. I'm gonna slip into Miss Watson's kitchen and get me some."

"What if'n you wake Jim?"

"I ain't gonna wake nobody. Thunder can't even wake a sleepin' nigger. Don't you know nuffin? Thunder, nor lightning, nor roarin' lions. I hear tell of one that slept right through an earthquake."

"What you suppose an earthquake feels like?" Huck asked.

"Like when you pa wakes you up in the middle of the night."

The boys sneaked awkwardly, crawled knees over fists, and none too quietly across the complaining boards of the porch and inside through the Dutch door of Miss Watson's kitchen. I heard them in there rifling about, opening cabinet doors and drawers. I kept my eyes closed and ignored a mosquito that landed on my arm.

"Here we go," Tom said. "I gone jest take three."

"You cain't jest take an old lady's candles," Huck said. "That's stealin'. What if'n they blamed Jim for that?"

"Here, I'll leave her this here nickel. That's more'n enough. They won't 'spect no slave. Where a slave gonna git a nickel? Now, let's git outta here befo' she shows up."

The boys stepped out onto the porch. I don't imagine that they were hardly aware of all the noise they made.

"You shoulda left a note, too," Huck said.

"No need for all that," Tom said. "Nickel's plenty." I could feel the boys' eyes turn to me. I remained still.

"What you doin'?" Huck asked.

"I'm gonna play a little joke on ol' Jim."

"You gonna wake him up is what you gonna do."

"Hush up."

Tom stepped behind me and grabbed my hat brim at my ears.

"Tom," Huck complained.

"Shhhh." Tom lifted my hat off my head. "I's jest gonna hang this ol' hat on this ol' nail."

"What's that s'posed to do?" Huck asked.

"When he wakes up he's gonna think a witch done it. I jest wish we could be round to see it."

"Okay, it be on the nail, now let's git," Huck said.

Someone stirred inside the house and the boys took off

running, turned the corner in a full gallop and kicked up dust. I could hear their footfalls fade.

Now someone was in the kitchen, at the door. "Jim?" It was Miss Watson.

"Yessum?"

"Was you 'sleep?"

"No, ma'am. I is a might tired, but I ain't been 'sleep."

"Was you in my kitchen?"

"No, ma'am."

"Was anybody in my kitchen?"

"Not that I seen, ma'am." That was quite actually true, as my eyes had been closed the whole time. "I ain't seen nobody in yo kitchen."

"Well, here's that corn bread. You kin tell Sadie that I like her recipe. I made a couple of changes. You know, to refine it."

"Yessum, I sho tell her."

"You seen Huck about?" she asked.

"I seen him earlier."

"How long ago?"

"A spell," I said.

"Jim, I'm gonna ask you a question now. Have you been in Judge Thatcher's library room?"

"In his what?"

"His library."

"You mean dat room wif all dem books?"

"Yes."

"No, missums. I seen dem books, but I ain't been in da room. Why fo you be askin' me dat?"

"Oh, he found some book off the shelves."

I laughed. "What I gone do wif a book?"

She laughed, too.

THE CORN BREAD was wrapped in a thin towel and I had to keep shifting hands because it was hot. I considered having a taste because I was hungry, but I wanted Sadie and Elizabeth to have the first bites. When I stepped through the door, Lizzie ran to me, sniffing the air like a hound.

"What's that I smell?" she asked.

"I imagine that would be this corn bread," I said. "Miss Watson used your mama's special recipe and it certainly does smell good. She did inform me that she made a couple of alterations."

Sadie came to me and gave me a kiss on the mouth. She stroked my face. She was soft and her lips were soft, but her hands were as rough as mine from work in the fields, though still gentle.

"I'll be sure to take this towel back to her tomorrow. White folks always remember things like that. I swear, I believe they set aside time every day to count towels and spoons and cups and such."

"That's the honest truth. Remember that time I forgot to put that rake back in the shed?"

Sadie had the corn bread on the block—a stump, really—that served as our table. She sliced into it. She handed portions to Lizzie and me. I took a bite and so did Lizzie. We looked at each other.

"But it smells so good," the child said.

Sadie shaved off a sliver and put it in her mouth. "I swear that woman has a talent for not cooking."

"Do I have to eat it?" Lizzie asked.

"No, you don't," Sadie said.

"But what are you going to say when she asks you about it?" I asked.

Lizzie cleared her throat. "Miss Watson, dat sum conebread lak I neva before et."

"Try 'dat be,' " I said. "That would be the correct incorrect grammar."

"Dat be sum of conebread lak neva I et," she said.

"Very good," I said.

Albert appeared at the door of our shack. "James, you coming out?"

"I'll be there directly. Sadie, do you mind?"

"Go on," she said.

I WALKED OUTSIDE and over to the big fire, where the men were sitting. I was greeted and then I sat. We talked some about what happened to a runaway over at another farm. "Yeah, they beat him real good," Doris said. Doris was a man, but that didn't seem to matter to the slavers when they named him.

"All of them are going to hell," Old Luke said.

"What happened to you today?" Doris asked me.

"Nothing."

"Something must have happened," Albert said.

They were waiting for me to tell them a story. I was apparently good at that, telling stories. "Nothing, except I got carried off to New Orleans today. Aside from that, nothing happened."

"You what?" Albert said.

"Yes. You see, I thought I was drifting off into a nice nap about noon and the next thing I knew I was standing on a bustling street with mule-drawn carriages and whatnot all around me."

"You're crazy," someone said.

I caught sight of Albert giving me the warning sign that white folks were close. Then I heard the clumsy action in the bushes and I knew it was those boys.

"Lak I say, I furst found my hat up on a nail. 'I ain't put dat dere,' I say to mysef. 'How dat hat git dere?' And I knew 'twas witches what done it. I ain't seen 'em, but it was dem. And one dem witches, the one what took my hat, she sent me all da way down to N'Orlins. Can you believe dat?" My change in diction alerted the rest to the white boys' presence. So, my performance for the boys became a frame for my story. My story became less of a tale as the real game became the display for the boys.

"You don't says," Doris said. "Dem witches ain't to be messed wif."

"You got dat right," another man said.

We could hear the boys giggling. "So, dere I was in N'Orlins and guess what?" I said. "All of a sudden dis root doctor come up behind me. He say, 'Whatchu doin' in dis here town.' I tells him I ain't got no idea how I git dere. And you know what he say ta me? You know what he say?"

"What he say, Jim?" Albert asked.

"He say I, Jim, be a free man. He say dat ain't nobody gone call me no nigga eber 'gin."

"Lawd, hab mercy," Skinny, the farrier, shouted out.

"Demon say I could buy me what I want up da street. He say I could have me some whisky, if'n I wanted. Whatchu think 'bout that?"

"Whisky is the devil's drink," Doris said.

"Din't matter," I said. "Din't matter a bit. He say I could hab it if'n I wanted it. Anything else, too. Din't matter, though."

"Why was dat?" a man asked.

"Furst, 'cause I was in dat place to whar dat demon sent me. Weren't real, jest a dream. And 'cause I ain't had me no money. It be dat simple. So dat demon snapped his old dirty fingas and sent me home."

"Why fo he do dat?" Albert asked.

"Hell, man, you cain't get in no trouble in N'Orlins lessen you gots some money, dream or no dream," I said.

The men laughed. "Dat sho is what I heared," a man said.

"Wait," I said. "I thinks I hears one dem demons in the bushes right naw. Somebody gives me a torch so I kin set dis brush alight. Witches and demons don't lak no fires burnin' all round 'em. Dey start to melt lak butta on a griddle."

We all laughed as we heard the white boys hightail it out of there.

AFTER STEPPING ON them squeaking boards last night, I knew Miss Watson would have me nailing down those planks and fixing that loose step. I waited till midmorning so I wouldn't wake any white folks. They could sleep like nobody's business and always complained to wake up too early, no matter how late it was.

Huck came out of the house and watched me for a few minutes. He hovered around like he did when something was on his mind.

"Why you ain't out runnin' wif yo friend?" I asked.

"You mean Tom Sawyer?"

"I guessin' dat da one."

"He's probably still sleepin'. He was probably up all night robbin' banks and trains and such."

"He do dat, do he?"

"Claims to. He got some money, so he buys himself books and be readin' all the time 'bout adventures. Sometimes I ain't so sho 'bout him."

"Whatchu mean?"

"Like, he found this cave and we goes into it and have a meeting with some other boys, but we get in there it's like he gotta be the boss."

"Yeah?"

"And all because he been reading them books."

"And dat sorta rub you da wrong way?" I asked.

"Why people say that? 'Rubbing the wrong way'?"

"Well, the way I sees it, Huck, is if'n you rake a fish's back wid a fork head ta tail, ain't gone matter much to him, but if'n you go ta other way . . ."

"I git it."

"It seem sumtimes you jest gotta put up wif your friends. Dey gonna do what dey gonna do."

"Jim, you work the mules and you fix the wagon wheels and now you fixin' this here porch. Who taught you to do all them things?"

I stopped and looked at the hammer in my hand, flipped it. "Dat be a good question, Huck."

"So, who did?"

"Necessity."

"What?"

" 'Cessity," I corrected myself. " 'Cessity is when you gots to do sumptin' or else."

"Or else what?"

"Else'n they takes you to the post and whips ya or they drags ya down to the river and sells ya. Nuffin you gots to worry 'bout."

Huck looked at the sky. He pondered on that a bit. "Sho is pretty when you jest look at the sky with nothin' in it, jest blue. I heard tell there are names for different blues. And reds and the like. I wonder what you call that blue."

" 'Robin's egg,' " I said. "You ever seen a robin's egg?"

"You right, Jim. It is like a robin's egg, 'ceptin' it ain't got the speckles."

I nodded. "Dat be why you gots to look past the speckles."

"Robin's egg," Huck said, again.

We sat there a little longer. "What else be eatin' you?" I asked.

"I think Miss Watson is crazy."

I didn't say anything.

"Always talkin' 'bout Jesus and prayers and such. She got Jesus Christ on the brain. She told me that prayers is to help me act selflessly in the world. What the hell does that mean?"

"Don't be swearin' naw, Huck."

"You sound like her. I don't see no profit in askin' for stuff just so I don't get it and learn a lesson 'bout not gettin' what I asked fer. What kinda sense does that make? Might as well pray to that board there."

I nodded.

"You noddin' that it makes sense or don't make no sense?"

"I'm jest noddin', Huck."

"I'm surrounded by crazy people. You know what Tom Sawyer did?"

"Tells me, Huck."

"He made us take an oath in blood that if'n any of us tells

gang secrets, then we will kill that person's entire family. Don't that sound crazy?"

"How you take a blood oath?" I asked.

"You're supposed to cut yer hand open with a knife and shake with everybody else what done the same thing. You know, so your blood gets all mixed and mashed together. Then you're blood brothers."

I looked at his hands.

"We used spit instead. Tom Sawyer said it would do the same thing and how could we rob a bank wif our hands all cut up. One boy cried and said he was going to tell and Tom Sawyer shut him up wif a nickel."

"Ain't you tellin' me yo secrets right naw?" I asked.

Huck paused. "You're different."

" 'Cause I'm a slave?"

"No, taint that."

"What it is, den?"

"You're my friend, Jim."

"Why, thank ya, Huck."

"You won't tell nobody, will ya?" He stared anxiously at me. "Even if we go out and rob us a bank. You won't tell, right?"

"I kin keep me a secret, Huck. I kin keep yo secret, too."

Miss Watson came to the back screen and hissed, "Ain't you done with that step yet, Jim?"

"Matter fact, I am, Miss Watson," I said.

"It's a miracle with this here boy yakking your ear off. Huckleberry, you get back in this house and make yer bed."

"I'm jest gonna mess it up agin tonight," Huck said. He shoved his hands in his britches and swayed there, like he knew he'd just crossed a line.

"Don't make me come out there," she said.

"See ya later, Jim." Huck ran into the house, running by Miss Watson sideways like he was dodging a swat.

"Jim," Miss Watson said, looking back into the house after Huck.

"Ma'am?"

"I hear tell Huck's pappy is back in town." She stepped past me and looked at the road.

I nodded. "Yessum."

"Keep an eye on Huck," she said.

I didn't know exactly what she was asking me to do. "Yessum." I put the hammer back in the box. "Ma'am, what I s'posed to keep my eye on, zackly?"

"And help him watch out for that Sawyer boy."

"Why fo you tellin' me all dis, missum?"

The old woman looked at me and then out at the road and then up at the sky. "I don't know, Jim."

I studied on Miss Watson's words. That Tom Sawyer wasn't really a danger to Huck, just a kind of little fellow sitting on his shoulder whispering nonsense. But his father being back, that was a different story. That man might have been sober or he might have been drunk, but in either of those conditions he consistently threw beatings onto the poor boy.

CHAPTER 2

THAT EVENING I sat down with Lizzie and six other children in our cabin and gave a language lesson. These were indispensable. Safe movement through the world depended on mastery of language, fluency. The young ones sat on the packed-dirt floor and I was on one of our two homemade stools. The hole in the roof pulled the smoke from the fire that burned in the middle of the shack.

"Papa, why do we have to learn this?"

"White folks expect us to sound a certain way and it can only help if we don't disappoint them," I said. "The only ones who suffer when they are made to feel inferior is us. Perhaps I should say 'when they don't feel superior.' So, let's pause to review some of the basics."

"Don't make eye contact," a boy said.

"Right, Virgil."

"Never speak first," a girl said.

"That's correct, February," I said.

Lizzie looked at the other children and then back to me. "Never address any subject directly when talking to another slave," she said.

"What do we call that?" I asked.

Together they said, "Signifying."

"Excellent." They were happy with themselves, and I let that feeling linger. "Let's try some situational translations. Something extreme first. You're walking down the street and you see that Mrs. Holiday's kitchen is on fire. She's standing in her yard, her back to her house, unaware. How do you tell her?"

"Fire, fire," January said.

"Direct. And that's almost correct," I said.

The youngest of them, lean and tall five-year-old Rachel, said, "Lawdy, missum! Looky dere."

"Perfect," I said. "Why is that correct?"

Lizzie raised her hand. "Because we must let the whites be the ones who name the trouble."

"And why is that?" I asked.

February said, "Because they need to know everything before us. Because they need to name everything."

"Good, good. You all are really sharp today. Okay, let's imagine now that it's a grease fire. She's left bacon unattended on the stove. Mrs. Holiday is about to throw water on it. What do you say? Rachel?"

Rachel paused. "Missums, that water gone make it wurs!"

"Of course, that's true, but what's the problem with that?"

Virgil said, "You're telling her she's doing the wrong thing."

I nodded. "So, what should you say?"

Lizzie looked at the ceiling and spoke while thinking it through. "Would you like for me to get some sand?"

"Correct approach, but you didn't translate it."

She nodded. "Oh, Lawd, missums ma'am, you wan fo me to gets some sand?"

"Good."

" 'Gets some' is hard to say." This from Glory, the oldest child. "The *s*'s."

"That's true," I said. "And it's okay to trip over it. In fact, it's good. You wan fo me to ge-gets s-s-some s-sand, Missum Holiday?"

"What if they don't understand?" Lizzie asked.

"That's okay. Let them work to understand you. Mumble sometimes so they can have the satisfaction of telling you not to mumble. They enjoy the correction and thinking you're stupid. Remember, the more they choose to not want to listen, the more we can say to one another around them."

"Why did God set it up like this?" Rachel asked. "With them as masters and us as slaves?"

"There is no God, child. There's religion but there's no God of theirs. Their religion tells that we will get our reward in the end. However, it apparently doesn't say anything about their punishment. But when we're around them, we believe in God. Oh, Lawdy Lawd, we's be believin'. Religion is just a controlling tool they employ and adhere to when convenient."

"There must be something," Virgil said.

"I'm sorry, Virgil. You might be right. There might be some higher power, children, but it's not their white God. However, the more you talk about God and Jesus and heaven and hell, the better they feel."

The children said together, "And the better they feel, the safer we are."

"February, translate that."

"Da mo' betta dey feels, da mo' safer we be."

"Nice."

HUCK CAUGHT ME as I was hauling sacks of chicken feed from the buckboard to the shed in the back of the Widow Douglas's house. He was studying on something intently and I could tell he wanted to talk.

"What be on yo mind, Huck?"

"Prayers," he said. "Do you pray?"

"Yessir, I prays all the time."

"What do you pray fer?" he asked.

"I prays for all sorta things. I pray once that the lil' girl February would get better when she be sick."

"Did it work?"

"Well, she be better now." I sat on the buckboard and looked at the sky. "I pray fer rain once."

"Did it work that time?"

"It did rain, sho nuff. Not right away, but 'ventually."

"Then how you know God done it?"

"Reckon I don't. But don't God do everything? Who else make it rain?"

Huck picked up a rock, studied it in his hand for a bit, then hurled it at a squirrel high on an elm branch.

"Wanna know what I thinks?"

Huck looked at me.

"I thinks praying is for the people round you what wants you to pray. Pray so Miss Watson and Widow Douglas hears you and ask Jesus for what you knows dey wants. Make yer life a sight easier."

"Maybe."

"Ever' now and den toss in something like a new fishin' pole or like dat so they can scold you."

Huck nodded. "That makes sense. Jim, you believe in God?"

"Why, sho nuff I does. If dere ain't no God, den how we get this here wonderful life? Naw, you run on and play."

I watched as Huck ran on down the street and turned out of sight around the corner in front of Judge Thatcher's big house. Old Luke came up behind me as I was about to hoist the last sack up on my shoulder.

"You startled me," I said.

"Sorry about that." He hopped up and sat his short body on the wagon bed. "What did that little peckerhead want?"

"That boy's all right," I said. "He's just trying to figure things out. Like the rest of us, I guess."

"Have you heard about that McIntosh brother down in St. Louis?"

I shook my head.

"Free man. Light like you. He got himself into a scuffle at the docks and the police came and got him. He asked what they were going to do to him for fighting. One of the police said they were probably going to hang him. The brother believed him. Why wouldn't he? He pulled out his knife and cut them both."

A white man walked up and for some reason studied the horse hitched to the wagon. Luke stopped talking. We tried to not make eye contact with the man. We had been talking, so we had to keep talking.

"Go on," I said to Luke.

"Okee. So, blue gum monkey on up da alley jes lak Lucifer done bit on da broomstick. And dem charlies be down on him like white on rice. I means dey be on 'em lak dem bubbles on soap."

I nodded.

"Hey," the white man shouted.

"Suh?" I said.

"This here horse belong to Miss Watson?"

"Naw, suh. The buckboard be belonging to Miss Watson. Da horse be dat of Wida Douglas."

"You think she wanna sell him?"

"I wouldn't know dat, suh."

"You ask her when you see her," he said.

"Yessuh, I sho will."

The man looked at the horse one more time, spread the animal's lips with his fingers and then walked away.

"What do you suppose a fool like that wants with a horse? He doesn't know anything about horses," Luke said.

"This creature is hundred years old and can barely pull this wagon when it's dry and empty."

"White people love to buy stuff," Luke said.

"So, what happened to McIntosh?" I asked.

"They caught up to him and chained him to an oak tree, piled sticks under him and burned him alive. I heard he screamed for somebody to shoot him. Men yelled they'd shoot the first person who tried to save him from his misery."

I felt sick to my stomach, but it wasn't so different from many stories I'd heard. Still the day felt hotter and I realized how sticky with sweat I was. "A terrible way to die," I said.

"I suppose there's no good way," Luke said.

"I don't know about that."

"What do you mean?" Luke asked.

"I mean, we are going to die. Maybe all ways to die aren't bad. Maybe there's a way to die that will satisfy me."

"You're talking crazy."

I laughed.

Luke shook his head. "That wasn't the worst part. Colored people die every day; you know that. The worst part was that the judge told the grand jury that it was an act of a multitude and so they couldn't recommend any indictments. So, if enough people do it, it's not a crime."

"Good Lord," I said. "Slavery."

"Got that right," Luke said. "If enough of them kill you, they're innocent. Guess what the judge's name was."

I waited.

" 'Lawless.' "

"Do you think we'll ever get to go to someplace like St. Louis or New Orleans?" I asked him.

"When we's gets to heaben," he said and winked.

We started to laugh and then we spotted a white man up the road. There was nothing that irritated white men more than a couple of slaves laughing. I suspected they were afraid we were laughing at them or else they simply hated the idea of us having a good time. Whatever the case, we were slow to hush and so captured his attention. He'd heard us and walked our way.

"What you boys gigglin' like little girls 'bout?" he asked.

I'd seen the man before, but I didn't know him. He tried to strike a pose like a dangerous man. That made me more and less afraid of him.

"We was wonderin' if'n it be true?" Luke said.

"What be true?" the man asked.

"We be's wonderin' if'n dem streets in New Orleans really is made a gol, lak dey say," Luke said and looked at me.

"And if'n it be true dat when it flood, it flood da streets with whisky. I ain't never tasted no whisky, nosuh, but it sho nuff look good." I turned to Luke. "Don't it look good ta you, Luke?"

It was at this point that I imagined, for a second, that he saw we were making fun of him, but he laughed big and said, "It looks good 'cause it is good, boys." He walked away howling.

"He's going to get drunk now, not so much because he can, but because we can't," I said.

Luke chuckled. "So, when we see him staggering around later acting the fool, will that be an example of proleptic irony or dramatic irony?"

"Could be both."

"Now that would be ironic."

CHAPTER 3

THE SPRING SNOW caught everybody by surprise. Miss Watson had me chopping wood all day, so that she could have enough for weeks. But there wasn't much and she wasn't suggesting that I or any other slave might take some home. We collected what we could from the ground and secretly felled some small trees near the quarters. That wood was, of course, green and smoked terribly and was hard to keep going, but it gave some heat. I managed to stash some seasoned logs under Miss Watson's porch. I would return for them in the night. The old slaves April and Cotton needed them. Some folks might have called what I was doing stealing. So would I, and I didn't particularly care. I had worked up a sweat and had my shirt off, even though it was cold.

"That's a lot of wood," Huck said. He startled me. "Did I scare you?" he asked.

"A lil' bit, I s'pose. Where you comin' from?"

"I just sold all my worldly possessions to Judge Thatcher. He give me this here dollar fer all of it."

I whistled. "A whole dollar. I din't know you had so much."

I split some more wood and caught Huck staring at me.

"How you be lakin' school?"

"I reckon you kin say I'm getting used to it."

"I wouldn't mind me sum learnin'." I split a couple more logs.

"You know, you ain't much darker 'n me."

"I be dark nuff."

"How come you're a slave?"

" 'Cause my mama was one."

"What about your pa?" he asked.

"Prolly not. But it don' matter. If'n dey know one o' yo kin colored, den you colored. Don' matter what you looks lak."

"I seen some tracks in the snow," Huck said.

"I s'pect dere be lotta tracks in da snow. Dat be where folks leaves 'em."

"One of them tracks had a cross in the heel."

"Whatchu mean, cross?"

"You know, like Jesus—that kinda cross."

"I wouldn't study on dat too much," I said. I didn't like seeing the boy troubled like that. I knew what he was thinking.

"So, you think it's him, too." He was talking about his father. "You think he's back, too."

"I din't say dat."

"But you thought it. I could tell that you thought it. What does he want, Jim? You know stuff."

I reached into my pocket and pulled out a ball of hair from a mule's tail that I always saved for those white children. "You know what dis here be?" I held it up so that the sunlight caught it.

"What?"

"It be a hairball from da belly of an ox. You know what dat make it?"

The boy shook his head. "Magic," I told him. "Dis here hairball be magic and it can talk ta me."

"What does it say?"

I put the ball up to my ear. "Yeah, I hears it. It be talkin'. It say your pappy gots two angels what folla him round in dis world, one dem black and da other one white. They be telling him different things. One be bad and one be good and da man don' know what one will win out. He don' know what he gwyne to do. Leave or stay. This here ball s'posed to know, but it don't."

"That don't help none."

"Wait, da ball talkin' 'gin."

Huck tried to listen with me.

"Yeah, yeah. It say you gone be awright. You gonna git hurt and den you gonna be awright. Dere be two womens hangin' round you. You gonna marry yersef a poor woman and den a rich 'un. But whateber you does, stay way from da water. That riber be da death of you."

"It say all that?"

I nodded. "It be sleepin' naw."

Miss Watson came to the door. "Huck," she called, "get in here and wash up for supper." She looked at me. "Boy, ain't you done with that wood yet?"

"Be a mess of it, missums."

"Well, stop now 'cause it's too loud. My head hurts."

"Yessum."

LUKE CAUGHT UP to me as I was walking home. "Slow down so an old man can keep up," he said.

We walked quietly for a while. I knew I was being extra quiet, but I couldn't help it. I kicked at a rock.

"What are you fretting over?" Luke asked.

"Nothing," I said.

"Are you worried about the logs you stashed under the porch?"

"You saw those?"

"I did."

"No, I'm not worried about the wood."

"You worried about that boy," Luke said. When I looked at him, he said, "Huck. That boy, Huck."

"Well, he's got a drunkard father that won't leave him alone."

"What's that to you? That's white people's business."

I nodded. "He's still a child."

"Yeah, a free child." He pointed at me. "There is something about that boy. Something about you and him."

"He's got a heap of trouble," I said. "Sad as that may be, I'm still a slave and I can't help him at all."

CHAPTER 4

THE WEATHER REMAINED unseasonably cold and I found myself pilfering wood for not only April and Cotton, but also my family and a couple of others. I was terribly concerned that the wood might be missed, and that fear worked its way into reality one Sunday afternoon. Sadie came to me.

"What's the matter?" I asked.

She peeked out the shack door, looked at the nine-year-old and then at me. "What are you going to do?" she asked.

"What are you talking about?"

"I heard Miss Watson talking to Judge Thatcher."

"Yes?"

Sadie sniffed.

I put my arm around her. "Settle down."

Nothing could have prepared me for what she said next. She said, "Miss Watson told Judge Thatcher that she was going to sell you to a man in New Orleans."

"What's that mean?" Lizzie asked. "Papa, what does that mean?"

I walked to the door and looked out.

"Jim?" Sadie said.

"Papa?"

"Did she say all of us or only me?" I asked.

"Just you, Jim," she cried. "What are we going to do? They're going to split us up and we won't know where you are."

"What?" Lizzie gasped.

"No, they're not," I said. I grabbed a big rag and laid it out.

"What are you doing?" Sadie asked.

I put bread and dried meat on the cloth and folded it up. "They can't sell me if they don't have me."

"You can't run," Sadie said. "You know what they do to runaways."

"I'll hide out. I'll hide out on Jackson Island. They'll think I've run north, but I'll be here. Then I'll figure out something."

"You can't do that. They'll find you for sure. Then they'll treat you like a runaway. They might even—" She stopped.

"Even what?" Lizzie asked.

"Well, I'm going to go out there until I can figure out what to do," I said. I took a knee and looked at Lizzie, held her tight. "Listen, everything is going to be all right. Okay, do you hear me, sweetie?"

She cried.

I stood and kissed Sadie. "Don't tell anyone where I've gone. You can't even tell Luke."

"Okay."

"Did you hear that, Lizzie?" I said.

"Yes, Papa."

I moved toward the door.

"Papa?"

"I'm okay, baby." I felt Sadie's hand land on my shoulder. I kissed her. "I'll come back for you."

I left my family and slipped into the woods. It was perhaps stupid to attempt escape during the light of day, but I didn't know when they might come for me. I didn't run. Running was something a slave could never do, unless, of course, he was running. No one noticed as I passed through the Widow Douglas's backyard and down the steep hill to the river. I waited there against an undercut bank. I couldn't venture out onto the water during the day. Too many ferries and riverboats and folks fishing along the shore. I was as much scared as angry, but where does a slave put anger? We could be angry with one another; we were human. But the real source of our rage had to go without address, swallowed, repressed. They were going to rip my family apart and send me to New Orleans, where I would be even farther from freedom and would probably never see my family again.

AT DUSK I was eaten alive by mosquitoes. I pulled a log from the bank and slid it into the frigid, muddy water. I pushed off and kicked my way straight across, knowing that the strong current of the Mississippi would suck me downstream. I could just barely see the island in the dark and I hoped I wouldn't glide right past it. Luckily, no riverboats ever navigated the channel between the shore and the island. But I couldn't be sure some peckerwood wouldn't paddle by in a canoe or on a raft.

I could finally see the island, but I felt a tugging on my leg. I couldn't shake loose of the snag. I didn't believe in river monsters, so I quickly figured I'd gotten hung up in somebody's trotline. Getting untangled was difficult, and for a brief time I thought I was going to miss the island or drown or both. It, however, turned out to be good fortune. When I yanked the line free of its tether, I pulled with it three large catfish that I could eat that night, which was good because my bread was ruined. Also, I could reuse the line and the hooks. This thinking was good because it distracted me from just how exhausted I was. I hit the rocky beach of the island and lay on my back, the fish on my chest. It was the fish smell that woke me. As my exhaustion wore off, I began to shiver uncontrollably. I was freezing, but there was nothing I could do about that. I wrestled out of my soaked rag of a coat and my clothes. I took my little knife from my pocket and gutted the catch. I cut off the heads and discarded them because I could not stomach their faces. I couldn't risk a fire in the darkness. I would cook them and eat in the morning. I had to get myself dry and warm and find some sleep. I moved into the trees, out of the wind, and buried myself in fallen leaves. I put my wet coat on top of the plant matter and closed my eyes. The weight of the garment at least made me imagine that I was warmer.

MORNING CAME AND I crawled into my drier, but frozen, clothes. The coat was still wet, so I laid it over a bush. I hopped around to get warm, waiting for the sun to get high enough for me to use my piece of glass to start a fire. I heard rustling in the trees. It sounded like a human, so I had to assume it was a white human.

"What dere be in dem woods? Dat be a ghost? You stays away from me, you ol' shade."

"Jim? Is that you, Jim?" It was Huck.

"I swear, you lak to scared me to def."

"What you doin' out here?" the boy asked.

"Furst off, I'm freezin'," I said. "What you be doin' on dis ilan? And why you got blood all ova ya?"

"I kilt myself," the boy said.

I looked him over. "You din't do a good job."

"Well, Miss Watson, that damn judge and Pap think I'm dead and that's all that matters. They think I was murdered."

"Why dey think dat?" I asked.

"I kilt a pig and spread his blood all round Pap's cabin. I made a mess like there had been a fight in there."

In my head I was doing the math. Huck was supposedly murdered and I'd just run away. Who did I think they would suspect of the heinous crime?

"But what you doin' out here, Jim?"

"I be hidin'."

"Why?"

"Well, I be hidin' causin' Miss Watson got a notion to sell me down the riber. And now . . ." I shook my head.

"And now what?"

"And now causin' I kilt you. Least dat what dey gone think." I looked at his eyes. "You needs to go back."

"I cain't," Huck said. "Pap will kill me for sure."

"I reckon dat's tru nuff." I looked through the trees at the channel we'd crossed. "Lawd, hab mercy."

"What's your plan, Jim?"

"I was gonna live out heah on dis here ilan for a spell, but naw dey lookin' fer a killa and a body."

"What you mean, Miss Watson gonna sell you down the river?"

"I be a slave, Huck. She kin sell me if she want. And 'parently, she want. I had to run fo' she done it."

"But you got a family."

"Don' mean nuffin if'n you a slave."

Huck sat and studied on that.

The sun was up and slicing the trees, burning off a bit of the chill. I pointed to the catfish. "Leaseways we got breakfast," I said. "You got matches?"

"No."

"Den I use my magic glass," I said. I took the round bottom of some bottle I'd found a long time ago from my pocket.

"Magic?"

"Magic," I repeated. "It take light from da sun and mixes it round and gits all narrow and turns inta fire."

I moved us to a small clearing and used the glass and got some kindling of dry moss started and let the boy add sticks. A couple of logs later and we had it going nicely. The fire felt good. It probably was a bad idea, but we didn't peel the skin off the last fish.

"I got some bread," Huck said.

"I lost mine in da water. I figger my jerky gone dry out okay." I looked at the fish. "I reckon dat skin gone burn 'way, awright."

"Pap jest eats the skin."

"Hmmm."

I watched the smoke rise. It seemed to disperse pretty well before it reached the treetops.

Huck enjoyed the fish. "How did you catch 'em?"

"Din't really," I said. "I gots snagged in sumbuddy's trotline and dey was already caught."

"Lucky," he said.

I nodded.

"I cain't believe Miss Watson gone sell you. I mean, she likes you."

"I reckon she likes money mo'. Mos' peoples likes money mo' 'n anythin' else. White folks, anyways."

"Not me," Huck said. "I told the judge to take all that money I found."

"How much you reckon it be?"

"Thousands," Huck said. "Money ain't nothing but trouble. Don't you think, Jim?"

"I woodn't know. Ain't never had no money."

Huck nodded.

We heard a boom and lay flat on the ground. We crawled to the edge of the trees and saw a ferryboat passing by. Judge Thatcher and his daughter, Bessie, were aft. Tom Sawyer's aunt Polly was leaning over the side. A man I'd never seen was readying a small cannon to fire another shot. He lit the fuse and cracked the air with another boom. The ball splashed into the water.

"Why they doin' that, Jim?"

"Dey's tryin' to get yo dead body to float up to the top o' da water."

"Be funny if some other body float up," he said.

"Hilarious," I said.

"What?" He looked at me.

"I say da 'he harry us.' "

"What's that mean?"

"What? Looky naw," I said.

The boy turned back and we watched the man at the bow float something into the water. I was relieved to be able to redirect his attention. In all my life that was the first time I had ever had a language slip. That had to be an indication of just how addled and agitated I was.

"What's that?" Huck asked.

"I reckon dat be a loaf a bread wif the quicksilva in it."

"What's that do?"

"It s'posed to find it way to a corpse."

"Does that work?"

"White folk believe all sorts a stuff I don't know about. Dey is the stupidstitiousest people in da world."

"You mean 'superstitious.' "

"Dat what I say." We watched the ferryboat disappear around the bend. "They sho' nuff thinks you dead." As I said it, that wave of fear washed over me again. I might have been better off drowning in the river or freezing to death in the night. One thing was certain: I had to make sure Huck didn't become the corpse they were looking for. More to the point, I had to make certain I didn't become the corpse they were looking for.

CHAPTER 5

WE RAN A TROTLINE across a little cove and so had plenty of catfish to eat, even the occasional crappie. We also found plenty of blackberries and gooseberries. The gooseberries were sour, but mixed with the blackberries and currants, they were quite good. The weather improved and we were living well enough that I wondered if Sadie and Lizzie and I could survive out there. But we would have to be running like fugitives, ducking and hiding. It was bad enough being a slave, but being fugitive slaves was worse. Being fugitive slaves hiding out under white people's noses would be intolerable.

Huck seemed happy, though, feeling safe from his father. We found a big cave near the center of the island and were safe enough there to have fires at night.

"Jim," the boy said one night, "why do you think my pappy hates me so?"

"Reckon I don' know, Huck. Whatchu think?"

"I know he don't like my head."

"What?"

"Well, my hairline. He don't like it. He's always grabbing me and he pulls back my hair and then slaps me."

"Hmmmph."

"Tells me I gots a widow's peak. I didn't even know what that was. Miss Watson told me when I asked and she said a lot of people got 'em. It's when yer hair points like an arrow." He pulled back his hair and showed me. "Heck, Jim, yer head does the same thing. Pull yer hair back."

"It do?" I touched my hair. "I reckon it do. What you s'pose a wida's peak mean? Is it good luck?"

"Sho ain't for me," Huck said.

After a spell of silence, I caught Huck staring at me.

"What?" I asked.

"Being a slave, you got to do whatever your owner say to do?"

"Whateber dey say," I said. "Wheneber dey say. Dey say, 'Jump,' I say, 'How high?' Dey say, 'Spit,' I say, 'How far?' "

"How kin one person own another person?"

"Dat be a good question, Huck."

"Look what I found." Huck showed me a length of snakeskin. He pushed it toward me, but I pulled away.

"Be bad luck to handle a snakeskin," I said. "Snake might come back lookin' fer his clothes."

"Who's superstitious now?"

"Dat ain't stupesition, dat's jest common sense."

Huck laughed. "What superstitions you know, Jim?"

"Don' walk under no ladder. I know dat one. Don' believe it."

"So, you would walk under a ladder."

"Nossir. Ain't safe to walk under no ladder, but it ain't bad luck. Black cats s'posed to be bad. White cats okay, black cats bad."

"What if'n you see an owl in the daytime?"

I was barely listening to him. I was worried about Sadie and Lizzie. "Owl?" I said. "Daytime? Lawdy, now dat dere is some bad bizness. Dat mean sumbuddy gonna meet his maker." I could see my answer made him happy. "But dat don' make me stuperstitious. Dat jest mean I gots mo' good sense, lak I say."

Huck laughed.

"Well, one thin' fer sho? It gone rain like crazy tomorrow, so we best to stow some food and get ready to hunkers down."

"Why you think it's gonna rain?"

"Seen lots of hawks flyin' round. Dey likes to hunt fo' it rain. And seen ants buildin' piles round dey holes."

"How do they know it's gonna rain?" the boy asked.

"Dey's a part of nature and weather be a part of nature and dem parts talk to each other."

"Ain't people a part of nature?"

"If'n dey is, den dey ain't no good part. Da rest o' nature don' hardly talk to no human peoples anymo. Maybe it try from time to time, but peoples don' listen. Anyway, gone be a big rain."

I watched as exhaustion came over Huck. His head dropped and he was asleep. I went out of the cave and collected lots of wood. We were going to have to keep the fire going. There would be no sun to use to start another one. I was serious about the rain. I could feel it in my joints.

MY PREDICTION WAS NOT only true, but turned out to be grossly understated. The rain was torrential, biblical. Our beach fairly disappeared. I managed to pull in our trotline, else it would have been lost for good. That a flood was coming was a foregone conclusion. The only question was how high. The river rose and rose, covering much of Jackson Island. Sheet lightning lit up the sky seconds at a time. Huck fretted that a twister might be coming, but I told him the winds were blowing in a rotation counter to such an event. What I said was "Dat wind be twistin' optsite of a tornada." It was nonsense, but it quieted the boy's fear. Then he pointed.

I looked. A house was floating down the channel toward us. It was a frightening sight. It was late afternoon, dark with no sun, and so it was difficult to see, but it was as big as what it was. It hung up against some trees and Huck and I had the same idea. Provisions. We dragged Huck's canoe from the cave to the water and paddled to the house. It was hard work. We tied the boat to a tree and climbed in through a smashed window. We waded through water inside the wrecked house, with clothes floating everywhere. It had settled at a severe angle so it was a bit of a climb to the kitchen cabinets. Huck opened one and squealed, ironically, like a pig, as he found a rasher of bacon. I turned and saw a boot between the stove and the wall, then it became clear the boot was at the end of a leg.

"What is it?" Huck asked.

"Take the bacon and get back in the canoe," I said.

Huck froze and stared at me.

"Does lak I say!"

I leaned over and got a good look at the man's face. It was a white man, deader than dead. His face was twisted and ugly and dead. I looked at the face for a while, my hands trembling not because he was dead, but because I was there while he was dead. A dead white man. I studied the face. All white men looked alike in a way, like bears, like bees, especially when dead.

"Is he dead?" Huck asked.

"Get on back in dat boat!"

"Who is it? You recognize him?"

"I ain't know him. Naw git. You don't need to see nuffin lak dat."

"I ain't no baby, Jim."

"You nuff o' one—naw let's git outta heah. Grab some dem clothes and git out dat winda."

While he was pulling garments into his arms I found a stack of papers wedged into the corner of a shelf. There was a bottle of ink. I pushed all of it into my trousers.

As we made it through the window and were trying to pull the canoe back to us, Huck asked me why I sounded so funny in the house.

"What you be talkin' 'bout? Git dat boat. Dis here house about to tear 'way from dem trees."

As soon as we had paddled away, the house did just that and roared by us.

"Woooweee," Huck said. "Look at that."

The house was quickly out of sight.

"Was he dead, Jim?"

"Yeah, he be dead."

"Who was he?"

I didn't say anything. I paddled us into the trees, and then we climbed out onto muddy ground.

"Who was he, Jim? I ain't never seen a dead person before."

"I ain't neber seed him fo'."

Back in our cave we listened to the storm. We might have heard lightning strike a tree. The thunder shook us hard. We chewed some bacon right off the rasher. It wasn't delicious, but the longer we chewed it, the bigger it got, and so it satisfied our hunger.

"I wonder who he was," Huck said.

"It be bad luck to study on dead folk," I told him. "You already stackin' dat bad luck after handlin' dat snakeskin."

"This bacon is awful," Huck said.

"Sho nuff," I said.

But we kept chewing.

"You heard the one 'bout not putting mirrors facing mirrors?" Huck asked. I looked at his young eyes and thought about Lizzie. I wondered just how scared she was for me at that moment, hated the idea of her feeling fear. I realized I hated it because I knew that feeling so well, every day, every night. I laughed to myself and I didn't know why.

"What is it?" the boy asked.

I couldn't use the word *irony* with him. "Sho be funny, ain't it?"

"What?"

"Here we is chewin' on dis terrbul bacon, me a runaway and you a dead boy. You know dey gone think I da one dat kilt you."

"I never thought of that," Huck said. "I never dreamed I could git you into trouble. Why would you want to kill me?"

"Dat don't matter none to white folks."

"I don't like white folks," he said. "And I is one."

"Sho look lak one."

Lightning lit up the outside at the cave's mouth and then thunder shook us again. The storm was right on top of us. I had been right about the weather, but I hadn't thought far enough ahead to remember that we might not be the only ones on the island trying to find a dry place. I reached back for another stick for the fire without looking and felt pain shoot through my hand. I screamed and jumped up.

"Jim," Huck shouted.

The rattlesnake that had been attached to my hand fell off into the fire, but it managed to wriggle free across the ground and out into the rain.

"Did he get you?"

" 'Fraid so." I walked over to the mouth of the cave and dropped to my knees. I took out my knife and cut the bite, gave a good suck and spat out the blood. Then I slapped some of the clay mud on it. "Git dat rag 'n' tie it round heah."

"What's this gonna do?" Huck asked.

"I's hopin' da mud will draw out the poison. Make it tight."

"Do you think it will work?"

"At least one of us gone know in da moanin'."

CHAPTER 6

MY FACE FELT FAT and numb and my hands and feet were without feeling, but where I was bitten was extremely painful. I felt weaker than I'd ever felt. If I had had any real food in me I might have vomited. My head was spinning, the world was spinning, and I didn't know if it was from the venom or from anxiety. I lay still, at first feeling the concerned stare of Huck, and then a spiraling into delirium, like down a whirlpool. I burned with fever, and the chills I was feeling were almost interesting. I saw Sadie and Lizzie. They stood on a little wooden dock, took vegetables from a little boat and piled them in big straw baskets. Then I was in Judge Thatcher's library, a place where I had spent many afternoons while he was out at work or hunting ducks. I could see books in front of me. I had read them secretly, but this time, in this fever dream, I was able to read without fear of being discovered. I had wondered every time I sneaked in there what white people would do to a slave who had learned how to read. What would they do to a slave who had taught the other slaves to read? What would they do to a slave who knew what a hypotenuse was, what *irony* meant, how *retribution* was spelled? I was burning up with fever, fading in and out of consciousness, focusing and refocusing on Huck's face.

François-Marie Arouet de Voltaire put a fat stick into the fire. His delicate fingers held the wood for what seemed like too long a time.

"I'm afraid there's no more wood," I said. "Which is fine, because I am hot enough. Too hot."

He reached in again and moved some charred pieces around. He looked at his blackened fingertips. "I'm like you," he said.

"How is that?"

He wiped his hands on his pants, left smudges. "You shouldn't be a slave," Voltaire said, sighing. He sat beside me, moved to feel my forehead with the back of his hand and then thought better. "Like Montesquieu, I think we are all equal, regardless of color, language or habit."

"You do, do you?" I asked.

"However, you must realize that climate and geography can be significant factors in determining human development. It's not that your features make you unequal, it's that they are signs of biological differences, things that have helped you survive in those hot, desolate places. It's those factors that stop you from achieving the more perfect human form found in Europe."

"Is that right?"

"The African can be easily trained in the ways of the European, of course. He can come to be more than he naturally is, to learn those manners and skills that will allow him to become equal."

"Yes?"

"That is what equality is, Jim. It's the *capacity* for becoming equal. The same way a black man in Martinique can learn French and so become French, he can also acquire the skills of equality and so become equal. But I repeat myself."

"I hate you," I said through my fever and chills. "You realize, of course, that I have been bitten by a snake. Only to have you come to me in this delirium."

"Well, yes, but all men are equal. That's my point. But even you have to admit the presence of, shall we call him—it—the devil, in your African humans." Voltaire adjusted his position and held his hands to the fire.

"You're saying we're equal, but also inferior," I said.

"I'm detecting a disapproving tone," he said. "Listen, my friend, I'm on your side. I'm against the institution of slavery. Slavery of any kind. You know that I am an abolitionist of the first order."

"Thank you?"

"You're welcome."

"You do not believe that humans are inherently bad?" I asked.

"I do not. If they were, they would kill as soon as they could walk."

"How do you explain slavery? Why are my people subjected to it, treated with such cruelty?"

Voltaire shrugged.

"Let me try this," I said. "You have a notion, like Raynal, of natural liberties, and we all have them by virtue of our being human. But when those liberties are put under societal and cultural pressure, they become civil liberties, and those are contingent on hierarchy and situation. Am I close?"

Voltaire was scribbling on paper. "That was good, that was good. Say all of that again."

"Jim? Jim?" It was Huck.

"Huckleberry?"

"You okay?"

The boy came into some focus. "I ain't as hot as I was." I glimpsed the mouth of the cave and saw daylight. "I guess Ima gone make it."

"You sho talk funny in yer sleep."

"I does?"

Huck nodded. He looked at me suspiciously.

"What I say?"

"Who is Raynal?"

I recalled some of my dream, wondered just how much talking I had done out loud. "He be a slave I knowed from way back."

"What does *hierarchy* mean?"

"What?" I said. "Ain't no such word."

"You said it. And a lotta other words. You didn't sound like you. Are you possessed, Jim?"

"Lawdy. I could be, I s'pose. Wouldn't dat be sumptin'. A snake is da devil, ain't he. I hopes he din't put no demons in my blood." I looked around the cave. "Where my lucky piece o' glass." I found the round glass and held it so the boy could see it. "My lucky glass will protect me."

I was still weak and I used fondling the glass as an excuse to get away from Huck's questions.

"You was sho talkin' funny."

"I'm habing dem chills 'gin." And in fact I was.

"Here, drink some water." Huck handed me the old can we'd been using for drinking.

"Thank ya, Huck."

"I'll go see if the storm ruined all the berries."

"You do dat. Ima gonna sleep sum mo'. Watch out for dem snakes."

As the boy disappeared into the bright light of the outside, I felt again how sick I was. I suspected at that moment that I would not die, but it was unclear whether I would be pleased about that fact. My head was swimming and I was in great pain. I was nauseated and still feverish. I tried to pull myself to my feet, but my limbs were numb and uncooperative. In truth, I was afraid to sleep again for fear of Huck coming back and hearing my thoughts without their passing through my slave filter. I was even more afraid of further unproductive, imagined conversations with Voltaire, Rousseau and Locke about slavery, race and, of all things, albinism. How strange a world, how strange an existence, that one's equal must argue for one's equality, that one's equal must hold a station that allows airing of that argument, that one cannot make that argument for oneself, that premises of said argument must be vetted by those equals who do not agree.

My chills returned and I thought again that I might die. I broke into a sweat and lay still for another couple of hours until Huck returned.

"Jim, you okay?"

"I's been betta."

"I found some blackberries what weren't ruined," he said and unfolded a cloth to show me. "I put our trotline out, so we should have some fish tonight."

"How big dat flood? Water go down?"

"Not that I kin see," the boy said. "We're a long way from the land now."

"Water might be movin' too fast to catch us dem catfish."

"You look a lil' better," Huck said. He stirred the fire and put some sticks in to get it going again.

CHAPTER 7

I STAYED SICK for a couple of days. My fever broke and slowly my appetite returned. A remarkable thing in itself, in that all we had to eat was catfish and berries. I finally ventured out to set a few traps for rabbits.

AT LAST we caught a rabbit and sat down to what felt like a real feast.

"I'm glad you didn't die," Huck said.

"Ima right pleased 'bout dat my own sef." I stared into the fire. "Dyin' can ruin a good time."

"What is it, Jim?"

"I be worried 'bout my fambly," I said. "I know dey be worried 'bout me. You gonna have to go see if'n dey awright."

"I cain't go there. I'm supposed to be dead."

"Sho would help me some if'n you wasn't," I said. I looked at the clothes he'd taken in such a hurry from the washed-away house. "What if'n you wore dat dere dress and make lak you be a gurl?"

"I don't look like no girl."

"You would if'n you was in dat dress. You kin tie you hair back like dem white gurls does."

"No."

"I needs to know if'n my fambly's okay."

"I suppose I should find out what's going on, too. What should my name be? My girl name."

"Sumptin' simple," I said.

"What about 'Mary'?"

"Dat a good name."

"What about my last name? What about 'McGillicuddy'?"

"Kin you spell it?"

Huck looked at his feet. "No."

"Sumptin' simple," I said, again.

" 'Williams'?"

"Sho."

Huck took his clothes off and put on the dress. His young face was effeminate enough that he might have been taken for a girl in passing. He wouldn't bear a close look. His posture was all wrong.

"How do I look?" he asked.

"Stan' up straight-lak and don't hunch lak a bear."

"Like this?"

I nodded.

"Why, I do declare," he said in a falsetto that was actually lower than his speaking voice. "Lordy, but it's hot in here."

"You s'posed to be a gurl, not no ol' woman."

"This ain't gone work," the boy said.

"Sho it will."

THOUGH WEAK, I helped Huck get the canoe from the cave to the river. The flood had receded considerably, but it was clear that the mainland had acquired a new contour. Because of this change it was difficult for us to know just where Huck should put ashore. We made a guess, but as Huck paddled out, it was clear that his hitting anywhere near our selected spot was hardly likely. I watched him for only a short time before I dragged myself back to the cave and the fire.

For the first time in my life, I had paper and ink. I was beside myself. I found a straight stick and shaved it to a point and scratched a groove on one side. I put the paper on my lap, dipped my stick into the ink and wrote the alphabet. I printed letters as I had seen them in books, slowly, clumsily. Then I wrote my first words. I wanted to be certain that they were mine and not some I had read from a book in the judge's library. I wrote:

> *I am called Jim. I have yet to choose a name.*
>
> *In the religious preachings of my white captors I am a victim of the Curse of Ham. The white so-called masters cannot embrace their cruelty and greed, but must look to that lying Dominican friar for religious justification. But I will not let this condition define me. I will not let myself, my mind, drown in fear and outrage. I will be outraged as a matter of course. But my interest is in how these marks that I am scratching on this page can mean anything at all. If they can have meaning, then life can have meaning, then I can have meaning.*

CHAPTER 8

I WAS HAPPY ENOUGH to send Huckleberry off on his mission to the mainland. My pleasure in seeing him off was threefold. If he was unsuccessful and discovered, he might be accused of having helped me escape, rather than my being seen as a runaway. And I might no longer be suspected of his murder and/or kidnapping, the punishment for either being torture and death. Finally, if Huck was able to find his way back without detection, he could bring me much desired and needed news of my family's condition.

I was proud of the way he used all the strength in his small body to paddle against the current. The morning fog was fairly burned away as he stood on the shore. He was just barely visible as he tied the boat to a tree and covered it with brush. He scrambled up the bank in his dress and was gone. I returned to the cave, ate some dried fish and fell into a nap, during which I did not dream.

I KNEW FROM EXPERIENCE that the snake bite was not likely to kill me. My main concern was the site of the bite—the wound, not the venom. The twin punctures had scabbed over and there was no puffiness. That relief allowed me to sleep. That I could sleep so much was slightly alarming, but I continued to improve. I felt stronger every time I awoke. Strong enough to become impatient. I collected wood and kept the fire going. I collected catfish from the trotline, ate some and hung strips over the smoke to dry. I imagined that I would be running through back country, with or without Huck, for some time. I became nervous and vigilant after the second day. I pulled more tree limbs up to conceal the cave and fashioned a place to sit from which I could look out. Not that I had any idea what I might do if I spotted anyone's approach. The boy had the canoe, so I spent some hours tying together branches, not quite a proper raft. A proper raft would need constructing near the water's edge, and I couldn't chance that.

I considered the notion of telling Huckleberry that the body I had seen in that flooded house was his Pap. I imagined that the knowledge might allow him to feel safe again in the house of Miss Watson. To tell the truth, I didn't know why I had kept it to myself. Perhaps, fearful of him or not, I had some concern that grief could overcome the boy if his father, hated or not, was dead. Selfishly, I wondered how Huck's incapacitation might affect me, but I felt only momentary guilt for that. Now that I had withheld the information for several days, Huck might become angry with me. He might betray me and cause my capture.

About dusk on the third day, I observed a column of smoke on the other side of the island. It was a terrifying sight. Maybe they were fishermen or hunters, though I was hard-pressed to know what game was there. I'd seen sign of some wild pigs, but they were plentiful on the mainland. I had seen only birds, snakes, squirrels and rabbits. I tensed and plotted which way I would run if I saw anyone, or, rather, if they saw me. I heard crunching footfalls on the forest carpet of dead leaves, and I was about to employ that route when Huck's voice cut through the trees.

"Jim," he called out, but not loudly.

"Here I is," I said.

"We gotta go," he said.

"I knows." I pointed at the smoke.

"I made that fire. I thought some men was following me, so I built that to draw 'em off while we git."

"Dat be good thinkin'," I said.

"I put the canoe on the south point."

"You sho dey comin'?"

"They was behind me, that's all I know. I think they was followin' me. I ain't for certain sure."

"Reckon we gotta leave, den. Cain't be takin' no chances."

I put our food together while Huck changed out of his dress and back into his trousers and shirt. I wanted to hear his report, but I'd have to wait.

We cut through the center of the island to remain under cover. Not all of the floodwater had receded, so we found ourselves knee-deep in silty water. I had no doubt that we would be pulling leeches off each other. Huck was high-stepping because of his short legs, disturbing the water. I imagined that his splashing might ward off cottonmouths. Hoped more than imagined. We froze when we heard voices echoing through the woods. We carried our food and sparse gear over our heads.

"You best stop all dat splashin', Huck."

"I reckon so."

"You know who dem is?"

“No, Jim. I don’t even know if’n they after us.”

“I sho nuff don’t wanna find out.”

We found the canoe and pushed it out into the water. We shivered, as we didn’t climb into the boat, but stayed in the water to keep a low profile. Soon we were away and in the current.

CHAPTER 9

WE CLIMBED INTO the canoe and lay down. I asked the boy if he was okay and he said he was cold. I told him to take off his wet clothes and cover himself with the rag I'd used to pack the dried fish. I took off my shirt and tried to wring it out as much as I could.

"Did you see my fambly?" I asked.

"From a distance," he said. "They looked awright. They looked sad."

"What else you see? What you find out?"

Telling his story was allowing him to forget how cold and miserable he was. "First I landed on the beach, that little one just below the Stinson place, you know, where them grapes cover that fence."

"I knows the spot."

"Well, there was this lady in a shack. I don't know if'n she was a Stinson or not. She was tall, near tall as you. To tell the truth, she sho looked like a man. She had big ol' hands. I guess I got kinda wet and muddy 'cause she called me to her. She called me 'gal.' Kin you believe that?"

"She did?"

"But I don't think she really believed it. She kept staring at me. But she liked to talk and she told me that folks was looking for my murderer. She didn't say 'my murderer,' she said 'Huck's murderer.' She said at first people blamed Pap and almost hanged him."

"They din't," I said.

"No. How'd you know?"

"Guess."

"She say then that they thought it was you what killed me."

My heart sank.

"I kept thinkin' that she knew it was me she was talkin' to. Anyway, they started thinkin' it was Pap Finn again. I guess it was because he run away from town and ain't nobody seen him. There is a two-hundred-dollar bounty on his head." He paused.

"What?"

"And there is a three-hundred-dollar reward for you."

I said nothing.

"I sneaked into town to see if'n I could find Tom Sawyer. I thought maybe he could help us. But all the kids was locked inside on account of there bein' a boy killer on the loose. At least, that's what I figured."

"Did ya hear anybuddy talkin'?"

"I heard the Judge Thatcher talkin' to some feller, but they was sayin' what I already done heard from that lady."

"But you din't talk to no slaves?"

He shook his head. "I slept in Miss Watson's shed the one night. I sneaked into the kitchen and got us some candles and matches. I had some cheese, but I lost it. Then I couldn't find the canoe. I hid out in that lady's barn, but I had the feeling she knowed I was there. When I found the boat and set out, I spotted some men followin' me. Least I think they was followin' me."

"How did my wife look?"

"Like I said, sad."

"My baby girl?"

"Sad."

I lay on my back and looked at the sky I couldn't see and thought about that. I would come back for my family, I promised myself.

WE MADE IT to the shore and hid in the woods. The next morning we ate some of our food. Berries and catfish. We saved our dried fish and the biscuits Huck had stolen. Keeping an eye for boats passing on the river, we fashioned a modest raft with a lean-to cover and lashed it to our boat.

"We does our trabelin' at night," I told him. "We kin fish, eat and jest rest during da daytime."

"That sounds right." Huck turned over the fish that was cooking on the stick he held over the fire. "Can I ask you somethin'?"

" 'Course."

"Why you think Pap hates me?"

"*Hate* be a strong word," I said.

"Well, what else you call it?"

"I reckon dat what you call it."

"He hates you, too," Huck said.

" 'Course he hate me. I's a slave."

"Why he gotta hate you 'cause you're a slave?"

"Just the way the world be, Huck."

"Naw, he got a special hate for you."

I nodded.

DUSK CAME ON, and with the fog we figured it was okay to set out. The Mississippi is swifter than it looks. It's scary, for that reason. You can mess around in some branches and backwaters and start to think it's gentle and then you get out into it and it's a different story. Because of the recent flood we had to get pretty far from the bank or else we'd get caught up in brush or debris. That made it even more harrowing. The riverboats couldn't see us, not that they would have steered to avoid us. And often, though they made plenty of noise, we couldn't locate the vessels in the fog until they were very near. Their wakes rocked us crazily, more so because our shelter had made us top-heavy and lopsided. We spent much time baling water with the only two small cans we had. The work was exhausting.

The fog lifted and we could see the lanterns of the riverboats across the river. We saw Fourmile Island. It looked like it went on forever, and I realized just how far away my family was from me. Then Huck screamed and I looked back to see a huge riverboat right up on us. There must have been a problem with its engines because it made no sound. We paddled toward the shore as hard as we could. I could feel the draw of the water on us.

"Fasta, Huck! You gots to dig in!"

"I'm workin'!" he cried.

We listed precariously toward the boat and then, as if the ship had a mind to let us go, we righted. I looked at Huck and he, too, knew what was coming. The wake. We grabbed on to our little craft the best we could, not just to keep it from capsizing, but to hold it together. The wake hit us, a wall of water. We lost some of our shelter. The wave soaked us through and we rocked violently. Holding on with one hand, we baled with abandon.

"You believe in Jesus?" Huck screamed.

"Sho," I said. "But maybe you be the one to ax him fo help? He don't seem to pay no mind to the wishes of no slave."

The ship gone, we continued to bale. We rocked less violently.

"Did ya pray to da Lawd?" I asked.

"Never got a chance to," Huck said. "We made it anyway."

"I reckon we did."

CHAPTER 10

We made our way downriver for a few days. Once we had drifted past Saverton, there wasn't much to see. Still, we traveled by night and foraged during the day. We trolled a line a couple of times, but Huck nearly pulled a cottonmouth into the boat once, so we gave that up. The river split and narrowed and we determined that we could travel some by day. That plan was short-lived. We came back to the wide channel and saw some men pointing at us from the deck of a small riverboat. That scared us back into the dark.

One night, our fire burning, Huck asked, "Why don't you just make me take you across that river? In Illinois you be a free man."

I had thought of it, but somehow it just seemed like I'd be that much farther from family. Slavery didn't recognize imaginary borders. I needed money. "I thinked on it, Huck. But you and me be friends. I cain't just leave you." And I meant that. Huck was just a boy.

Huck nodded. "You know where we goin'?" the boy asked.

"Ain't got no idee. But we's on our way."

NIGHT CAME and we set out. About an hour later a storm came up and started knocking us about like we were a toy in the water. Lightning flashed south of us, but it was clearly headed our way.

"Whatcha think?" I asked.

"Dunno."

"Stay in the wata wif lightnin' ain't a good idee."

"Look!" he said. He pointed.

Ahead of us, grounded on a shoal, was a wrecked steamboat. It leaned at nearly forty-five degrees. Huck paddled us forward while I used my oar as a rudder and tried my best to turn us away.

"What are you doin', Jim?"

"Ain't no good idee to be goin' in dere."

"Sure it's a good idea. Who knows what we might find? Might even be some treasure. Gold and silver and diamonds and like that. Maybe we'll find us a lamp with a genie in it."

"Kin you think of anythin' that kin get a slave killed faster than havin' him some gold? And the genie sho nuff won't grant a slave no wish."

"Maybe there's food, cans of beans and like that. More bacon."

He had a point, but still I shook my head.

"Well, I'm going aboard."

I gave in and helped him paddle us near the wreck. Once close, we could see that the boat wasn't quite fully lodged on the shoal, but tethered to a big tree. Huck tied us to some bushes down the bank.

I stopped at the back of the boat where the big paddle lay

dead and motionless. A broken spoke pointed toward the sky and another toward the far bank. The name of the boat was written across its back.

"Wha dat says?" I asked.

"*Walter Scott,*" Huck said.

"Wonder who he be."

"That be the name of the boat, Jim."

"Oh."

"You not coming aboard?" he asked.

"Ima stay right heah. I be keepin' watch."

"That's a good idea," Huck said. "Give a signal whistle if'n there's danger or somebody's comin'."

I watched as Huck climbed up the slippery deck. I then ducked under the tilted hull to get out of the rain.

BECAUSE OF THE WIND, my cover was hardly cover at all. I was fairly soaked through. I tried to think but couldn't. Then Huck came careening down the deck and slid off into the water. He was shaking.

"We have to get out of here," he said. "We've got to get out of here. We gotta run, Jim."

"What is it, Huck? What be da matter?" I asked as we made our way to where we'd tied our boat.

Before he could answer, we saw that our craft had come undone and had drifted far out into the river. "I reckon I did a poor job of tying," the boy said. "We got to hide. We need to hide."

"Why?"

"There was some robbers in that boat. They was splittin' up their loot and then one of 'em said they was gonna have to kill another feller. I didn't see him. I don't know where that 'un is."

"I done told you not to go in, din't I." I shook my head. "Well, cain't change nuffin naw."

We heard deep voices from the *Walter Scott*. I pulled Huck into the bushes. We watched as the men put their takings into a skiff. Then a big wave came and lifted the *Walter Scott* and dropped it with a thud. Lightning flashed and thunder shook us. The storm was on us.

The men went back into the riverboat. I knew we had to get out of there. Our boat was gone. When I looked at Huck I saw he had the same notion. We stayed hidden in the brush and worked our way close, then we dashed for the robbers' skiff. I untied the rope and the current snatched us out into the river in mere seconds. Another big wave lifted and slammed the wreck again. The robbers came running out onto the deck. We couldn't see them, but we heard them shouting and swearing. I took the oars and did little more than keep us from capsizing, which was enough work.

THE SKY UNTWISTED itself and the storm flashed north of us, the thunder just a rumble now. I managed the boat to the bank, not because day was breaking, but because I was exhausted. We pulled up into the trees and lay on our backs. We were plenty wet, but no rain fell.

Once it was light, we went through the robbers' booty, as Huck called it. The boy was highly excited by the adventure of it all. I admired that, was envious of it, to tell the truth, to be able to feel that in a world without fear of being hanged to death, or worse.

It turned out that the robbers didn't care much for eating, as there was no food in the cache. There was jewelry, clothing, cigars. And books. I had to hide my excitement about the discovery of books. As to the monetary value of books I had no knowledge, but their intellectual value was immediately evident.

Among them were copies of Voltaire's *Treatise on Tolerance* and *All for the Best* and Rousseau's *Discourse on Inequality.* These were books I had seen on Judge Thatcher's shelves and was eager to read. There was also a Bible and a book about training horses. And one pamphlet. I held it and studied the worn cream-colored cover. *The Narrative of the Life and Adventures of Venture, a Native of Africa: But Resident Above Sixty Years in the United States of America.* The slim volume felt soft, as if handled by sweaty hands. The work purported to be "related by himself." *Related.*

"Maybe we kin sell the jewels," Huck said.

I nodded.

"Why you holdin' them books?" Huck asked.

"Dey feels good," I said.

"That's funny. How kin a book feel good?" He grabbed the Rousseau and thumbed through it. "It ain't even got pictures."

"I likes the weight of 'em," I said.

Huck stared at me for a long few seconds. "I guess I don't understand niggers," he said.

Somehow that word seemed strange coming out of Huck's mouth. I think he heard it, too, because we shared an awkward silence.

"Mebe I learn m'self to read wif dese books," I said.

"You could probably find somethin' better to start with

than these." He noticed that I had pushed aside the Bible. "You don't want this 'un? The Bible?"

I felt cornered. "No," I said. "Kin I keep dese?"

"I sure as shootin' don't want 'em."

I put them in the sack they'd come in.

"You is a mystery to me, Jim, a sho nuff mystery."

"I reckon I is, Huck."

"First you don't wanna go to Illinois where you kin be free and then you start collectin' books causin' they make you feel good. I swear I don't understand."

CHAPTER 11

"I SHO LOVE that story about the genie," Huck said. "Just imagine that feller what lives in a lamp."

"A lamp?"

"Yeah, but instead of oil inside it, there's a man."

"A lil' man, I s'pose," I said.

Huck shook his head. "No, I reckon he ain't little. As I heard it, he come out like smoke and then just appears like."

"How you knows dis?"

"Tom Sawyer told me," Huck said.

"Well, dere you hab it," I said.

"What do you mean?"

"When be da last time Tom Sawyer telled you anythin' true? 'Member when he told you 'bout dat gold and da rainbo?"

"Anyway, the genie comes out the lamp and gives you three wishes. Anything you want. You just ask. But just three."

"Kin you ax for more wishes?"

"You know, that was what I said, but it seems you cain't have but three. What would you wish fer?"

Entertaining such discussions in character was exhausting, but I had thought about such a thing many times before and, just like a story I'd read in the judge's library, I could see that anything I thought was good could entail some bad consequences. For example, living forever would mean you'd have to watch everybody you loved die. The question I played with, but certainly couldn't share with Huck, was what would Kierkegaard wish for. "I dunno, Huck. I reckon I'd be scared to wish fer anything."

"Think about it."

"I reckon the genie be white. I ain't got no need to wish fo sumptin' dat ain't gone happen. Good story or no."

Huck let that sink in, then he looked at the sky. "I kin tell you what I'd wish fer. First, I'd wish fer some adventure." He smiled big. He looked at me. "Then I'd wish dat you was free like me."

"Thank ya."

" 'Course. Well, I'd wish all slaves was free."

I nodded.

"Don't every man got a right to be free?" Huck asked.

"Ain't no such things as rights," I said.

"What say?"

"I ain't said nuffin."

He looked at the sack. "Don't know what you want with them heavy books, but sure. I suppose if some real treasure come along, we kin just drop 'em."

"Like a lamp wif one dem genies," I said.

"Yessir," said Huck.

The boy and I fell silent. We lay back on the wet carpet of leaves. I could sense exhaustion overtaking Huck. He was snoring softly in a short time. I stared up through the canopy of sycamore branches. I'd always liked how the bark of the tree curled and peeled away.

I really wanted to read. Though Huck was asleep, I could not chance his waking and discovering me with my face in an open book. Then I thought, *How could he know that I was actually reading?* I could simply claim to be staring dumbly at the letters and words, wondering what in the world they meant. How could he know? At that moment the power of reading made itself clear and real to me. If I could see the words, then no one could control them or what I got from them. They couldn't even know if I was merely seeing them or reading them, sounding them out or comprehending them. It was a completely private affair and completely free and, therefore, completely subversive.

I pulled my sack of books closer, reached in and touched one. I let my hand linger there, a flirtation of sorts. The small thick book I'd wrapped my fingers around was the novel. I had never read a novel, though I understood the concept of fiction. It wasn't so unlike religion, or history, for that matter. I pulled the book from the bag. I checked to see if Huck was still sleeping soundly and then I opened it. The smell of the pages was glorious.

In the country of Westphalia . . .

I was somewhere else. I was not on one side of that damn river or the other. I was not on the Mississippi. I was not in Missouri.

CHAPTER 12

THAT LATE AFTERNOON we were surprised to find our canoe and raft hung up in some brush just down the beach from where we'd landed earlier in the day.

"What luck," Huck said.

"I think we bet' take our own boat," I said.

"Why?"

"It ain't stole, fer one thin'. And nobuddy be looking for our canoe."

"I reckon you're right." He looked at my sack.

"Let's be gittin'," I said.

"I reckon we're getting close to the Ohio."

"Could be."

It was dusk by the time we shoved off, I in the canoe and Huck on the raft. We were dry, and that was a good thing. There was no fog that night and few clouds. The stars hovered above us.

"Look at all dem stars," I said.

"Yeah," Huck said with wonder. "Reckon a feller could count all of them?"

"I knows I cain't."

"I got a question for you, Jim."

"What's dat?"

"You ain't got no last name, right?"

"Dat yo question?"

"No," Huck said. "My question is, if you could choose yourself a last name, what would it be?"

"I got to gib it to ya, Huck. Dat be a good question."

"How you go 'bout gettin' a slave name if you ain't got one to begin with?" the boy asked.

"Reckon you just picks one."

"Gotta be more to it than that. Else people be callin' themselves somethin' different every day."

"Who to say dey don't?" I asked. "I hear tell dat dem Indian folk get dey names after folks know sumptin' 'bout dem. Lak 'Swift Deer' or 'Yeller Hands' or 'Fast Arrow' or 'Runs From Bear.' "

"Are those real names?"

"I jest made dem up."

"I like that. I could be 'Hawkeye.' What about you, Jim?"

I studied the sky, saw a shooting star. " 'Golightly,' " I said.

"What?"

"Dat be my name. 'Golightly.' "

"Jim Golightly," Huck said. "Sounds good."

"James Golightly."

I steered us down the river. Huck shivered himself to sleep on the raft. I dozed off myself for a few minutes and was awakened by the wild racket of a party on a steamboat. I looked up at the lamplit deck, crawling with people. Not only didn't they see me, but they couldn't see me. For some reason, this notion struck me as funny and I chuckled, then caught myself. My laughter had not woken Huck. And the reason for that was that he was not there. Somehow our raft and canoe had become disconnected. I worried immediately that the raft might not be river-worthy.

"Huck!" I called out, softly at first, then more urgently. "Huck!" Now I was screaming. The empty quiet of the river itself was enough to swallow any sound I made, but the music, laughter and sloshing of the big wheel from the riverboat made certain that Huck would never hear me.

I looked for shadows moving on or through the water, listened for any sound, searched for any disturbance in the water and found nothing. We were separated, and I wondered, in spite of my concern for the boy, if that was a bad thing.

After a while, with the river black, deep and lit only by the moon, I, quite miraculously, spied Huck kneeling on the raft. I could tell from the constant swiveling of his head that he was in a panic looking for me. I pointed the canoe toward him and lay back, leaned against the thwart and pretended to be asleep. I listened as he tied the two vessels back together, then pretended to wake.

"Huck, you is alibe," I said, excitedly.

"Of course I'm alive—what else would I be?"

"Well, drownded, for one."

"How that gone happen?"

I could see the prankster mind at work in the boy.

"How that gonna happen when you right here with me?" he persisted.

"But, Huck, we been seprated for a spell."

"What are you talking about, Jim? You been asleep this whole time. I been watching you."

"Nawsuh, we be seprated, you an' me. Dis big ol' riverboat come by and when I looked down you be gone wif the raft."

"Tweren't no riverboat."

"Sho dere was."

"No, Jim, you been sleepin' this whole time."

"No," I said. "I fell 'sleep, sho, but dat was after."

"You dreamed all that," the boy said.

Having me on was giving the boy much pleasure. "Sho nuff seemed real. Dem people on dat boat, dey wasn't real?"

"No, Jim."

"Lawdy, Lawd, Lawd," I said. "Sho was a scary dream."

Huck started laughing. He pointed at me and laughed harder.

"You mean you was pullin' on my leg?" I said. He was enjoying himself and that was all right with me. It always made life easier when white folks could laugh at a poor slave now and again.

"I had you goin'," Huck said.

I acted like he'd hurt my feelings. White people love feeling guilty.

"I'm sorry, Jim. I just thought it was funny," he said.

"Yeah, it be funny, Huck, sho nuff funny." I pushed out my lower lip a bit, an expression I displayed only for white people.

"I din't mean to hurt you none."

It could have been my turn to experience a bit of guilt, having toyed with the boy's feelings, and he being too young to actually understand the problem with his behavior, but I chose not to. When you are a slave, you claim choice where you can.

We drifted, steering clear of other boats.

"Jim, you belong to Miss Watson, right? I mean you her property, right?"

"Dat right," I said.

"So, truth is I'm stealin' you from her."

"Well, Huck, now you din't zackly take me from her, did you? We sort of come dis way tagether."

"But I didn't give you back to her, did I?"

"No, you din't."

"So, that's like stealin', right? If'n I took a mule from the side of the road and I knowed who it belonged to, wouldn't that be stealin'?"

"I ain't a mule, Huck."

We drifted on.

"Ain't I doin' wrong, though?" Huck said. He was troubled. "How am I s'posed to know what good is?"

"Way I sees it is dis. If'n ya gots to hab a rule to tells ya wha's good, if'n ya gots to hab good 'splained to ya, den ya cain't be good. If'n ya need sum kinda God to tells ya right from wrong, den you won't never know."

"But the law says . . ."

"Good ain't got nuttin' to do wif da law. Law says I'm a slave."

We drifted on, our silence becoming quieter.

"LISTEN TO DAT," I said to Huck.

"What?"

"Listen."

"I don't hear nothing."

"Dat's it, Huck. Dat's da riber talkin' to hersef."

"What she sayin'?" the boy asked.

"Dat's fer her to know and fer us to figger out." I looked downriver. "Dere's anudder voice."

Huck closed his eyes and listened. "I don't hear it."

"It's the Ohio, Huck. She be tellin' dat ol' Mississip 'bout freedom. I'm gonna get me a job and save me sum money and come back and buy my Sadie and Lizzie."

"Then they will belong to you?" Huck asked.

"Naw, dey jest won't belong to nobuddy else. Dey won't belong to nobuddy. Dey be free."

CHAPTER 13

THE QUIET of the morning and the drone of the river caused me to let down my guard. I had fallen asleep while we were still afloat. I cracked open my eyes and found daylight staring back at me, but it was a voice that had awakened me. Men's voices and Huck's, very near, right over me. I assessed my situation and determined that I was on our raft and covered by a tarp. I figured that Huck had thrown it over me, as I had no recollection of pulling it over myself. I lay still.

"What's yer name, boy?" a man asked.

"Johnny, sir."

"What you doing out on this river all by yerself?"

"Looking for a good place to fish."

"You from round here?"

Huck paused. "Yessir."

"What you fishing fer?" another man asked.

"Catfish."

"You sho in the right place."

"You seen a nigger hereabouts?" the first man asked.

"No, mister. Why?"

"He's a runaway."

"A runaway slave," the second man said.

"What else could he be?" This from the first man.

"Well, it could be we talkin' 'bout a runaway prisoner. Right? Ain't that right, Johnny? Tell him."

"Could be a prisoner," Huck said.

"But it ain't," the first man said. "It's a black slave nigger what belongs to some woman up in Hannibal."

I could hear the wheel in Huck's little head turning.

"Seen anybody, boy?" the first man asked again.

Huck paused. I listened to his pause. Water lapped at the sides of the canoe and got me wet through the slats of the raft floor. The chill of the water must have made me move an inch or so.

"Boy?"

"No, I ain't seen nobody."

"Who you got under that tarp?" The man's voice was louder.

"That there is my sick uncle," Huck said.

"Oh, yeah?"

I felt something snag the raft, maybe a hook, maybe a hand.

"Yeah," Huck said. "I bring him out for air every day. He's got the smallpox."

The raft was let go.

"And you there with him?" the second man asked.

"I never touch him. I'm afraid to touch him."

"Smallpox," the second man repeated. His voice grew fainter.

"He sleeps most of the time," Huck said. "We keep thinkin' he gone die, then he just don't."

The first man harrumphed.

"I ain't messin' with no pox," the second man said.

"Git," the first man said.

"Yessir," Huck said.

"What you using for them catfish, boy?" the second man asked.

"What I kin find. Nightcrawlers, crickets."

"Git yoself some cheese. They love them some cheese."

"Go on, boy," the first man said. "Watch out for that nigger. They say he's a dangerous one."

"Yessir, I sho will."

"Here's some money," the first man said. "Boy out fishin' with his almost-dead uncle needs some money."

"Why, thank you, sir!" Huck said. "Ya'll is sho kind."

"Go."

When we were well away Huck said we were clear. "That was close," he said.

"Closer den I likes," I said.

"Kin you believe it? That man up and give me ten dollars."

"Dat a fortune. Wha ya gone do wif all dat money?"

"I dunno. Buy somethin', I reckon. I could buy some food."

"We got food. We catch food."

"I dunno, then. What would you buy?"

"I reckon I dunno how much my wife and child be costin'." I looked at the light of day, at the people on the boats. "We gotta git off'n dis riber. We knows naw dat dey's lookin' fer me."

NIGHT FELL. When we slogged through muddy grass to where we had hidden our boat, we found our canoe gone.

"It's been stole," Huck said.

"What is we gone do?" I said. "I reckon we just gotta move on wif da raft. What other choice we got?"

"I reckon you right, Jim."

There was an unusual amount of traffic on the river that night. We tried to stay out of the lanes, but steamboats and ferries seemed to be everywhere. We bobbed on the wake of a big ship to find another coming in the opposite direction. We didn't have the time or strength to paddle and steer clear. We were caught by the next passing hull. After so much abuse, our raft broke apart.

"Huck!" I watched the boy's head bobbing in the river. Then I got sucked under by the riverboat. I admit that I entertained briefly the thought that I was going to drown to death. Drowning to death always made a person more interesting, but I wanted, at that moment, to be, to remain, as boring as possible. I resurfaced someplace, disoriented, focused only on keeping my head above water and finding a bank. I had lost Huck.

CHAPTER 14

I DIDN'T SO MUCH swim to shore as the river spat me out. Spat me out into a terrible bramble of blackberries. Unripe blackberries, so the insult was complete. I was afraid for Huck, but the situation was hopeless. I couldn't very well roam the land asking about the whereabouts and condition of a white boy, this while being the subject of a manhunt myself. My only solace was that my sack of books and paper had been strapped over my shoulder. Morning came and I crawled into a clearing. I splayed open my books as best I could so the sun could dry the pages.

I fell asleep in that little meadow, the sun shining down on me. I wasn't hidden at all, but I was so tired I couldn't even crawl to hide beneath a shrub. I was also sick with worry over Huck and ashamed to feel such relief for being rid of him. My eyes opened and I could immediately tell that it was late afternoon, as the sun was far across the river. I could also see that I was not alone. Four men sat on the ground near me, observing me. I breathed and felt my body relax as I noted they were black.

The clearly oldest of them was touching my books, seeming to fan out the pages to help them dry.

I looked at them in turn and lay back to stare at the cloudless sky. "Where am I?" I asked.

"You're in Illinois," the old man said.

"So, I'm in a free state?"

The men laughed. "Boy, you're in America," a muscular man said.

The old man put down one of my books. "We're in Illinois, true enough, and Illinois is supposedly a free state, true enough, but the white folks around here tell us we're in Tennessee."

"Maybe they believe it," I said.

"What are we going to do?" the big man asked. "Take a map to the courts and say, 'Look here—we're actually free'?"

A lean, squinty-eyed man stared at me. "Just who are you?"

"My name is Jim. I escaped from upriver. There are people looking for me everywhere, I fear."

Squinty Eyes looked at my books. "What are you doing with these?"

"I stole them, I suppose."

"You can read?" the oldest man asked.

"I can."

"I can read some," the big man said. He reached over and shook my hand. "I'm Josiah."

"Josiah."

"Old George," the old man said.

"Young George," said the younger man, who looked just like Old George.

There was a pause and then the last man, the lean man, said, "Pierre." He seemed suspicious, though I could not think up why he would be worried about me. Perhaps he simply believed that I would bring them trouble and poor luck. As I considered that, I decided that it was a reasonable fear.

Young George had an instrument in his lap. A carved wood neck attached to a gourd with some strings. "Is that a banjo?" I asked.

"I made it," Young George said. "But I dare not play it here. Ain't nobody around, but sound travels, you know? Especially music. People can hear music miles away and then they try to find it."

"Especially music," Old George agreed.

"Especially music," Josiah repeated.

"How far did you come?" Pierre asked.

"Quite far. Hannibal, Missouri."

"That is a long way," Pierre said. "How did you make it so far, with people looking for you and all?"

"I was in a canoe."

"A lone black man on the river like that? Some white man would have shot you dead just for sport."

"Yeah, it's called hunting," Josiah said.

"Josiah has escaped three times and he didn't get ten miles away," Pierre said. "And he can run fast."

I studied Pierre's face. "I didn't run over ground. I drifted down the river. And I did it at night."

Pierre chuckled.

I considered mentioning Huck, but refrained. I'm still not certain why, but at the time I didn't know how to bring it up and doubted whether it mattered anyway.

"Do you know if there's a reward for you?" Josiah asked.

"I know."

"You're going to keep moving, I reckon," Young George said.

I looked around. "A lot of people live around here?"

"Not so you could tell," Old George said. "Some slaves. A few white people. Owner, overseers."

"And those crazy white people," Josiah said.

"The Grangerfords and the Shepherdsons," Young George said, appearing to enjoy the words. "They hate each other. Always killing each other. They don't care how, either. Guns, knives."

"Fine with me," Pierre said. "It's good to have the whites kill whites. The fewer the better."

"I think I'm going to hide out in these woods for a few days," I said. "You think I can do that?"

"If they don't come looking with dogs," Old George said.

"It's the dogs," Josiah said. "Once the dogs are on your scent, you might as well just give up."

"Three times?" I asked.

"No more, though," the big man said. "I'm not running anymore."

"The dogs?" I asked.

"No. The first two times they caught me, brought me back and worked the bully on me." Josiah pulled up his shirt and turned to show me the angry scars on his back. "The third time, they beat me and then some of the others."

"A woman, too," Old George said.

Pierre glanced away when I looked at him.

"I don't want to get any of you in trouble. So you'd best stay clear of me."

"You'll need food," Old George said.

"No, he's right," Pierre said. "If they find out we helped there's no telling what those bastards will do."

"There is telling what they will do," Josiah said. "There's lots of telling what they will do."

I looked at Old George. "They're right. I can fend for myself. I've done it this far—I can keep doing it."

Pierre looked at my books. "What's all this about, anyway?"

"They give me comfort," I said.

"I can understand that," Old George said.

Pierre appeared to soften in that moment. "We'd best get back before they start counting," he said.

"There is one thing I need," I said. I hated to bring it up since I had just told them I didn't want to be a liability.

"What's that?" Pierre asked.

"A pencil."

"What? A pencil?" Pierre looked at the others as if to say, *I told you so.* "What in hell does a slave need a pencil for? You gonna write a letter? Who the hell is a slave going to send a letter to?"

"The president?" Josiah joked.

"I can get you a pencil," Young George said. "Can you really write?"

I nodded.

"Okay," Pierre said. "Young George will get you a pencil." He looked at me. "A pencil."

CHAPTER 15

FORAGING WAS NOT DIFFICULT. I was a slave. I knew how to scratch and claw. And I had accustomed myself to life on the river. Crappies and catfish and berries. No one came by the spot I had chosen as camp. I listened for dogs, but that awful sound never came. Two days passed, and I considered possible strategies for searching for Huck, but none made sense. I read. I never felt more exposed or vulnerable as I did in the light of day with a book open. What if I had been spotted by one of the local plantation's overseers? Or a slave who might have been frightened by the sight? Or a slave who simply wanted to ingratiate himself to his master? There were those slaves who claimed a distinction between good masters and cruel masters. Most of us considered such to be distinction without difference.

I read and read, but I found what I needed was to write. I needed that pencil. I could not keep track of my thoughts. I could not follow my own reasoning after a while. This was perhaps because I couldn't stop reading long enough to make space in my head. I was like a man who had not eaten for a season and had then gorged himself until sick. And my books, once read, were not what I wanted, not what I needed. The so-called self-related story of Venture Smith became more infuriating the more I examined the work, wondering how a five-year-old could have remembered so much detail that made such neat sense. I had already come to understand the tidiness of lies, the lesson learned from the stories told by white people seeking to justify my circumstance. I appreciated Voltaire's notion of tolerance regarding religious difference and I understood, as absorbed as I was, that I was not interested in the content of the work, but its structure, the movement of it, the calling out of logical fallacies. And so, after these books, the Bible itself was the least interesting of all. I could not enter it, did not want to enter it, and then understood that I recognized it as a tool of my enemy. I chose the word *enemy*, and still do, as *oppressor* necessarily supposes a victim.

It was raining lightly at dusk, so the mosquitoes were quieted. A serious relief. And so were the sounds of the woods quieted. I didn't hear the approach of Young George, and he startled me.

"Sorry, Jim," he said.

"It's not your fault. I've become lazy. I have to listen better."

He looked up at the sky and let the rain hit his face.

"What are you doing here?" I asked.

"I brought you something."

Young George dug down into his pocket and came back with a stub of pencil. The pencil sat on his big hand like a small bird.

"Good Lord," I said.

"It's not real big," he said.

"Young George, it's huge. It's amazing. Thank you."

"You're welcome."

"How did you get it?"

"I stole it."

He saw the look of panic on my face. "Young George."

"Nobody saw me."

His smile was truly a child's smile, his joy infectious. "You took an awful risk," I said.

"It was easy. The master was sitting on his porch writing something and a breeze came up and blew his papers all over the place. I was there digging a hole for an azalea and I ran over and helped him with the papers. I pocketed his pencil in the confusion. When he couldn't find it, guess what I did?"

"What?"

"I helped him look for it."

We laughed together.

"And you can *write*. If you can write, you need a pencil. I wish I could. What are you going to say, Jim?"

"I don't know."

"Tell your story," he said.

"What do you mean, Young George? Tell my story? How do you suggest I tell my story?"

He looked at his feet. I did, too. They were bare, his toes grabbing the wet grass. He looked at my face. "Use your ears," he said.

"What's that?"

"Tell the story with your ears. Listen."

"I'll try, Young George."

And he was gone. It was night now. He'd made an impression on me, and though I didn't know what he was asking me to do, I understood his advice to be profound. I also didn't know, had no inkling, what I would write or why I would write it, but I would, as instructed, use my ears.

I held my pencil. It might have been three inches long. It felt like a dense stone in my hand.

DEEP IN THE NIGHT from deep in the forest, I heard the barking and howling of hounds. I pulled myself into an even tighter ball atop the tree roots that had become my bed. There was a mama raccoon that lived in the tree. She had taken to walking past me nonchalantly in the darkness. Tonight she stayed in the tree, high above me, listening to the dogs. We were both animals and we didn't know which of us was the prey. We accepted that we both were. I considered running, leaving my raccoon friend, but in which direction does one run from lightning?

CHAPTER 16

MY NAME IS JAMES. I wish I could tell my story with a sense of history as much as industry. I was sold when I was born and then sold again. My mother's mother was from someplace on the continent of Africa, I had been told or perhaps simply assumed. I cannot claim to any knowledge of that world or those people, whether my people were kings or beggars. I admire those who, at five years of age, like Venture Smith, can remember the clans of their ancestors, their names and the movements of their families through the wrinkles, trenches and chasms of the slave trade. I can tell you that I am a man who is cognizant of his world, a man who has a family, who loves a family, who has been torn from his family, a man who can read and write, a man who will not let his story be self-related, but self-written.

With my pencil, I wrote myself into being. I wrote myself to here. My hiding place had become a safe place, and I stayed for longer than I imagined I would. I didn't know how to set out because I had no plan. A runaway could not use roads or trails, and I had no boat. The men who had first visited me stopped by now and again. Often they would bring me scraps, but it turned out more times than not that I had more food to offer than did they. I had a store of dried fish and I kept berries nearby. Pierre grew less and less suspicious. Old George seemed older. Josiah was again considering trying to escape.

"But I can't stand the idea of them whipping my people," he said.

"But if you make it," Old George said, "no whipping in the world can undo the hope you will give us."

"That's bullshit," Pierre said. "A lashing is a lashing. No thought in the world will stop the bleeding and the scarring. Not even Jim is eager to risk it."

"I don't know how to leave," I said. "The farther I run, the farther I am from my family. I want to come back and buy their freedom."

"You can't do that," Old George said. "You're a runaway. You can't buy anybody's anything if you're strung up from a limb."

"You'd have to get some white man to come buy them," Pierre said. "That doesn't seem likely, does it?"

I agreed with my silence.

"You just have to go north and find a life. God will take care of your family."

We looked at Pierre. He flashed a smile.

"Damn, I thought you'd turned," Old George said.

"Believing would be nice," Josiah said. "But we all be jest slaves."

"You sho nuff be rat," Old George said.

"Oh, Lawdy, Lawd, Lawd," I said.

"What are you going to do?" Young George asked.

"Run," I said.

DURING THOSE DAYS under my tree, I had woven a bag out of flat grass and reeds. I stuffed it with fish and set out. I waited, of course, until dark. Traveling by night had worked so far, river wrecks notwithstanding, and it seemed poor judgment to abandon that strategy now. Night on the land might not have been darker than night on the river, but it was thicker, more oppressive, scarier. Perhaps because the mere act of moving was more of an effort, one carefully measured step at a time. Perhaps because the land is where white people live. I also had to entertain the thought that I missed young Huck. I worried for his safety, felt responsible for him.

Those woods were dense, but I had some moonlight to work with. Half a mile in, I became aware of a familiar sound. It echoed around me. A slap. A crack. I saw firelight in the near distance. The noise drew me closer. Louder as I approached, sick thuds full of bad rhythm and punctuation. I came to a thicket and stared from there.

Slaves were gathered around a large and sad circle. A smattering of white overseers' faces dotted the congregation. A white man stood in the center of it all, a long, coiled bullwhip in his hand. He let go with another thunderous strike. Facing me, tied to a post, was Young George. He grimaced after another lash across his back and settled deeper into the post. The punisher stood nearly ten feet away, dragged the end of his whip through the dirt back toward him.

"Steal a pencil from the master, will you!" the man with

the whip shouted. He struck Young George again. "Do you want me to stop, nigger?" He drew the leather back slowly so that the sound became a part of the torture.

I flinched with Young George. The whip stung me as if it were my back, opened me. I saw Josiah in the crowd in the glow of the fires. He was stoic and stiff, as if trying to give Young George strength, certainly feeling the blows just like me. But our sympathetic suffering was nothing like Young George's. That hurt most.

Young George found my face in the thicket. I had the pencil. It was in my pocket. He was struck again, and I winced. We stared at each other. Young George seemed to smile until the whip found him again. Blood was dripping down his legs. He found my eyes and mouthed the word *Run.*

I did.

CHAPTER 17

I MADE MY WAY through the dark as quietly and as swiftly as I could. My heart couldn't seem to slow to a normal rhythm. Sunrise approached and the worst of my fears pressed against me, that I would not be able to find a place to hide. A place in the light of day removed from human traffic. Part of that problem was that in the dark I couldn't identify frequently used footpaths or animal trails.

I heard yelling. Angry men's voices. I couldn't make out the words. In the midst of the arguing I heard a higher voice, a familiar voice. I got down on my belly. I did not crawl toward the ruckus—it came to me.

"You ain't nothing but horse pucky!" a man shouted. "Damn Shepherdson! Sophia, you step away from Harney!"

"She ain't steppin' nowheres! She and me are gonna git hitched!" Harney yelled.

"Like hell!" the first man said.

"You gotta run, Sophia!" It was Huck's voice, a voice I knew so well. I couldn't see him.

"Ima gonna fill you fulla lead, Grangerford."

"Have at, you lily-livered sheep-fucker!"

"Run, Sophia," Huck screamed.

I saw a young white woman run across the open field and into a stand of trees. Then I spotted Huck crab-running his way across the ground toward me. He was just feet from me when the pistol flashed. I reached out from the bushes and pulled Huck to me. He startled, of course, and tried to fight me off.

"Huck, it's me, Jim," I whispered.

"Jim?"

"Yes."

There were more flashes and deafening pops. The pistol fire stopped as abruptly as it had begun. There were no sounds, no voices in the field. We stood up.

"You reckon they all dead?" Huck asked.

"Sure sounds like it," I said.

The sun was just beginning to rise. We stepped out into the meadow. Four bodies were flat on the ground, splayed out like they were trying to be washed by a rain.

"They're dead, Jim. All of them."

"We've got to get out of here, Huck."

"How'd you find me?" the boy asked.

"Luck. I just happened upon you."

"They're all dead."

I pulled the boy with me toward the trees.

"No, this way," he said.

I followed him the opposite way, through a wall of poplar trees and down a steep hill toward the river.

"Is this a good way?" I asked.

"You ain't gonna believe what I found," Huck said, almost laughing. "You just ain't gonna believe it, Jim."

He was right. I didn't believe it. "Is that our raft?"

"Washed up a couple of days ago. I relashed the logs and fixed her up."

The world was lit by now. "On the river in the daytime?" I thought out loud. I looked back in the direction of the killing. Dead white people in the vicinity of a black man never worked out well for the black man.

"Get on the raft, boy," I said.

We climbed aboard and pushed off into the flow.

"Jim," Huck said.

"What?"

"Why you talking so funny?"

"Whatchu be meanin'?" I was panicking inside.

"You were talkin'—I don't know—you didn't sound like no slave."

"How do a slave sound?"

He stared at me.

"I only knows one way to talk, Huck. Naw you got me scared. What you mean, I sounds funny?"

"You don't now, but I could have sworn you did."

"How 'bout naw, Huck? How does I sound naw?"

"You sound okay now."

"Lawdy, that's good."

Huck cut me another suspicious look.

CHAPTER 18

THE RIVER WAS WIDE down there, nearly a mile and a half in places. On occasion, as we traveled at night, the river was all ours. It was a vast highway to a scary nowhere. The riverboats favored the side far from us and they looked so small as to not appear dangerous at all. Huck told me the story of the feuding Shepherdsons and Grangerfords with much relish, about the ongoing battle between the families, about how he'd been taken in. Exhausted, I listened without much interest.

"That Papa Grangerford was a fine man, Jim. He reminded me of Judge Thatcher a little bit. 'Ceptin' I don't think he ever read no books, but he acted like the sort of man what reads books. You know what I mean?"

"I reckon," I said.

"And that Sophia, she was sho nuff pretty. But she sho had it bad for that Harney Shepherdson. I din't see it myself, what she seen in him."

"Why dey hate each other so much?"

"I dunno. But even I could see that Sophia and that Harney gettin' together weren't gonna come to no good."

"It sho din't," I said.

Huck fell silent.

ONE MORNING, after we'd tied our raft up to branches in stagnant water under a towhead, Huck and I found a sandy beach at the mouth of a creek to swim and perhaps get cleaned up a bit. It was there that we found a canoe. It seemed to have been hidden there for ages, as it was filled with leaves, dirt and spiderwebs. But it floated.

"Can you believe it?" Huck said. "We lose a canoe, we find a canoe. Everythin' evens out, don't it?"

"Sho do," I said.

We cleaned the vessel and Huck said he was ready for a side adventure.

"What say?" I asked.

"I reckon I should take the canoe up this crick a ways and test it out. Wouldn't want to get out on the big ol' Mississip with a bad boat."

I could see that the child in him needed to play. "I reckon you right," I said. "Ima wait heah and tend ta our trotlines."

"Okay, I'll be back."

I helped him shove off. I could see that the business with the warring families had troubled him. Killing is hard to see up close. Especially for a child. To tell the truth, I hadn't seen much killing myself, except that I lived with it daily, the threat, the promise of it. Seeing one lynching was to see ten. Seeing ten was to see a hundred, with that signature posture of death, the angle of the head, the crossing of the feet.

Somewhere along the way my books had again become

soaked and fairly ruined. I tried to let the pages dry as much as possible. The blank places at least left me room to scribble with my prized possession. I studied the small stick that had cost so much. I had no way of knowing whether Young George's beating had stopped short of his death. I knew I owed it to him to write something important. The pencil lead was soft and made a dark mark. I resolved to use it with a light touch to have it last as long as possible. Stamped on it was the name FABER. Perhaps that would be my last name. James Faber. That didn't sound too bad.

I closed my eyes, and when I opened them I saw a gaunt, but not-too-tall, figure walking out of the water toward me. His angular face might have been distinguished, but I reserved such valuations for after I'd heard someone speak.

"If it isn't John Locke," I said.

"James."

I knew I was dead asleep and dreaming, but I didn't know whether John Locke knew that.

"I've been thinking about you," I said. "I've been pondering hypocrisy."

"Don't start up with that now," he said. "It was a job. After I wrote the constitution for Barbados, the Carolinians asked me to write them one, too, and I wrote it."

"What you're saying is that if someone pays you enough, it's okay to abandon what you have claimed to understand as moral and right."

"When you put it that way," he said.

"When I put it that way what?"

"They wanted a constitution that would justify their behavior. If I hadn't written it for them, someone else would have. What in the world would be different if that had happened?"

I looked at him. “You tell me,” I said.

“Some might say that my views on slavery are complex and multifaceted.”

“Convoluted and multifarious.”

“Well reasoned and complicated.”

“Entangled and problematic.”

“Sophisticated and intricate.”

“Labyrinthine and Daedalean.”

“Oh, well played, my dark friend.”

“Jim! Jim!” Huck’s voice split the air.

Locke disappeared back into the water.

Huck paddled up with two white men. I was terrified until I detected the looks of terror on their faces. They were so frightened that they didn’t pause to regard my skin color. Then I heard the dogs.

“C’mon heah, Huck. Let’s tie up dat raft to dis canoe and we kin git.”

The sounds of the dogs had me acting out of fear. Neither of the two visitors leaned in to offer a hand. But quickly enough Huck and I got the boat and raft away from the towhead and into the swift current of the river.

“We best git to da udder side,” I said. “Not so many people on da udder side.”

“You sho is right,” Huck said.

One of the men was old, perhaps seventy, perhaps more. He was wheezing something awful and I suspected he might die. The other man was considerably younger. Both of them squinted in the bright sunlight and finally noticed me.

“You got yerself a slave, eh?” the young man said.

“Jim ain’t my slave, he’s my friend,” Huck said, sternly.

“I see. What’s yer name, boy?”

"Huckleberry, but folks calls me Huck. And this here is Jim."

"Yes, I know," he said. "Your friend."

I was afraid of the men, but I was considerably more afraid of the dogs I'd heard coming our way. I could only imagine that they were after me, and so I was left confused by the presence of these two white men in our boat. Adding to the absurdity was the fact that they were opposite in nearly every way. The older man was very tall and gaunt, while the younger was nearly as short as Huck and fat. The younger had a head full of dark hair. The older was completely bald. Older, bearded. Younger, clean-shaven. Blue-eyed, brown-eyed. They had in common that they were white and shifty-eyed. The old one carried a ripped and soiled carpetbag.

The old one looked at the younger. "What got ya into trouble, friend?"

"I reckon it because of a defective product. I was sellin' this paste what takes the tartar off'n yer teeth. Works real good, too."

"How'd that cause you trouble?" Huck asked.

The younger man sighed. "Turns out it takes the enamel off along with it."

"That ain't no good," I said, without thinking.

The man tossed me an angry look. "I know."

I looked away, realizing that spending time with Huck alone had caused me to relax in a way that was dangerous.

The younger man continued his tale. "If'n I had lit out of there that same day I would have been clear of trouble." He turned to the older man. "That there is my story. What's yours?"

"I was runnin' a little meetin' about the evils of the devil's juice. The revival business is a reliable one and if'n you tap into the disgruntled womenfolk you kin raise a pretty penny."

"So, what happened?"

The older man cleared his throat. He was a talker. "Well, I was rakin' in five or six dollars a night, a dime a head, children and niggers got in free. Then one night, ironically—her name was Penny and she was pretty—she caught me partakin' from my private jug. Then all hell busted loose. They asked of me the impossible."

"What was that?" Huck asked, hanging on every word.

"They asked me to return all their money. I am constitutionally unable to do such a thing. Since that wasn't gonna happen, I ran."

"Least you kept yer take," the younger man said.

"Yep, I've got it right here." That was when the older man discovered the big rip in the bottom of his bag. His head dropped. "I reckon the Lord done seen fit to punish this old sinner."

"Hey, old man," the younger said. "You ever think of workin' with a partner? We could double-team it for a while and see how it goes."

"I don't disagree with the notion. Tell me, just what are you 'bout, possible partner?"

"I'm a journeyman printer and none too good at it, possibly because, though I knows my letters, I cain't connect them in such a way that I kin read. Of late I have done a little in patent medicines. I been a actor, though, again, the readin' reared its head. And I done stabbed at mesmerism and some head-bump readin'."

"Ah, phrenology," the old man said. "That a good 'un."

"What about you, old-timer?"

"I done a lot of doctorin', but people git a bit bent outta shape when you make things worse. Especially when it's significantly worse. Especially when somebody sorta dies. So, I take on now and again to the layin' on of hands. You know, for cancer and paralysis and like that."

"I bet you told a fortune or two in yer day,"

"Yeah, but revivals is my real go-to. I can preach them women right outta their corsets before I take a breath."

I could believe it, I thought, pretending, in slave fashion, not to be there. After being cruel, the most notable white attribute was gullibility. As evidenced by Huck's reaction. He said, "You fellers are amazin'."

"Hardly, boy," said the older man. "Look at how low I done sunk in life, look at the company that the good Lord done left me with. But there ain't no one to blame but my own self. Nothing personal."

"I do take it personal," the younger man said. "But I reckon I might be sayin' the same thing."

"But I said it first, didn't I." The old man looked at the other man and then at Huck, then even at me.

"I will share with you all a secret," the younger man said.

Huck leaned in.

"Do you promise not to whisper what I'm about to tell you to a soul? Not even if somebody offers you a dollar?"

"I promise," Huck said.

He looked at the older man, who nodded.

"What about you, nigger? Kin you keep a secret?"

"I reckon I kin."

"My great-grandfather, the oldest offspring of the Duke of Bridgewater, escaped to this country so that he could be free. He took a wife here and died here. He died about the same time as his daddy and so his younger brother seized the estate and the title. The real duke was forgotten, run over by history, but I am his descendant, and therefore"—he paused—"I am the rightful heir to that title. I am the Duke of Bridgewater."

"Lawdy," Huck said. "A duke. A real duke. Right here on our little raft. You hear that, Jim?"

"I heard it, Huck. Lawdy, Lawd, Lawd."

"How am I supposed to address you?" Huck asked. " 'Your Dukeship'?"

" 'Your Lordship' is customary," the man said.

"The Duke of Bridgewater," Huck said to the air.

"You kin call me Bridgewater," he said to the older man. "What's in a title, anyway?"

"Indeed," the older man said.

Bridgewater gave him a sidelong glance.

"Listen, Bilgewater," the older man said.

"Bridgewater."

"You ain't heard my story yet. You ain't the only one what was birthed with a secret. Mine is even sadder than yourn." The old man looked at each of us in turn.

"What's yer secret, mister?" Huck asked.

"Bilgewater, I know I kin trust the child and the nigger, but kin I trust you with my secret?"

"It's *Bridgewater*, and yes, you kin."

"To the bitter death?"

"Yes."

The old man held his breath for a second, then said, "Child, gentleman, nigger, I am the former Dauphin."

"You are what?" Bridgewater asked.

"Indeed, my friend, it is the truth, sitting here on this raft with you on this mighty Mississippi River is the disappeared

Dauphin. I is Louie the Seventeenth, son of Louie the Sixteenth and Marie Antoinette. I was sneaked out of France in a barrel used for some kind of stinky cheese. I couldn't stand myself for months."

"Lordy," Huck said. "You hear that, Jim?"

"Yes, my friends, I is the rightful King of France."

"Jim?" from Huck.

"I done heard," I said to the boy.

The Dauphin tossed his face into his palms and wept. "Here I is," he said. "So dreadfully far away from my home and don't nobody even call me 'Yer Majesty' or 'Yer Highness.' "

"Don't be too sad, Yer Highness," Huck said. "At least them dogs and temperance people didn't catch up to you."

The old man's tearless face popped out of his hands. "You know, you're right, son. I'm on the loose. In part, thanks to Bilgewater here. Friend, what do you say we tie in together and ply our trade, two royals."

I shared a look with Huck. I suspected he suspected that the Duke and the King were liars, but he was transfixed by the adventure of it all. Regardless, they were with us and we could not easily shed them.

CHAPTER 19

THE MEN INTERROGATED us quite fairly. Where were we from? What was Huck's last name? Did we have any money? Huck had the good sense to not reveal the ten dollars that had been given to him. Then the questions turned to me.

"Is the nigger a runaway?" the Duke asked.

"I done told you he's my friend," Huck said.

"A runaway kin be a friend," the King said.

"Cain't the nigger talk?" the Duke said.

"His name is Jim," Huck said.

"I remember," the Duke said. "You a runaway, boy?"

"Naw, suh."

Huck looked at me. I cast my eyes downriver and then back at him. "What kind of runaway would be headin' south instead of north?" he asked.

"Boy's got a point," the King said. "Of course everyone would be lookin' for a slave to run north. Skidaddlin' south would be the smart move."

"So, he's yer slave?" the Duke asked.

Huck looked at me and I gave a slight nod.

"I guess so. I reckon he is," the boy said. I could see how it caused him pain and discomfort to say it.

"That don't explain what you two doin' on the river," the King said. "A boy and a slave all alone."

I regarded Huck's face and I could see him lean into the whole thing. His eyes brightened and, perhaps inspired by the lies of the men, he started. "My people is from Pike County in Missouri. I was born there. All my family died of some strange plague, all except me, Pa and my little brother, Ike. Pa was poor, 'specially after all them funerals. Did you know you gotta pay a preacher to introduce your dearly departed to that man at the pearly gates? Well, Pa had a bunch of debts to pay off, and once he was done doin' that, all he had left was a few dollars and Jim here."

"That's terrible," said the King.

"Anywho, Pa got him a brother down in Orleans, my uncle Ben. He got a little one-horse farm and Pa figgered we go help him."

"Sounds reasonable," said the Duke.

"I should say," said the King.

"Pa couldn't afford to book us no deck passage on a steamboat, but he struck it lucky one day when he found a raft."

"You mean he stole a raft," the Duke said.

"He found an abandoned raft," Huck said. "Right, Jim?"

"Sho nuff did, Huck. A 'bandoned raft," I said.

"We climbed aboard and set off. I guess we got lazy and just let the river carry us willy-nilly 'cause next thing we knowed, there was a riverboat right on us. It was terrifyin'. That big paddle was just choppin' up that water like yer granny beatin' eggs."

"Lordy," the King said.

"Pa was drunk, like he was always drunk, and I lost sight of him right off. I tried to swim for my little brother, but I got swept under. Last thing I seen before the world went dark was Jim here swimmin' like crazy for lil' Ike."

The Duke looked at me and nodded. "Good nigger," he said. "But you couldn't save the boy, huh?"

"Lawd knows I tried," I said. "Paddle hit me in da head."

Huck cleared his throat. "Jim and I come up clingin' to what was left of our raft. I lost my pa and my baby brother in a flash." He contorted his face and offered what I thought was an unconvincing cry.

It turned out that con men are the easiest people to con. As soon as Huck started into weeping, the two men joined him. Had I been thinking, I might have added my voice to the chorus for effect, but I was more astounded than anything.

"I ain't never heard such a sad story as that in all my dishonest and sneaky days," the King said.

"Poor lil' Mike," the Duke said.

"Ike," Huck corrected him. "Anyway, we took to traveling at night because every time we was out in the daylight somebody would row a skiff out to us and try to take Jim away from me."

"People are the worst, ain't they?" the King said.

"I'm just tryin' to figger a way for us to cover some miles in the daytime. Let me consider it awhile," the Duke said. With that, he leaned back and closed his eyes, let the sun bake his face. "I'll cipher on it a bit."

"You know that sounds like a good use of time. Reckon I will, too," the King said and closed his eyes as well.

When night fell and we'd normally consider setting out, a strong storm came up. Heat lightning flashed low and we decided to rest on the shore and wait it out. No need to get fried. When the lightning let up, we cast off. Our normal sleeping spots on the raft were taken by the Duke and the King. In fact, Their Majesties covered much of the deck of our vessel and left us with little room to find comfort. Huck and I sat close together just under the edge of our roof, not enough cover to keep from getting soaked, but at least our backs remained dry.

The rain ceased in the middle of the night. The royalty stretched and yawned and looked around for food. We shared our dried fish with them as we floated down the river.

"A human person cain't live off this," the King said. "We need real food. Eggs and a rasher of bacon."

"We need money to buy it. We need a town," the Duke said.

"We cain't be goin' into no town," Huck said. "They'll try to take Jim."

"Not if'n I say he belongs to me," the Duke said.

"Nobody will believe you own a slave," the King said. "You don't carry yerself like you rich enough to own a human being."

"And you do?" the Duke asked.

"Why, son, I'm the King of France."

"Well, okay, King, the next time we come to town, we'll set ashore and you kin put on a show fer the people and make us some money. What kin you do?"

"I know the lines of some plays. I kin string somethin' together and you pick up a few things, if'n you catch my drift."

Huck inserted himself into the conversation. "You cain't be telling folks that Jim belongs to you."

"And why not?"

"Causin' he don't. How do I know that once you start sayin' that, you won't try to sell him to somebody?"

The King and the Duke looked at each other.

"I cain't have it," Huck said.

CHAPTER 20

JUST BEFORE DAYBREAK the fires of a little town appeared. The Duke urged us farther toward the middle of the river.

"We'll get south of this little hamlet, then tie up. We'll walk into it and start some business. Sound good, Yer Highness?"

"Indeed, Yer Majesty," said the King.

"We'll wait with the raft," Huck said.

Both men laughed.

"And that will surely be the last we see of you and this nigger," the Duke said. "No, boy, I reckon you two will stay with us."

"He's right," the King said. "You two would be down that ol' Mississip faster than a minnow can swim a dipper."

They watched while Huck and I secured the raft to a stand of willows. I considered tossing a rat snake I saw in the grass onto them, pushing Huck onto the raft and trying to get away, but the water was so shallow for so far out that they would have been able to run us down. That would have created a dynamic in our relationship that would not have boded well for Huck and certainly not for me.

"Tie it good and tight there, nigger," the King said.

"Ya, suh."

"You wouldn't study on escapin', would you, Jim?" the King asked.

"Na, suh."

"Anybody ask, who you belong to?"

"You, suh."

"Very good."

"Are we ready?" the Duke asked.

"Let's go," the King said. "Boy, you and my slave lead the way."

WE DID. We broke brush until we came to an animal path and then we found ourselves on a wagon road. I made sure to look closely at the junction of the road and the path. I didn't want us getting lost trying to find our way back but I didn't want to mark the trail. There was a huge sycamore there that showed rope scars on a thick branch. My heart sank as I thought of Young George.

"What's wrong, Jim?" Huck asked.

"Nuffin," I said.

"I love walkin' on a country road," the King said. "There's just somethin' about it, the air, the openness."

"All roads is the same," the Duke said. "They takes you out and they takes you in and they takes you out agin."

We made our way to the backyards of some houses at the edge of town. There was not a soul to be seen.

"This place is dead," the Duke said. "If I was a different sort of crook I'd just rob me a house or two."

"That wouldn't be good," Huck said.

Then the King spied a man walking down the middle of the street. "Sir, may I trouble you?"

The man looked the King up and down.

"Might you tell me where all the good folks of this town has gone off to? It seems a might overly quiet."

My first fear, as always of late, was that he had heard of my flight.

"That yer nigger?" he asked.

"Why, yes, he is," the King said. "As sorry a slave as you will ever meet, but he's mine. A waste of food and air."

"So, where is everybody?" the Duke asked.

"Everybody at the revival. Some old preacher's aholdin' 'em spellbound with healin' and such. Damn clown, if'n you want my opinion. Gullible fools just bleedin' money into them baskets." He kept his eyes on me.

"I see you're interested in my slave," the King said. "Perhaps you'd like to make me an offer."

"You just said he was sorry."

Huck was about to make a ruckus, but I gave him a look.

"Sorry, but not completely worthless," the King said.

"I don't need no slave. I ain't got no farm. I ain't got no shop. I'm just an old man." With that he appeared to become preoccupied with his own pitiful plight and started away, muttering to himself. "My life ain't worth a hill of shit. Why on earth would I want another mouth to feed?"

"A revival?" The Duke's eyes lit up. "If I may, dear partner, have a play with the crowd we are about to encounter?"

"Though it is my specialty, please, have at it," the King said.

As we walked out toward the edge of town, Huck said to

the King, "You ain't got no right to be talking about selling Jim."

"I suggest you shut up, child."

"How come you ain't got an accent?"

"What say, boy?"

"You don't sound French. Kin you even speak French?"

"I'm not one fer showin' off, boy. I wouldn't want to set a bad example. Besides, French is a very complicated language. Hearing it might cause yer ear a consternation from which you might never recover. So, I employ the language sparingly."

There must have been more than three hundred white people standing out in the sun on a hilltop meadow. Some ladies had brought folding chairs and were seated there knitting or fussing with needlepoint. Some younger folks had paired off and were hiding out in the trees and were kissing and touching. In front of the crowd was a small tent, under which stood a large, heavy-set white man. He was dressed in all white and cut a striking figure there, standing flanked by two much shorter men, also clad in white. The big man's voice boomed. "May we have our next sinner?"

A couple of broken-down women walked another, even more broken-down woman to stand before the big man.

"What ails you, sister?"

"She cain't hardly walk," one of the women said. "A stiff wind kin blow her over like she's a leaf."

"She kin move one leg long and one leg short," the other woman who was holding her said.

"Which leg be the long one, chilluns?" the preacher asked.

The two helping women conferred. "This 'un here," one said, pointing to the woman's right leg.

The big man slapped a giant hand on the ailing woman's head. "Lawd!" He stopped. "What yer name, sister?"

"Jeanette Booth," the woman said.

"Lawd! Jeanette Booth also got herself uneven legs. Jesus, Lawd, God Almighty, Jeanette Booth needs yer spirit to ring through her, to strengthen this body and even out these here mismatched legs. Heal! Jeanette Booth, heal! Accept Jesus the Lord Christ Almighty into yer giant heart."

Jeanette Booth slithered her left foot inches ahead and then tossed her left foot high into the air and brought it down with a thump.

"That's a girl, Jeanette Booth. Take yerself another step. Even it out, sister. Even it on out."

Jeanette Booth walked, short step, long step away from the preacher, then turned to come back. Her right foot reached out and her left foot followed.

People clapped. Some women sang. One man made unintelligible sounds with his mouth and strangely long, flapping tongue. A fat woman fainted.

The smaller, white-clad soldiers of the preacher moved through the crowd with baskets and, just like the old man on the street had described, people parted with their money like they didn't like it.

"Lawdy, this is a gold mine," the Duke said. "Watch me, old man."

"Who do we have here?" the big preacher asked. "Do we yet have another ailing, downtrodden sinner?"

Huck leaned close to me and whispered, "They is all big phonies."

"Sho nuff," I said.

The Duke raised his arms. "No, Reverend, though a sinner,

I am not here as one at this moment. I have been inspired by your meeting here, dazzled, you might say, flabbergasted. It has moved me near to tears. These are indeed good folks assembled here under yer modest tent."

"Why, thank you, stranger," the preacher said.

"I am reminded of the revival what saved my life. It turnt me around, it did." The Duke stood at the front with the preacher, and now the stage was his. "You see, my friends, I used to be the worst of men. I was a pirate."

The crowd gasped.

"A pirate on the high seas, where I stole and killed and did all sorts of other nefarious deeds that decent folks don't talk about."

"Where's yer eyepatch and yer parrot?" someone yelled out, and there was a smattering of laughter.

"Oh, I had me one, brothers and sisters. I had one, right on this here eye, but the Lord, just like He done today fer some of ya'll, He put the sight back in my dead eye." That hushed them all up. "I was a bad, bad man. Then I landed in a revival meeting, just like this one here, exceptin' it was under an enormous tent, a white tent, like a cloud, and I found the Lord God Almighty Jesus Christ, our savior."

"Oh, he's good," Huck whispered.

"Ya gots to give it to him," I whispered back. I looked around to see what effect the Duke was having on the crowd. They were hanging on his every word. Then I noticed something odd, something that I should have noted right away. There weren't any Negroes around. No slaves. Then I remembered that scarred sycamore limb on the road, and I felt fear creep into my belly.

The Duke carried on. "I been to many a place and seen lots

of kinds of folks, heathens and pagans, harlots and whores, card sharks and even some out-and-out devils. At that meeting, under that white cloud of a tent, the Lord Jesus breathed His awesome spirit into my lungs and I put down my lustful, evil ways and determined to devote my life to the conversion of them heathens, pagans, gamblers, whores and devils into good God-fearin', Jesus-lovin', Christian people."

The crowd yipped and applauded.

"Take my nigger over there," the Duke said, pointing at me. "He's a savage from Borneo. I found him there gnawin' on the bones of the poor missionary what preceded me. And look at him now—you can also see the Christian light glowin' all around him. It's probably hard to see in this bright light. Come on up here."

I did as instructed, leaving Huck standing where he was.

The Duke laid his hand atop my head. "Have you ever seed such a light come off a nigger?" he asked. "You'd hardly know he was a slave. That's because he's a slave to the Lord."

It was then that being seen as incidental in the white world paid off, as the Duke forgot my name and introduced me as Caesar. "Caesar here is an example of my good work, the Lord's work. Won't you help me save other heathens, pagans and devils of the world?" He nodded to the King.

The King snapped open a sack and handed it to Huck. "Go on now, boy, and collect the money." Huck took the bag. "And linger," he said to the boy. "Don't be rushin' through them folks—give 'em time to get nervous and to be seed by their neighbors."

The Duke continued. "While you dig deep for whatever you can give, I will have my missionary partner entertain you with a bit of theater from that English feller Shakespeare. I know you heard of him, that songwriter from the old country what writes poems, plays and such like. Mr. Bilgewater?"

The King cut the Duke a hard glance. He stood in front of the crowd and filled his chest with air. The bright light bounced off his bald head. "I reckon I will use it as fish bait," he said, his voice deeper than before. "If it will feed nothin' else, it will feed my revenge. He hath disgraced me and hindered me half a million, laughed at me, mocked my gains, scorned my country, messed up my bargains, cooled my friends and heated up my enemies, and what's his reason? I am a Jew. Hath not a Jew eyes?"

The Duke made a face, leaned in close to the King. "Jew? What are you doin'?" he whispered.

"It's the only speech I got memorized," he whispered back.

"Well, it ain't good."

"I'll try somethin' else," the King said. He cleared his throat and shook his head clear, studied the now-confused audience. "What lady is that over there, what makes rich this knight's hand? Oh, she doth teaches the torches to burn bright in the dark night, her hanging there upon the cheek of night, like a rich jewel in, in somebuddy's ear, beauty too rich fer use, fer earth too dear! So, show a snowy dove—"

Someone shouted out, "Did he say he's a Jew?"

"I reckon that's what I heard," said another.

"You must understand," the Duke said. "Those were lines from a play meant to loose the ropes of your minds."

The big white-dressed preacher stepped back into the front, obviously irritated by the fact that his enterprise had been usurped. He saw his chance to regain control. "But he said quite clearly that he's a Jew."

"No, that's what Shakespeare said," the King said.

"Shakespeare was a Jew?"

"No, Shylock was a Jew."

"Who the hell is Shylock?" the preacher asked.

"He's the fella what says that speech in the play," the King said.

"Were you really a pirate?" the preacher asked the Duke.

It was clear to me that the preacher was immediately sorry he'd opened that door, because the Duke jumped in and attempted to reclaim the crowd.

"There I was, aboard the good ship *Whiskey Mack* with its horrible captain, the wooden-legged Ahab. We had just plundered a Spanish galleon, taken its food and gold and ravished the few women aboard."

The women in the audience gasped.

"I didn't personally, mind you," the Duke said. "As even when I was a heathen, I was a chivalrous gentleman." He made eye contact with a few of the ladies. "In fact, it might be said that it was a woman as much as that revival what brought me back to the fold. Her name was Annie."

A couple of women sat up to listen.

"Okay, that's enough," the preacher said. "This here is my revival."

Huck had made it up to where we stood with the bag full of money. The King took it from him without so much as a glance down.

"O'course, Preacher, Reverend, I apologize, but yer congregation here is such a handsome crowd of folks that I was pulled in by them. I want to thank you all for aiding me in my missionary endeavor."

"That's good," the King whispered.

"Hey," a broad-shouldered man shouted. "That nigger of yourn don't look like he's from Borneo."

"Do you know where Borneo is?" the Duke asked.

"Why, no."

"Neither do I," the Duke said. "This poor nigger does, because that's where he comes from. Ain't that right, Octavius?"

"I thought you said his name was Caesar." This from a woman in the front.

"It is customary for niggers in Borneo to have two, sometimes three names," the King said.

"I don't believe a word of it," the broad-shouldered man said. "I want to have my money back."

Huck sidled up close to me. A strange reaction, because I was the one person who could offer him no protection.

"Liars!" the crowd shouted. "Charlatans!"

"We ain't had a hangin' in a week," a man screamed.

"You always talkin' about hangings," a woman yelled at the man.

"So?" the man shouted back. "These liars deserve it."

CHAPTER 21

FASTER THAN YOU can say Old Ben Franklin, I had Huck running with me toward the buildings of the town. From the sounds of commotion behind us, it was evident that the Duke and the King were making haste as well. I turned and saw that the tent awning had been half ripped down and that it was causing considerable confusion, as it had blown into some of the crowd. By the time we'd reached the edge of town, I could sense that Huck was tiring. Then he leaned away, pulling back on me.

"What is it?" I asked.

The boy had slid to a halt at a storefront, where we observed a poster nailed to the wall. I looked and found a drawing of a black man's face.

"That could be you, Jim," Huck said.

Under the drawing was written RUNAWAY.

"There could be another runaway, right?" Huck asked. "Slaves run away all the time."

"I'se afraid it be me," I said. "Even if'n it not, it look a whol lot lak me."

"There's a three-hundred-dollar reward for you, Jim."

"We gotta git," I said and pulled Huck along. Out of the

corner of my eye I caught a glimpse of the King and Duke pausing at the same poster. I could hardly breathe. My mind fell back to poor Young George strapped there under the whip, back to the three times I had seen slaves hanging in trees, back to the sight of that scarred sycamore branch on the road. I ran head-down, harder, if not faster, and now I was carrying Huck.

I said nothing, just huffed and puffed my way between buildings, trying now to put more space between us and not only the townspeople, but our royal friends as well. I was yet another bounty for them.

"Jim?"

I put the boy down to catch my breath.

"I'm afeared the Duke and the King might look to turn you in fer the reward money. Did you think of that?"

I looked at the boy's eyes and feigned surprise. "You be right, Huck. I thinks dat jest what dey might do."

"I saw them lookin' at that poster."

We were on the same road we had followed into town. We couldn't see or hear anybody behind us.

"You reckon them people caught up to the Duke and King?" Huck asked. "Lawd help 'em if they did."

"I dunno," I said, hoping that they had indeed been snared.

"What will they do to them?"

"We gots to keep movin', Huck."

We made our way down the lane until I spotted the landmark sycamore. I steered us into the woods.

"How do ya know this is the way?" Huck asked.

"I kin feel it."

I ran back to the road and used some brush to cover our tracks. I was fairly certain that neither of the con men had noted our trail junction. It started to rain, lightly at first and then hard enough to make the animal path slick. We slipped and slid downhill toward the river, then searched for our raft. It took a while, but we found it. The Duke had tied one side up with an unsolvable knot. Huck couldn't get it undone so I started working at it.

Then we heard angry shouting and screaming in the woods. I turned around and untied the raft end of the knot. I pulled Huck aboard and pushed us out until I was waist-deep. We were well out into the flow when the Duke and the King shouted for us from the bank to come back.

"Should we save them, Jim?"

The boy was so innocent.

"Huck, I reckon if'n we save 'em, dey gonna turn me in. What you think?"

The boy studied on that for a spell. "I reckon you're right. But what will them folks do to them?"

"I don't know, Huck. Maybe dey jest pay a fine. Maybe dey get tarred and feathered. I don't know."

"That seems right awful."

"I s'pose it do. But dey was stealin' from dem folk. Tellin' lies lak dey was. He weren't neber no pirate."

"Yes, but them people liked it, Jim. Did you see their faces? They had to know them was lies, but they wanted to believe. What do you make of that?"

"Folks be funny lak dat. Dey takes the lies dey want and throws away the truths dat scares 'em."

The river put its full pull on us and we watched the men grow smaller.

"I reckon I do that, too," the boy said.

"What say?"

"I kin see how much you miss yer family and yet I don't think about it. I forget that you feel things jest like I feel. I know you love them."

"Thank you, Huck."

THE RAIN MADE US less nervous to be on the river in daylight, and soon it was dusk. The rain stopped and we stripped down to dry our clothes.

"I knowed yer mother, Huck."

"You did?"

"Yes, she were real nice. It was sad when she died. She din't know you long, but she loved ya. You should know dat."

Huck didn't say anything.

"Just thunk you should know."

"Was she pretty?" he asked.

"I dunno. I reckon. It's a scary thing for a slave to think such things."

"Why is that?"

"Jest the way the world is."

"You think this here river is pretty?" Huck asked.

"I reckon I do," I said.

"Then why you cain't say if my mama was pretty?"

"River ain't a white woman."

"What about Sadie, yer wife? She's pretty. You think she's pretty."

"I do, but, Huck, I'm a slave. You don't neber forget dat. I ain't no nigger, but I is a slave."

After some quiet: "Was she nice? You kin say whether she was nice."

"She was nice, Huck. We was young 'uns."

"Was you friends?"

"Looky dere," I said.

"Lawdy."

Across the river, a steamboat was on fire. Flames leaped high into the sky. People jumped off the decks into the river. Small boats circled, pulling people in. If there was screaming, the wind carried it away onto the far shore and we heard none of it, so it played out like a sort of weird dream. A man on fire hurled himself from the upper deck and fell like a firework into the water.

CHAPTER 22

WHEN PASSING SOUTH between Missouri and Illinois, before meeting the Ohio River, the Mississippi makes a couple of massive bends so that at one point she's actually heading slightly northwest, then loops back around and heads south again. All I really wanted was the Ohio. Now that traveling south had failed to throw off pursuers, I needed to get to the Ohio to travel north. Traveling only at night made going slow. Somebody riding the current day and night could travel twice as fast. Another way to say it would be that the King and the Duke could cover the same distance in half the time. I point out this fact because that is precisely what happened.

We concealed ourselves and slept under the sun and we came out of our daytime hide to find the Duke and the King sitting on our raft, waiting for us.

"If it ain't Hucklelarry and his nigger," the Duke said.

"That's Huckle*berry*. How did you get here?" Huck asked.

"We're thieves," the King said. "We stole a boat." He pointed to a skiff tied up to some willows down the bank.

Seeing them there was like a bad dream. It was as if they

had appeared out of thin air. They were so assured and pleased with themselves.

"How did you get away from that mob?" Huck asked.

"Oh, we ducked into a shop and waited 'em out," the Duke said.

"Always pays to wait," the King added.

"What he said." The Duke looked up the hill that was behind us. "I wouldn't think 'bout makin' a run fer it. There's a road up'n that way and I might start shoutin' 'runaway.' " He pulled a paper out of his pocket and unfolded it, showed Huck and me my picture. "*Runaway.* That's such an ugly word. Ain't it, Dolphin."

"That's Dauphin, *Dough*-fan, Bilgewater."

"That's Bridgewater." The Duke looked at me. "Anyway, the King and I have come up with a new business."

"What's that?" Huck asked.

"We goin' into the slave-sellin' business," the Duke said.

They smiled. "It's beautiful. See, we sell ol' Caesar here. He escapes and we sells him again. He's already a runaway, so it should make no never mind to ya'll. He ain't worth much dead. They cain't lynch you but once, but we kin sell you a bunch of times."

"It's genius and I come up with it," the Duke said.

"Actually, it was my idear," the King said.

"You couldn't come up with a good idear if ya et one. You ain't come up with a good idear in yer life."

"You ain't knowed me but for a couple o' days," the King said.

"And in all that time."

"Listen, Bilgewater . . ."

I gave Huck a nudge and we started to try to slide-step our

way out of their reach, but the Duke saw us and shook his head. "Don't even think about it."

"He don't belong to you," Huck said. "He's my slave. He don't belong to neither one of you."

"See, boy, you're a minor and there's a state law that says a minor cain't own no slave," the Duke said.

"And our story was that he be belongin' to me," the King said. "That's the story we come up with and you din't stick to it. Nothing worse than fellas won't stick to a story. The nigger was supposed to be mine if'n anyone asked. So, he belong to me. Possession is nine-tenths of the law."

"What's that mean?" Huck said.

"Story goes that I own Caesar, so, in real life, I own Caesar."

"Anyway, he run from us and we cain't have that," the Duke said. He took off his leather belt. I, of course, saw this as a bad sign and instinctively took a step back. "See, he be at it again. I guess it's just his nature to run. Well, you ain't runnin' from this. Pull down them britches, nigger."

"He will not," Huck cried and jumped in front of me.

The Duke slapped Huck away so that he landed awkwardly and cried out. I moved to him, but the King blocked me.

"I see," the Duke said, smiled. "Tell you what, I kin beat you or I kin beat the boy. How will you have it, nigger?"

"You kin whoop me," I said. "But I ain't droppin' my draws."

"What did you say?"

"I say I ain't droppin' my draws."

The Duke swung his belt and caught me at my knees. It did hurt. He laughed and did it again. I didn't wince.

"You see that?" the King said. "I say, did you see that? They don't even feel like no human man."

"He feels it," the Duke said. He hit me again. Again. Ten times or so around my thighs. I felt my flesh tear. It was a burning pain that brought me to the ground on my knees. The Duke had worked up a sweat. Huck was crying.

"Don't tear him up too much," the King said. "We gotta be able to sell him. We cain't get a dime fer him if'n he's torn all asunder."

"Hell, man," the Duke said. "He ain't no proper people. He don't feel pain like we do. He need a lesson he kin remember. Nextwise, he'll get it into his head to run again. That's the way these creatures is built."

"Stop it," Huck cried.

"There might be a little left over for you, boy," the Duke said.

Huck caught my eyes telling him to back away.

CHAPTER 23

We didn't travel that day, as the river was choppy and wild. The King claimed he was bound to be sick on such a rough sea. The Duke and the King sprawled out in comfort while Huck and I caught a mess of fish. The two men sat out in the open, unafraid of being seen. That was new to me and Huck. A boy and a Negro attracted suspicion, but grown white men and a Negro, that was normal.

Huck and I were hauling in catfish while those two yakked. "I ain't never seen two fellas talk so much and say so little," Huck said.

"You be almos' thinkin' dey be preachers," I said.

"You know what I could go fer, Bilgewater?"

"What's that, Dolphin?"

"A taste. Oh, I know I was preachin' temperance to them fine ladies in Illinois, but there ain't nothin' wrong with that nice, warm feelin' that only a big round jug of corn licker kin give ya."

"As much as it pains me to agree with ya, on sheer principle, I has to agree with ya. Next town we find, into the saloon we go," the Duke said.

"Next town. That's a funny one and good fer our plan. There be a town near here that's half in Missoura and half in Illinois. So, they don't know whether they's a'comin' or goin'. I reckon we can sell the nigger on one side of town and help him escape to the other."

"Sounds like my kind of town. I wish I had me a seegar."

The King hummed, then said, "If'n my blood was whisky and my nose a seegar, I'd run my whole life and never get far."

"If the ladies would love me as much as I them, I would, I would . . . I cain't remember the rest," the Duke said.

"Too bad," said the King. "Started like a good 'un."

"How you figger this town will be good for our con?" asked the Duke.

The King pretended to draw with his imaginary cigar.

"Put another catfish on the fire," the King said. He stared at me.

I looked away from his eyes. "There's something about you, Caesar," he said.

"His name is Jim," Huck said.

"Whatever." The King waved a dismissive hand. "Caesar, Jim, April, Boyboy, Mandingo, don't make no diff'ence. Tell you what, though, you run and you get worse than last time. Somethin' about you," he said again.

WE WALKED A LONG WAYS to the outskirts of a town. Slaves, mostly women and children, dug potatoes out of the dirt and tossed them into sacks. I watched a small old woman trying to drag a bag as big as she was over the rows. It was sad that the sight of them caused me to relax, as if that picture were the reality that was normal. I realized that I was limping from the beating my legs had taken from the Duke. He walked slightly behind me while the King led the way.

"Don't gimp it," the Duke said. "Boy, I'm talkin' to ya."

I looked back at him. "Suh?"

"Walk straight. Don't be limpin'. How I am s'posed to get a good price for a crippled nigger?"

I tried to walk evenly.

The King waved his arm. "All the town on the south side of this road is Missoura. Looks the same, but taint. I reckon we could run a couple of games at the same time in this here town. I could tell fortunes, maybe."

"That's always a good one," the Duke said. "Don't do that speech again. Either one of them."

We stopped outside a tavern. There was out-of-tune piano music playing inside. The Duke gave Huck a little slap on the face. "Listen, boy, we're gonna have ourselves a little libation and you and the nigger are gone wait right here. Not down there." He pointed. "Not over there. But here." He looked at both of us. "Where will you be?"

"Right here," Huck said.

" 'Cause if you ain't here Ima gone to show you that there's somethin' to fear other than death. Ya'll understand?"

"We understand," Huck said.

"Dolphin, let's go."

They stepped into the saloon. Huck looked at me. "Do we run?"

"I reckon if'n we run they gone catch us and beat you and hang me." I looked up and down the dusty and forlorn street. "Wif ma leg lak dis, I cain't run but so fast. Dat was a long hike from da riber."

"We could just run to the other side of town," Huck said.

"Dat don't matter none, Huck. Free state, slave state. Ain't no diff'ence one side ta other."

"I don't much like them," Huck said.

"Me, neither," I said.

WE SAT in our assigned seats for a long time, off to the side of the saloon, down on a step to an alley. A couple of men walked into the bar, but none troubled us a look or even seemed to notice us.

"What happens if'n they sell you and you cain't get back?" Huck asked. "What do we do then?"

"Den I belongs to some other white folk. Maybe dey beat me, maybe dey don't. Not like my life gone be dat diff'ent."

"I don't like it," the boy said.

I shrugged. I thought on our situation. "If we could find out a shortcut to da riber, den maybe we could git away."

"How we gonna find that out?" he asked.

"I s'pose you could jest ax sumbuddy," I said.

"I could, couldn't I."

Just as we were pondering that, a man came from the bar. He leaned against the wall and stared blankly at us. He was drunk.

"Hey, you're a nigger," the man said. "Why you ain't diggin' taters?" He hiccuped. "Make sense, though. Even niggers got a right to sit and rest." He laughed. "That ain't true."

I nudged Huck.

Huck looked at me and then at the drunk man and slowly came to understand. "Hey, mister."

"Yes, young man?"

"Kin you tell me the fastest way to the Mississippi?"

"The Mississippi River," the man said. "The Big Muddy, the Big River, Ol' Man River, Old Blue. What you goin' do with a river, son? It's wet and big and deep. That's where I lost my wife and my money on a riverboat called the *Chester.* The Mississippi River. Who wants the river?"

"I do," Huck said.

"The Gathering of Waters. The Mississippi. Who wants to know?"

"I do, mister."

"Is that yer slave?" the man asked.

"Yes," said Huck. "The river. Which way is it?"

"What ya want with it?"

"We wanna go catch us a mess of catfish."

The man closed his eyes and tilted back his head. "Hmmm, catfish. That sho sounds good. I know how to cook 'em up jest right, too. You bring me some catfish and I sho will fry 'em up for ya. I like to fry 'em in old bacon grease. That sound good to you?"

"Which way is it, mister?"

"Which way is what?"

"The river, the Mississippi."

"You gotta knife? You gonna need a knife to clean 'em."

"Yes, I got a knife," Huck said. "Please, mister, which way?"

The drunk man pointed north, but said nothing.

"S'pose we takes da short way to da riber? Wifout dat raft, dey ain't much fer us to do when we get dere," I said.

"We could steal a boat," Huck said.

I personally didn't have a problem with stealing a boat if it was going to get me away from these men and up the Ohio, but I knew it was unlikely. If I was caught, it would be the end of a rope for me. The warped wooden steps were making my butt numb.

"I hate just sittin' here," Huck said.

The drunk man came to. "So, you want the river."

Huck and I looked up at him.

"Yes, it's that way." He pointed north again. "And it be that way." He pointed east. "And that way." West. "Come to think of it, the only way to miss it is that way." He pointed south, but his finger was against the wall of the tavern. " 'Course I don't mean in this here saloon."

"I understand."

"The Grandaddy of Waters."

"Yes, sir."

The man turned, leaned against the wall and started snoring.

"Is he asleep?" Huck asked.

"I reckon he is," I said. "If'n we was gonna run anyways it should be back da way we come. Dat's whar our raft might be."

"Like you said, that's a long way, Jim."

"Yeah, but we don't know how fer the riber be dat way or dat way or dat way. Dat white man weren't no help, but he made dat clear. A distance you know is shorter den one you don't."

"I reckon that's right," Huck said. He looked at the sleeping man. "Jim, I'm thinkin' I ain't got no runnin' left in me today."

"Ain't dat da truth."

I reached down and felt the injuries on my legs. My pants were sticking to the blood and making the wounds burn. I didn't express my thoughts to him, but I knew I could run. I could always run. But running and escaping were not the same thing. I could be like Josiah and run and end up back where I started, again and again. As it stood, I had no plan, but it was clear that I needed one. I had to ask myself and answer honestly, *How much do I want to be free?* And I couldn't lose sight of my goal of freeing my family. What would freedom be without them?

CHAPTER 24

HUCK AND I dozed off sitting there on those boards. With a little rest I felt even more like running, and had Huck's head not been resting on my shoulder, pinning me down, as it were, I might have lit out without him. Before I could consider that further, the saloon doors sprang open and out came the Duke and the King.

"Looky," said the Duke. "Nappy time."

"A nigger nap, slave slumber," said the King in an exaggerated Shakespearean accent. "Chattel coma." He was drunk and proud of his wordplay.

"Shut up," the Duke said. "Barkeep said there's some rooms up the road."

"What about them?" the King asked, pointing to us.

"Livery. We'll take them to the livery."

The Duke led the way down the middle of the street. It was dark now. A few lamps burned in windows. We found the livery at the other side of town. The King rang the bell and an old black man came out.

"Where's the blacksmith?" the Duke asked.

"I'se the blacksmith," the man said.

"What's yer name, boy?"

The man rubbed his eyes and said, "My name be Easter."

"Were you born on Christmas?"

"Nah, suh. I'se born on Easter."

The King and the Duke laughed.

"You got a shackle and a chain in here?" the Duke asked.

"I does."

"Well, slap 'em on my slave here so we kin go git some sleep."

The old man looked at me, and I nodded to him with my eyes. I could feel Huck watching our interaction. "You ain't got to chain him up. Jim won't run nowhere."

"He definitely won't if'n he's chained," the King said.

"Lock him up and give me the key," the Duke said.

The old man left us to find what he needed.

"You got something to say, nigger?" the Duke asked me.

"Nawsuh," I said.

"Good."

Easter came back. "Whar you wan it, suh?"

"Slap it on his leg there. The bloody one."

"Yessuh." Easter knelt down and put the metal device around my ankle. It was a nostalgic terror that I felt. I couldn't remember when I had last been shackled, but my body recognized the feeling. If ever I was ready to run, it was right then.

Huck was trembling. "Don't do this."

"The key." The Duke held out his hand and Easter dropped the key into it. The Duke stuffed the key into the little pocket of his waistcoat.

"Nighty night," the King said.

Huck was fit to be tied as they walked away. I held him back by his shoulder. Easter observed this.

"I sho is sorry," Easter said.

I nodded.

"I hate them," Huck said.

Easter looked at me and gave a questioning nod toward Huck.

"He okay," I said.

Easter reached into his pocket and pulled out a key. "You'll prolly sleep better widdout dis chain."

Huck laughed. "Two keys?"

"I got fitty key dat fit dat lock. Ya'll go ov'r dere and sleep on dat hay. I lock ya up 'gin in da mornin'."

"Thank you, Easter," Huck said.

The old man smiled. " 'Magine dat, white person say thankya to a slave. Haw, haw. What'll be the next thin'."

" 'Magine dat," I said.

Huck and I walked over to the pile of hay. We were near dead, but thankfully not dead. In no time, the boy was fast asleep. I was as exhausted as he was, but I couldn't sleep a wink. All I could think about was running.

"You won't outrun anyone with that leg," Easter said.

"You're right about that," I said. I leaned over to look at Huck's face. "He's sound asleep."

"What's your name?"

"Jim," I said.

"Pleased to know you."

"Same. Thank you for your help."

Easter shrugged. "We does wat we need to does."

We laughed.

"Tell me, Jim, what's this boy to you?"

"He's my friend," I said. It felt strange to say and must have been stranger to hear. "He's trying to help me escape."

Easter regarded Huck. "Hmmm."

"What?"

"White boy?"

"Excuse me?"

"Is he white?" Easter asked.

"Look at him."

"I see a lot of things in that face. I see—"

"Do you have water?"

"Bucket's over there."

I got up and walked over to the barrel of water. I splashed my face and drank some from my cupped hands. I looked past the barn doors at the dark road that led out of town, then went back to my bed of hay.

"Don't mind me," Easter said. "Just know that white folks don't see like we do. They can't or they don't want to."

I nodded.

"I'm putting the lantern out now," the old man said.

"Okay, Easter."

He put out the light and walked away into the back of the livery. Huck stirred beside me.

"Is Easter gone?" he asked.

"Yeah, he be gone."

Huck sat up.

"You don't trust me, do you, Jim?"

" 'Course I trusts ya, Huck. Why you say dat?"

"I was listening to you and Easter talkin'. You weren't talkin' like you talk to me."

I said nothing.

"Why is that, Jim? I thought we was friends. I thought you trusted me."

"I does trust you, Huck. Cain't you see dat? I trusts you wif my life."

"I'm going back to sleep," the boy said. "Just one thing?"

"Yeah, Huck?"

"I understand why you talk the way you do."

"What do you mean?" I asked.

"I mean it makes sense."

I studied his face. He was talking with his eyes closed, as much fighting sleep as losing to it. There was a lot of this in that face. "You be a smart boy, Huck."

"Goodnight, Jim."

"Goodnight, Huck."

CHAPTER 25

"WHAT IN TARNATION!" A voice split my sleep like a bad dream. It was the Duke. He was standing over me as I lay in the hay. The King was behind him. "What that old nigger's name?" he asked.

"Easter," the King said.

"Easter!" the Duke shouted. "Easter, git yer black ass in here!"

"Easter!" The King called him, too.

Easter shuffled in. "Suh?"

"What you know about this?" the Duke asked.

"Lawdy," Easter said. "How did he git aloosened?"

"I'm askin' you that," the Duke said.

"I did it," Huck said. "I couldn't let Jim sleep all chained up like that."

"How'd you git it off him?" the King asked.

"It just slipped off."

"Then it weren't put on good, was it now, Easter?"

"You seen me put it on 'im, suh."

The Duke grabbed a buggy whip from a nail on a post.

"But he didn't run," Huck said.

I could see in the Duke's eyes that I was not his target this time. I looked at Easter and saw the fear in his eyes.

"No," I said.

The Duke looked at me. The King looked at me. Huck looked at me. But mostly Easter looked at me. I had said *no.* The Duke appeared to forget about Easter and laid his stare into me. "Boy, this here gonna be a real one. King, tie this slave to that thar post."

The King looked around for a length of rope.

But the Duke had not forgotten Easter. The whip's crack pierced the room and Easter fell to the ground. The leather had caught him around his chest and upper arm. His thin skin gave up blood immediately.

"What the hell!" another voice rang out. "Easter!" A man had come into the livery and knelt by the fallen slave. "Who hit this man?"

"I did," the Duke said.

The man was big and white, white hair and white beard, all white. "Easter is my slave," he said. "Who are you to hit him." He snatched the whip away from the Duke and glared at him. The big man hovered over him.

I saw the fear in the Duke's face and I have to admit I enjoyed it. His eyes could have been Easter's. The King had retreated a few steps.

"He let our slave go in the night," the Duke said.

"This here slave?" the man asked, pointing at me.

"He's the one."

"But he's right here. He didn't run nowhere."

"Jim ain't his slave," Huck said. "He belongs to me."

"You're just a child," said the big man.

"Don't listen to that boy," the Duke said. "He's teched. He thinks he's friends with this nigger."

The white-bearded man shook his head, perhaps angry,

perhaps confused. "All I know is that you was beating my Easter. You ain't got the right."

"I'm sorry, Mr.—"

"Wiley."

"Mr. Wiley."

"You okay, Easter?" Wiley asked. He peeled back the man's shirt and looked at the wound. "That ain't no good," he said. "That ain't no good at all. How is my man supposed to work now? Tell me. Are you a farrier?"

The Duke said he wasn't.

"This here slave know anything about blacksmithin'?" Wiley asked.

"Jim can do anythin'," Huck said.

"That true?" Wiley asked, looking at me.

"I reckon I kin shoe a hoss," I said.

"Kin you forge a shoe?"

"I reckon I kin."

"But you see, we jest passin' through," the King said from his distance.

"Well, you fellas and the boy is welcome to keep passin' on through. You kin go where you want, but this nigger here will be workin' until I don't need him."

"I don't think so," the Duke said.

"We kin let the sheriff sort it," Wiley said.

"I shouldn't have hit yer property," the Duke said, looking at Easter. "I'm dreadful sorry about that. We got some business next town over. We'll take care of it and come back for our slave."

Wiley nodded.

The Duke cut me a hard look like all of it was my fault. "We'll be back," he said. Then he mouthed, "Don't run."

Huck came and stood next to me.

"What do you think you're doin'?" Wiley asked Huck.

"I'm staying with Jim."

"I'll say you're not," Wiley said. "You'll be goin' with them."

"I don't even know them," Huck said.

"Why of course you know yer ol' uncle," the Duke said to Huck. "Let's not play this game agin." He grabbed Huck by the arm. "You'll be acomin' with us."

Wiley helped old Easter up in a tender fashion that caught my eye. The Duke leaned into me and whispered in an evil tone, "We got this boy here, so I don't 'spect you'll be running off."

CHAPTER 26

THE THREE OF THEM, men and boy, disappeared down the road and around a bend. The extreme brightness of the morning felt incongruous with all that had just transpired. Huck and I had been violently separated, an event that was inevitable, but it was, nonetheless, jarring and unreal. And I was now, temporarily or not, the possession of yet another white person. I didn't know where my new owner lived, only that he possessed at least one other person, and that I was expected to make iron shoes and nail them onto horses.

Wiley glared at me and then slapped me on my back like a chum. "Hey, work good and I treat you good. Right, Easter?"

"Dat sho is raght, Massa Wiley," Easter said.

"I'm gonna git me some breakfast," Wiley said. As he walked away, he said to the air, "That's the easiest slave I ever got."

I looked at Easter.

"He's right. If he didn't own slaves I'd like to think that old Wiley was a decent fellow."

"If," I said.

"What's the story with you and your boy? Did you teach him how to pass?"

"What?"

"How to pass," Easter said.

"Pass? Easter, that boy's whiter than Wiley."

Easter smiled at me. "The boy doesn't know?"

"Doesn't know what?" I asked. "I knew both of his parents."

Easter shook his head. He winced as his new laceration caused him some pain. He traced it with his finger.

"Are you all right?"

Easter laughed. "What if I'm not? What's going to change? What are you going to do about it? What would *all right* look like?"

His point was well taken.

"What am I supposed to do here?" I asked. I looked around at the anvil and the steel rods.

"You're supposed to make three sets of shoes before sundown. That's twelve shoes. A lot of work. You don't know the first thing about blacksmithing, do you?"

"Not one damn thing."

"Well, I'll talk you through it. First, get that fire going real good and get a bunch of that coal into it, get it good and hot, hell-hot." He pointed to the bellows and told me to pump it. "When the coals are glowing red, shove a rod into them and get it red-hot, too. It will take a while."

While we waited, I sweated. The heat from the fire was intense and unrelenting, but distracted me from my worrying about Huck.

"There was a lynching upriver," Easter said.

"I'm sorry to hear that," I said.

"Guess what it was for?"

I wasn't going to guess and Easter didn't expect me to. I raked my brow with my forearm and looked at him.

"A pencil."

An ice-cold spear hit the back of my stomach. "A what?"

"A pencil. Can you believe that? A slave was accused of stealing a damn pencil and they hanged him dead for it. They didn't even find the pencil on him. What's a slave need a pencil for? Can you believe that?"

"It's hard to believe, all right." I could feel the pencil in my pocket. I was taken then by the fact that I thought of it as *the* pencil and not *my* pencil.

"It's a horrible world. White people try to tell us that everything will be just fine when we go to heaven. My question is, Will they be there? If so, I might make other arrangements." Easter laughed.

I laughed with him.

"And they named you Easter."

I looked at all the work there was to do. "This will take some time," I said. "That's good."

"White folks watch us work and forget how long we're left alone in our heads. Working and waiting."

I smiled. "If only they knew the danger in that."

"I don't believe they even know we talk to each other," Easter said.

"They can't accept it. They won't accept it. And they're always surprised. You hear about that Denmark Vesey? He almost took over there in South Carolina. Had guns and organization."

"What happened?"

"Hanged him. Of course, they hanged him. Found out his plans and hanged him," I said.

"How did they find out?" Easter looked at the door as if for Wiley.

I looked at Easter's face. "My people, my people."

"Think those men gonna come back for you?"

"I don't know." The rod in the fire was starting to glow. "Easter, if I was to run away, what do you think Wiley would do?"

"I don't know," the old man said. "He's got some dogs, but they're fat and lazy. I don't think they could track each other home."

"Maybe he wouldn't chase me. It's a lot of work chasing a man. I mean, I'm not even his property. Legally."

"I don't know. I don't know if that's how he thinks about it. I do know that if he saw you trying to run, he'd shoot you deader than dead in a heartbeat. He's known to shoot first and ask questions later."

"I don't like hearing that."

"He cares about what work gets done. Since I can't work the bellows or swing the hammer, he's going to be mad. If you can get those shoes done, then maybe he won't care so much when you run off."

"Or he'll like my work and decide I'm a good slave to hang on to," I said.

"Well, there's that."

"The end of this rod is red," I said.

"Good. Now put it over the fat, round part of the anvil and bang it with that hammer into a horseshoe shape."

"Like this?" I pounded the hot steel with the heavy hammer. The strikes against the anvil rang with a not-unpleasant music.

"Let the hammer bounce," Easter said. "It will feel good."

I followed his instruction. The bouncing somehow made

the hammer lighter, or at least provided a rhythm that urged me to the next blow. Soon it was the familiar semicircular shape.

"Stick it back in the fire," Easter said.

I did.

"Get it real hot and then you'll snap off the shoe."

"Sounds simple when you say it."

"How many folks know?" Easter asked.

"Know what?"

Easter smiled and shook his head, scratched it. "Use the bellows to make the fire hotter. It doesn't take that much to see it."

"Easter, I'm trying to make a horseshoe. Are you going to help me?"

"Of course, brother."

Easter guided me and I listened.

"Easter, do you remember when you first arrived here?"

"Here with Wiley or here in hell?"

"Hell."

"I don't remember much of my home, but I remember the ship. I remember the abuse. I remember the splashing. You?"

"Born in hell. Sold before my mother could hold me."

"You're not holding the hammer square," Easter said.

"Sorry."

"If you're not making mistakes, you're not learning."

THE SHOE NOW FORMED, I held it with long tongs. I appreciated what strength Easter must have had in his hands. I dropped the shoe into the quenching bucket. I had come to like the sound and the steam. I pounded it some more, the strikes reverberating through my arm and body, before sticking it back into the fire.

"Heating and cooling it like that will harden the steel," Easter said.

"Metaphor," I said.

"That's nearly all we have," Easter said.

I reached into my pocket and pulled out the pencil, showed it to Easter.

"Well, I'll be damned," he said.

"Young George stole it for me," I said.

"You can write." It was not a question or an accusation, more a discovery, perhaps a call to duty.

"I can write," I said.

"Then you had best write."

"I will," I said.

IT WAS MIDMORNING and I was still at work on the first shoe. Wiley came into the livery and looked at me. "How's this boy doin'?" he asked Easter.

"He knows a lil' sumptin'," Easter said.

I was drenched in sweat. Strangely, it felt as if I were having a good cleansing. I pounded the steel, finding the rhythm that Easter had taught me.

"Sing for me," Wiley said.

I looked at Easter. The old man nodded to me and started to sing.

Won't you ring, old hammer?
Hammer ring!

Won't you ring, old hammer?
Hammer ring!

Wiley looked at me and I joined Easter.

Broke dat handle on my hammer!
Hammer ring!
Broke dat handle on my hammer!
Hammer ring!

As much as I hated the idea of singing for Wiley, the song made the work easier, and I liked our sounds bouncing off the stable walls. I found myself singing harder, glancing at Easter and finding the song more pleasant for a shared irony.

Got to hammerin' in da Bible!
Hammer ring!
Got to hammerin' in the Bible!
Hammer ring!

"This slave kin sho nuff sing," Wiley said, looking at me.

"He certainly can," came a voice from behind Wiley.

There stood a short white man with perhaps ten more white men of varying sizes and shapes holding black cases of varying sizes and shapes. They were dressed alike in dark suits that made me hot just looking at them.

"And who are you?" Wiley asked.

"My name is Daniel Decatur Emmett. And we are the Virginia Minstrels."

CHAPTER 27

"STOP SINGIN', keep hammerin'," Wiley said. He turned to Daniel Decatur Emmett. "What are you fellas all goin' on about?"

"We're the Virginia Minstrels. We're musicians. We're playing at the town hall." Emmett handed Wiley some cards. "Here—tickets to our performance."

Wiley looked at the tickets.

"I came in here because of that slave's exquisite voice. You see, we've lost our tenor and that boy's voice is just perfect."

"What do you mean you lost your tenor?" Wiley asked.

"I mean, we simply can't find him. We were riding the train and it seems very likely that he, being drunk, not an unknown condition to him, fell off or out, however one dismounts a moving train."

"I see."

"As I was saying, your slave has a lovely voice. It is a better voice than our lost tenor's. His name was Raleigh Nuggets, but that hardly matters now, to us, you, and possibly him."

"And you call yerselves the Virginia Minstrels?" Wiley asked.

All of the men leaned toward a common point and hummed a chord that sounded quite lovely.

"How much?" Emmett asked.

"How much what?" Wiley asked.

"For your slave here. The one that can sing."

Wiley was thrown by the question. He must have considered the fact that, technically, I was not his property to sell. He had no bill of sale. But also he must have been thinking I was, in fact, in his possession and, as I had just heard and learned, possession was nine-tenths of the law. "You want to buy Jim, here?"

"If that's his name, yes."

Wiley looked at me. He was basically honest, his practice of owning people notwithstanding. But before he could say whatever he was going to say next, Emmett stopped him with a hand.

"Hear me out, my good friend. An excellent tenor is especially hard to come by. Believe it or not, I can find bass voices in every town. I'll give you two hundred dollars for him."

Wiley's eyes widened.

"Two hundred, but I can't go a nickel higher."

Wiley looked at Easter, as if for advice, but he offered none. He looked at me, as if with an apology.

"Well?" Emmett asked.

"How you reckon a nigger kin perform with you?" Wiley asked.

"We're a minstrel company," Emmett said. "We perform in blackface."

"Blackface?" Wiley asked.

"Yes, we put bootblack on our faces and pretend we're Negroes."

"Negroes." Wiley laughed at the word. "Boot polish on yer faces?"

Emmett nodded.

"What will they think of next."

"It's a good show," Emmett said.

"I'm sure it is," said Wiley.

"Two hundred dollars," Emmett repeated. "Two hundred and, like I said, not a nickel more."

"You're tellin' me this boy will be singin' onstage with you."

"Nobody will know. We'll put bootblack on his face, too. He ain't black enough as he is, anyway. Well?"

"You done bought yerself a nigger," Wiley said. "A Negro."

"I'd like a bill of sale," Emmett said.

"Of course." It was clear that Wiley really didn't want to leave any paper connecting him to this transaction, but he was stuck. He turned to Easter. "Go git me a piece a paper from the office."

Easter ran off.

"Just take a second," Wiley said to Emmett.

"No rush."

"You're gittin' yerself a good one," Wiley said. Easter was back with the paper and also a pen and bottle of ink. "Thank ya, Easter, that's very thorough of you." It was more of a complaint than a compliment. "Here we are. Here we go."

I looked at Easter. He knew what I was thinking. I had stood and listened to this transaction and never once was I asked for either opinion or desire. I was the horse that I was, just an animal, just property, nothing but a thing, but apparently I was a horse, a thing, that could sing.

Wiley handed over the paper.

"Thank you," Emmett said.

Wiley's beard parted to reveal a huge smile as Emmett

counted out the money. He held out his big paw and received it. "Jim," he said, "meet your new master."

"Daniel Decatur Emmett," the man said. He then did something that was stranger than anything I had yet seen. The sight of it froze Wiley and Easter. Daniel Decatur Emmett extended his hand to me as if to shake.

I looked at his hand and then to Wiley and then to Easter. Neither of them regarded the object of the transaction, but looked at the hand stuck out into space in front of me. I looked at Emmett's face. He was open and weirdly nonthreatening. I reached out and shook his hand.

"Don't that beat all," Wiley said.

"I like the way you sing, boy," Emmett said.

"Thank ya, suh," I said.

"I still don't see how you gone git him on a stage with you," Wiley said. "I mean, look at him."

"That's my problem now," Emmett said. "Come on, Jim."

Emmett slapped me on the back and then the rest of the Virginia Minstrels huddled around and slapped me on my back and they turned me around and we all walked out of the livery stable like we were one.

CHAPTER 28

THE VIRGINIA MINSTRELS had set up camp just outside town. The tents were pitched and a fire remained alive when we returned. A short man offered me a tin cup of brown liquid. I had never tasted, but only smelled, coffee. I nodded and took it. These white men scared me. They scared me because they weren't invested in my being afraid of them.

"How you like dat coffee," the man tending the fire asked. "Sho am good, ain't it."

I nodded.

"Everybody, Jim here likes our coffee," the man called to the others. Then only to me he said, softly, "Jimbo done tried it and he likes it."

I cocked my head like a dog, hearing him. It would have been easy enough to understand him as mocking me, but somehow he sounded more like he was practicing, or even trying to make me feel comfortable, which was at once evidence of some sort of kindness and terribly offensive. Not to mention that he, though loquacious, was hardly fluent.

"Sho is good," I said.

The man offered a wide smile. "My name is Cassidy. I play the trombone."

"What be a trombone?" I asked.

"It be a horn. I show it to ya later."

"Thanks fer the coffee, Mistuh Cassidy."

"Just Cassidy."

Emmett walked over to me, stepped back from the fire. "It's hot enough out here without standing next to that thing," he said.

"Wha ya'll want me to does, suh?" I asked, maybe laying it on a little thick, but I was confused about the situation. I was about to be more confused.

"I want you to sing," Emmett said. "When the time comes."

"Jest sing?"

"Yes. That's why I hired you."

"Hired me?"

Emmett looked at me and might have smiled. "I didn't buy you back there, I hired you. I hired me a tenor."

"You don't say," I said.

"Don't tell anyone around here, but I'm opposed to slavery."

"You don't say."

"I say." He looked around his camp at the rest of the troupe. "All of us are opposed to it."

"You mean youse be abalishnists?"

"I wouldn't go that far. We ain't working to get you free, we're just working. We needed a tenor."

A man brought a banjo to Emmett. The other men collected their instruments. Cassidy held a long horn that I believed to be a trombone. "Okay, Jim, are you ready to learn a few songs?"

I didn't say anything, but stared at him. He stared back at me and just started singing, a big, crazy grin on his face:

Ole Dan Tucker was a fine old man,
Washed his face with a fryin' pan,
Combed his hair with a wagon wheel,
Died with a toothache in his heel.

Git outen de way, Ole Dan Tucker;
You's too late to come yo supper.
Git outen de way, Ole Dan Tucker;
You're too late to git yo supper.

"Right now, you just worry about joining in on the chorus. That's 'Git out the way Ole Dan Tucker, you're too late to git yo supper.' Got it?"

I nodded. They started again and I sang with them. I enjoyed the sound of the band, the horns, the banjo, the guitar and the single drum.

Emmett started in on another song:

When I was young, I used to wait
On my massa and give him his plate,
And pass de bottle when he got dry,
And brush away da blue-tail fly.

"This is the chorus."

Jimmy crack corn, I don't care,
Jimmy crack corn 'n' I don't care,

Jimmy crack corn 'n' I don't care,
My massa's gone away.

When he go ridin' in da afternoon,
I follow behind him with a hickory broom,
The pony being rather shy,
When bit by the blue-tail fly.

Jimmy crack corn, I don't care,
Jimmy crack corn 'n' I don't care,
Jimmy crack corn 'n' I don't care,
My massa's gone away.

"That's a good one, don't you think?"

"Sho nuff," I said. I was still processing the situation. I quite frankly didn't believe him when he told me I wasn't his slave, having just watched him pay money for me. In fact, he had in his possession a bill of sale, which no doubt described me as a slave of light-brown complexion, about six feet high, having large feet and a scar on his forehead, having been bought from a man named Wiley. Not a bill of hire, but a bill of sale.

"Put this on," a tall, thin man said. He pushed a pile of clothes into my arms. "Put it on."

I looked at Emmett and he nodded.

"You can get dressed in that tent," Cassidy said.

I was, in no understated way, overwhelmed by their kindness and deferential treatment. I stepped into the tent and dressed as best I could. The woolen trousers made me hot and the fabric caused itching, but, worst of all, the rough material raked and clawed at the open wounds on my leg. I put on the white shirt and the vest. I knew that this one strap of cloth was called a tie, but I didn't know what to do with it. When I stepped back outside, the men laughed at me.

"Let me help you there," Cassidy said. He began to push my shirt down into my trousers, but I pulled away from him. He gently let me know it was all right. He tucked me in all around. Then he redid the buttons of the shirt, smiling at me all the while. "And now the vest. You'll probably find all of this hot, but you'll get used to it. Sort of."

"I is hot, you right," I said.

"We never button the bottom button on the vest," he said.

"Why?"

"I don't know." He took the tie, put it around his own neck, put a knot in it and then slipped it over my head.

Emmett came to us as Cassidy folded my collar over the tie. "Good. Not great, but good. Certainly good enough."

"Thank ya," I said.

Emmett looked down at my feet. "Only problem is shoes. We have no extra shoes. Our old tenor was wearing his when he abandoned us."

"Bare feet work for the act," a heavy-set man said from the other side of the fire. "We can just black them like the rest of him."

Emmett nodded.

CHAPTER 29

"SIT STILL. I don't want to get this in your eyes," the heavy-set man said. His name was Norman. He had large hands and used one of them to tilt my face this way and that. In his other big hand he held a flat tin.

"Wha's dat?" I asked.

"You need to put some white around his eyes and mouth first," Cassidy said.

"I was thinking I'd put the white on after," Norman said.

"You're the expert," Cassidy said.

"What's dat?" I asked again.

"This is bootblack, but you have a choice. I can use lamp black or soot or burnt cork. Different smells. All hard as hell to wash off."

"I dunno, suh."

"Then I'll just use the bootblack."

"Dis gone hurt?" I asked.

"Only if you move and I get it in your eye." Norman looked to see that Cassidy had wandered away. "And you can drop the slave talk."

" 'Cuse me, suh?"

"You can stop the *suh*s and *yeowza*s."

"How did you know?" I asked, suspiciously.

"A slave can spot a slave," Norman said.

"What?" I studied his face. I couldn't see it, but why would a person lie about such a thing, and how could a white person see through me? I thought that perhaps I'd slipped up with my language, as I had with Huck. That was a terrifying notion.

"You didn't slip," he said. "I'se jest knows." His accent was perfect. He was bilingual, fluent in a language no white person could master.

"Do they know?" I asked.

"They do not."

"What is this whole thing?" I asked. "Singing?"

He looked around. "The new thing is white folks painting themselves and making fun of us to entertain each other."

"They sing our songs?" I asked.

"Some. They also write songs that they think we might want to sing. That's strange, but not the worst."

"What, then, is the worst?"

"I'd better start putting this on you," he said, showing me the tin of polish.

I sat still and looked straight ahead.

"Ready?"

I nodded.

Norman tucked a towel around my collar. "Can't get this on your shirt." He smeared the black onto my forehead. "They even do the cakewalk."

"But that's how we make fun of them," I said.

"Yes, but they don't get that—it's lost on them. It's never occurred to them that we might find them mockable."

"Double irony," I said. "That is amusing. Can one irony negate another, one cancel out the other?"

Norman shrugged. "I know this stuff feels cold going on, but it won't stay like that. Especially when we're up there singing."

"Are you a singer?" I asked.

He put the bootblack under my chin.

"I play the drum."

"Why? Why are you with them?"

"I want money. I need money. I want to go back to Virginia and buy my wife," Norman said.

"They have no idea?"

"What kind of idea could they have? You think one of them is going to wake up one morning and say, 'Hey, you look like a Negro'?"

"No."

He stepped back to examine his work on my face.

"Will they pay me?" I asked.

"Can't say. Emmett's never done this before. None of these men own slaves, but they don't think we're like them."

"I see. Have they ever knowingly had a black person in the band before?" I asked, looking about the camp.

"No, you're the first. To tell the truth, I was surprised. But that tenor up and left. He was a strange one. He got caught up with some man's daughter in the last town and I guess he spooked. He was gone in the morning without a sound. Strange for a tenor."

"Emmett is coming," I said.

"I don't know if I need to add any white around his mouth. What do you think, Dan?" Norman turned to face Emmett.

"Looks pretty authentic," Emmett said. "Suit fits pretty well. Stand up."

I stood.

"Trousers a little short," Emmett said.

"Authentic," Norman said.

I was hot in the woolen pants, though amused by the fact they were not frayed below my knees. I didn't understand the complaint that the pants were too high. Pants were pants—they covered my ass.

"Blacken the top of his feet," Emmett said. "And maybe just a little white around his eyes."

"Will do," Norman said.

Emmett caught my eyes. "Keep singing. 'Jimmy crack corn and I don't care, Jimmy crack corn . . .' Keep singing until you know it. Norman, keep him singing."

"I will."

"Everyone, get blackened up. It's almost time to head into town." Emmett marched on through the camp like a commander.

"Help me understand," I said to Norman. "I'm to look authentically black, but I need the makeup."

"Not exactly. You're black, but they won't let you into the auditorium if they know that, so you have to be white under the makeup so that you can look black to the audience."

"Got it." I reached up and touched my face. "What about my language?"

"Don't talk at all—that's the best thing. And don't rub the makeup."

"What about the songs? I don't know them."

"They're simple. You'll learn them as they're sung. Believe me. Emmett's songs are music for idiots."

My mind was racing. The business about the performance was surreal and foreign, of course, but I couldn't leave alone the thought that Daniel Emmett might be paying me for my singing. I might be able to have the money to buy my wife and daughter.

"Jim, are you ready?" Emmett called to me.

I paused, unsure of my diction, whether to speak as myself or as a slave. I made the safe choice. "I is, suh."

CHAPTER 30

NEVER HAD A situation felt so absurd, surreal and ridiculous. And I had spent my life as a slave. There we were, twelve of us, marching down the main street that separated the free side of town from the slave side, ten white men in blackface, one black man passing for white and painted black, and me, a light-brown black man painted black in such a way as to appear like a white man trying to pass for black. The storefronts, a bank and a store and such, all looked flat and without depth, like I could just kick them over. It occurred to me that there was no telling which side was free and which was slave. Then I understood that it really didn't matter. We marched in step, then fell into a cakewalk stagger. Emmett belted out a song line and the rest of us repeated it.

Lawdy, Lawdy, slap dat mule, slap dat mule.
Lawdy, Lawdy, slap dat mule.
Massa keep his corn in a old brown keg.
Massa keep dat corn in a old brown keg.
Massa's chilluns run to school, act the fool.

Massa's chilluns run to school.
Ole Miss chase 'em with her wood'n leg.
Ole Miss chase 'em with her wood'n leg.

White people came out and lined the street, smiling and laughing and clapping. I made eye contact with a couple of people in the crowd and the way they looked at me was different from any contact I had ever had with white people. They were open to me, but what I saw, looking into them, was hardly impressive. They sought to share this moment of mocking me, mocking *darkies,* laughing at the poor slaves, with joyful, spirited clapping and stomping. I looked at one woman who might have been intrigued by me or taken with me, the entertainer. I saw the surface of her, merely the outer shell, and realized that she was mere surface all the way to her core.

The auditorium was a part of the town hall. In fact, it appeared very much like a courtroom. I had been in one once, as I had been sent to deliver a lunch to Judge Thatcher. We marched and sang our way onto the stage and belted the songs. As Emmett, Cassidy and even Norman had stated, I learned the songs quite quickly, as least enough to sing with them on the choruses. It was actually painful to watch those white faces laughing at me, laughing at us, but, again, I was fooling them.

Come listen, all you gals and boys, Ise from Tuckahoe,
Ima gone sing you a little song. My name is Jim Crow.

Wheel 'bout and toin 'bout and do jis so,
Ev'ry time I toin 'bout, jump Jim Crow!

I went down to da riber 'n' I dint mean ta stay,
But dere I seen so many gals I couldn't run away.

Wheel 'bout and toin 'bout and do jis so,
Ev'ry time I toin 'bout, jump Jim Crow!

After I been dere awhile, I tried to push my boat,
But I tumble in da riber and find my sef afloat.

Wheel 'bout and toin 'bout and do jis so,
Ev'ry time I toin 'bout, jump Jim Crow!

Den I go to Na'leans 'n' I feel so full a flight,
Dey put me in the calaboose 'n' keeps me dere all night.

Wheel 'bout and toin 'bout and do jis so,
Ev'ry time I toin 'bout, jump Jim Crow!

I whupped my weight in wildcats 'n' et a alligator,
I drunk da whol' Mississip and left a great long crater.

Wheel 'bout and toin 'bout and do jis so,
Ev'ry time I toin 'bout, jump Jim Crow!

I kneels to da buzzard and I bows to da crow,
And ev'ry time I wheel 'bout, I jumps jis so!

By the time we reached the end of that tune, the whole place was jumping, just like the song instructed. And then the show was over. All the white people were happy. We had done our job. However, we, the troupe, did not march away, but dispersed into the crowd. And why shouldn't they have? They were white. Norman chose to tend to his drum, and so I was left alone and helpless. I stayed in my chair waiting for him or any other member of the band to realize my predicament and get me out of there, when I looked up to find the face of the woman who might have taken a fancy to me on the street. She had yellow buckteeth and big blue eyes and never was I more frightened by a creature, human or otherwise. And I was a slave.

The woman looked this way and that and leaned in to be heard over the din. "What's yer name?"

I searched for help. A man had cornered Norman in conversation, asking about his drum. Cassidy was far across the room, showing someone just how far a trombone could be extended.

"Jim," I said. *One-word answers*, I told myself.

"I'm Polly," she said.

"Polly Wolly Doodle," I said. We had sung the song.

She laughed. "You sho is funny."

"Thanks."

"Where ya'll from?"

"Different places," I said.

"Lawdy, how I'd like to go to different places. See different places. Smell different places. This place is ugly and it stinks. Tell me where all you've been."

I was shaking. I took a deep breath and closed my eyes tight and when I opened them she was still there.

"You sho is quiet. I liked yer singin'."

"Thanks," I said.

I tried to find Emmett in the crowd.

"P-P-P-P-Polly, you should know something," I said.

"Tell me, Jim."

"I'm married. I have a wife," I whispered.

"Is she here?" Polly asked.

"No," I said.

"Have you been to Washington, D.C.?" she asked. "I would jest love to go there. I ain't even been to St. Louis. I bet you been to St. Louis."

A large white man with a white beard and a white suit and a white string tie and a disapproving look stepped toward us. "You sing right nice, young man," he said. "But Polly won't be takin up with no show-bizness folks."

"Oh, Daddy," Polly said. "We was jest talkin'. He was about to tell me all about St. Louis."

"Is that right?" Polly's father looked at my face. "That is some incredible makeup job." He reached a pudgy hand out and touched my hair. "Lawd, but that sho do feel like nigger hair."

"Some wig, isn't it?" It was Emmett. He came up behind the large man, actually gave him a start.

"That wig is very expensive and I wish you wouldn't touch it," Emmett said. He shared a glance with me.

"Your wig ain't like his," Polly's father said.

"We're not a rich troupe. We couldn't afford but that one and it happened to fit Jim here perfectly. Tell me, sir, miss, did you enjoy the show?"

"Did I?" Polly said. "It was just marvelous. A few times I could have sworn you was all darkies fer true."

Her father laughed. "Nice show, son. But none of ya'll had me goin'. You kin black up all you like, but you cain't fool me. I kin smell me a darkie from fifty country yards away. Cain't fool me."

"No, sir, I suppose we couldn't."

"Hell, son, I kin smell a slave from half a mile away. They got kinda a sweet smell. Especially the dark ones."

Norman finally made it over to me. "Come on, Jim. We've got some chores back at camp."

I nodded. I ducked my head and started to leave.

"Jim," Polly said.

I turned to look at her.

She pulled her skirts wide and curtseyed. I nodded, but said nothing.

Outside, Norman and I leaned against a wall, panting, sweating, too terrified to look at each other.

"I've never been that scared in my life," I said.

"Me, neither."

"Is Emmett crazy?"

"Maybe."

"I have to get away from here," I said. "Norman, you can pass. But look at me. They can't keep me made up like this all the time. It doesn't make any sense, my being here. I need to run."

It wasn't too long until the rest of the troupe came outside, led by Emmett. He put his hand on my shoulder. "Jesus Christ," he said. "I thought you were a goner." He laughed and slapped his leg. "What would they have done to you if they had figured out that you were exactly what you were pretending to be?"

Norman looked at my face. "What would they have done to all of us?" he said to Emmett.

Emmett stopped laughing. "That's a good point."

The troupe walked back across the muddy main thoroughfare toward camp. I found a new emotion as we trudged. A couple of new emotions. The woman's father had touched my hair. Slaves didn't have the luxury of anxiety, but at that moment, I had felt anxiety. Slaves didn't have the luxury of anger toward a white man, but I had felt anger. The anger was a good bad feeling. In addition, my feelings about Daniel Emmett were complicated, confused. He had bought me, yes, but reportedly not to own me, though he expected something from me—my voice, he claimed. I wondered what he would do if I tried to leave. In my head I could hear him shouting, "But I paid two hundred dollars for you." A man who refused to own slaves but was not opposed to others owning slaves was still a slaver, to my thinking.

CHAPTER 31

NORMAN AND I lay down to sleep in a tent with a clarinet player called Big Mike. Big Mike, a small man, of course did not know that Norman was black. But he didn't offer any objection to my presence. He was far more comfortable with my presence than I was with his. He performed what I imagined was his nightly ritual. He placed his cased clarinet very neatly and squarely at the foot of his rolled-out blanket, laid a cloth over it and then lay down to rest. Norman nodded to me and we, too, found our beds.

I don't know how long I had been asleep when I felt something touch my ear. I reached up to brush it away—a fly, a beetle—my eyes still shut. Again, the brush. I would not be disturbed by an insect and I held my eyes fast shut. On my third swat I found a hand. I leaped from my blanket and shouted, "Good Lord, what in the world!" loud enough to wake the entire troupe. I turned to find the fat father of the white girl Polly. I didn't know how or what to scream. To him, I had to sound white. To the rest of the troupe, I was to sound like a black slave. For my second shout I used the racially neutral "Lawdy! Oh, Lawdy!"

Emmett came running into the tent with a lamp. He nearly fell over when he saw the man in the white suit.

"I just had to touch that wig again," the man said.

"What?" Emmett looked at him as if he were ablaze. "What in God's name are you doing here?"

"I just had to touch that wig again," he repeated.

Emmett looked over at me. He was as confused as I was and perhaps even more afraid.

"It feels so real," Polly's father said. "Tell me, why does he sleep in the wig and in makeup?"

"It's too hard to wash off," Emmett said.

"You're washed."

"Why are you in here?" Emmett asked.

"You're washed," the man said again.

"Shall I send someone for the sheriff?" Emmett said.

"You certainly may," he said. "My nephew is a good lawman."

Emmett looked caged. He studied the man for a few seconds. "Shall I send someone for your daughter?"

"Excuse me?"

"Does she know you crawl around at night touching men as they sleep?"

Polly's father stammered, but came up with nothing.

"Where did he touch you, Jim?" Emmett asked. "Don't say a word," he instructed me.

"His hair," the man said. "I only touched his hair."

"Am I to tell your daughter you only touched this man's hair? That you crawled into a tent to touch a strange man's hair?"

"Sir, I don't much like your tone and I certainly do not approve of your offensive insinuation."

"What insinuation would that be? What is your name?"

The man backed his way toward the flap of the tent. "I'll be going." He shook his big head. "I know there's something amiss here. I just know it."

"What's your name, sir?"

The man ran.

Emmett looked around. He looked at me, Norman and then at Big Mike. He raised his arms and yelled, "Pack up! Pack up! That fool won't stay scared for long. He'll be back here to find out that's no wig. Pack up!"

"This is bad," Norman said.

I stood frozen. I could still feel the crazy white man's fingers on my hair.

Big Mike slapped a small hand on my shoulder. "Help me take down this here tent," he said.

Everyone worked to collect their things, large and small. Emmett stopped for a second and looked at me. He said something that confused me. Confused me because I wasn't quite sure what it meant. Confused me because I had never heard anything like it before. He said, "I'm sorry."

I had been about to help take down the tent, but this white man's apology screwed me to the ground.

"Let's go," Norman said.

I moved. The men were still pulling things together as we slogged and tramped through the wagon-rutted, muddy lane that led away from town. I walked in the lead, beside Daniel Emmett.

"This be my fault," I said.

"You might be the reason, but it's not your fault."

"Still, suh, I's sorry."

"Want to hear my new song?" he asked.

"Yessuh."

He cleared his throat and sang:

I wish I was in da land o' cotton,
Old times dere are not forgotten,
Look away, look away, look away Dixie Land.
In Dixie Land whar I was born
Early on one frosty morn,
Look away, look away, look away Dixie Land.

Oh, I wish I was in Dixie.
Hooray! Hooray!
In Dixie Land I makes my stand,
To live and die in Dixie.
Away, away, away down south in Dixie
Away, away, away down south in Dixie.

Emmett held the last note for an impressively long time. "I call it 'Dixie's Land.' What do you think?" he asked.

"Suh?"

"Do you like it?"

"It be a raght pretty song," I said.

"What do you know?" he said in a dismissive way.

"I knows I likes da song," I said, allowing him to think I was unable to understand his sarcasm.

"Thank you, Jim," he said, to shut me up.

Emmett looked behind us and seemed to be satisfied that we weren't being chased. "To tell the truth, I'm not even sure why we're running."

I didn't tell him that I knew why I was.

"Mistuh Emmett? Kin I ax you a question?"

"Of course."

"Does I belongs to you now? I mean, seein' as you bought me from dat fella back in da livery."

"No, you don't belong to me."

"You mean dat if'n I wanted to, I could jest run off through dem trees 'n' be gone, dat be okay?"

"Well, I did hire you to be my tenor. I paid two hundred dollars, and you ought to pay me back."

"So I understan'. I cain't run away and you be paying me, but you be keepin' da money untils I pay you back."

"Until I get my two hundred dollars."

"How much I be gettin' paid?" I asked.

"We didn't discuss that, did we? I think a dollar a day is fair, don't you? A dollar a day is a good wage, especially when you've never been paid before."

"Dat how much a tenor norm'ly make?"

"A nigger tenor, yes. I think that's a good wage," Emmett said, nodding his big head and humming his "Dixie Land" tune.

"A dollar a day," I said. "So, dat be two hunnert days."

"Two hundred performances," he corrected me.

"One hunnert ninedy-nine," I said.

Emmett's silence was palpable.

"Suh, I's tryin' to unnerstan'. You sayin' you is makin' a 'stinction 'tween chattel slavery 'n' bonded slavery?" I didn't think I'd meant to actually ask that question out loud, but I must have, because I said it in proper and appropriate slave diction.

Emmett looked at me askance. "Would you mind repeating that?"

"I reckon I would," I said.

CHAPTER 32

WE WALKED ON for a long way and the too-tight boots they'd finally found for me worked up several nasty blisters. My feet hurt to the point that I took off the shoes and continued barefoot. The wet of the track actually served to cool and soothe my injuries. I wondered every few steps where Huck was, if he was all right, if he had escaped those men. I knew he hadn't. If he had, he would have found his way back to me.

We came to a town, more an encampment, where logging seemed the primary interest. There were many thrown-together shacks and a couple of mills and that ever-present eggy mill smell. Black men sawed with long saws and short while white men stood around laughing and chatting. A couple of the white men held bullwhips at their sides. The backs of the shirtless slaves showed the results of their industry. In my pocket I wrapped my fingers around my pencil. I wondered if I might ever have paper again.

We marched through to the far side of town. We set to erecting the tents while Emmett walked back into town to arrange a performance.

"Does this town have a name?" Big Mike asked.

The trombonist laughed. "Yeah. Hell. Maybe Little Hell."

The other men laughed.

"I sure would like to be in St. Louis," a man said.

"New Orleans," said another.

"Yes, New Orleans. They know how to have fun in New Orleans."

"Ever been to New Orleans?" Big Mike asked me.

I shook my head.

He thought for a second. "You oughta go some day. Pull that line tight."

I did and watched as he pounded in a stake with a sledge. "I ain't neber been nowhere," I said.

He gave the stake a couple more strikes and stood straight. He looked at me as if to say we had nothing to talk about.

"Is Mistuh Emmett a good man?" I asked.

Big Mike looked around. "He's okay, I guess."

"He say you folks don't b'leeb in slavery. Dat true?"

Big Mike shrugged.

"Does you?"

"Some folks have slaves. Who else gonna do the work? I have no slaves. I don't have a dog, neither."

After the tents were up and coffee and food had been prepared, Daniel Emmett came back to us with his report.

"This is a rowdy place indeed, a downright scary lot. Being devoid of taste and any semblance of discernment, I feel it judicious, prudent, to see that our newly acquired tenor remains here while we perform this evening." He studied our faces.

"What did he just say?" the trombonist asked.

"He said these folks is likely to kill Jim here if they realize he's a nigger."

That was not how I would have put it, but correct nonetheless.

Emmett sighed. "We really can't afford to lose another tenor," said the man to whom I was in debt to the tune of 199 performances. I caught Norman's eye. Without shaking his head, that was just what he was doing.

I picked up and cleaned the dishes while everyone else blackened themselves for their performance. They hummed and sang and fussed with their collars and waistcoats while I did the slave work.

As they collected in formation to parade into the encampment, Norman gave me a look. He knew. He knew, as sure as everyone in the troupe was now blacker than me, that I would not be there when they returned. When they were out of sight, their cakewalk music not unpleasing, I grabbed some bread and the too-tight shoes and, much to my surprise and perhaps some shame, I grabbed Daniel Emmett's leather notebook, the one with his songs. I sprinted into the dense trees. No road or track or path for a runaway. I didn't know if I was running from Daniel Emmett or from the idea of remaining a slave or back to Huck. I knew only that I had about two hours to put distance between them and me. I knew also that I was now a double runaway slave, perhaps also wanted for kidnapping, perhaps wanted for murder, wanted certainly for an unpaid debt and now, again, theft. I was confident that they must have no idea in which direction I had run.

And run I did, like only a slave can run. My injuries ached, my feet complained, but I moved at top speed through trees, through dry creek beds, sloshed through branches of the river, climbed what small hills there were and damn near rolled down the other sides. I stopped when I couldn't see well enough to run anymore. I ate some bread and slept.

PART TWO

CHAPTER 1

A RUSTLING IN DRY LEAVES woke me just as the sky was tinged with dawn. A deer? A bear? Something smaller I could kill and eat? I sat up and tracked its movements by sound. In dry leaves even a foraging bird could come across as heavy. But neither bird, bear nor deer could call out, "Jim, Jim."

How had they tracked me? I heard no dogs.

"Jim, it's me."

"Who is me?"

"Norman."

"Over here."

Norman emerged, backlit by the dawn light, like the saddest of apparitions.

"What in the world . . . ?" I said.

"I just couldn't stay there. It was too much. Do you know what it's like to pass for white."

I cocked my head. "As a matter of fact, just recently I passed for white so I could pass for black."

"Exhausting, isn't it?" He moved, and I could see once he wasn't silhouetted against the sun that he was still made up in blackface.

"What are you doing here?" I asked.

"We came back and found you gone and all of a sudden Emmett sounded like every slaver I ever met. He was cursing darkies and yelling about how he was going to get a bully and beat you just before he hanged you from a oak."

"I knew he had it in him. How did you find me?"

"I ran. I ran like the runaway I am. While they scurried around in circles, I ran straight, leaping every log and rock I could to break up my track."

"Did you run all night?"

"I did."

"Sit down. Catch your breath. Do you think they saw which way you went?"

"I'm certain they didn't."

"Well, here we are," I said. "What now?"

"Do you have any idea where we are?" Norman closed his eyes and I could see that he was ready to fall asleep.

"None," I said. "You should just sleep. I'll keep watch."

He didn't answer. He was already gone.

NORMAN WOKE WITH A START and stared at me wide-eyed. "You're still here," he said. He sat up and rubbed his eyes.

"Where would I be?"

"I thought you might run off."

"Well, I didn't." I pushed the last of the bread toward him and he took it. "I've been thinking. You want to buy your wife, correct?"

"Yes."

"I want to buy my wife and daughter. My situation is complicated by the fact that I might be wanted for kidnapping and murder and I'm a slave. A slave can't buy a slave. If I show up to buy them—well, you get the picture."

"A mess," Norman said.

"But I have an idea. It's a crazy idea."

"Tell me."

"Have you ever had any problem passing? I know you said it's exhausting, but is it easy?"

Norman nodded.

"Has anyone come close to spotting you?"

"No."

"I want you to sell me."

"What?"

"I want you to be my white owner. I want you to sell me. I escape and we do it again. We save the money and you show up and buy my family. Then you take your money and go buy your wife."

"Are you insane?"

"No. However, I did get the idea from an insane person. Tell me what's wrong with the plan?"

Norman thought, tugged at his ear. "Aside from the quite obvious danger to you and then to me for stealing property, namely, you, I see nothing wrong with it. Yet the consequences of discovery will be severe."

"I appreciate you stating that so clearly, but I point out that we are slaves. What really can be worse in this world?"

"Right."

"We'd better get you cleaned up," I said.

There was a little creek below us. Norman stripped down and began to wash off the burnt cork. He had to scrub extremely hard, and it made his light skin red and angry. Lacking a brush, he used handfuls of leaves and sand.

"I'm starting to like your plan. I miss my wife."

"Do you know how much she will cost?" I asked. The question felt so strange in my mouth. "I ask because I have no idea what it will take to free my family."

"I'm guessing a thousand dollars," he said. "She's very pretty. She's wide-hipped and I heard them say she is good breeding stock." He was obviously disturbed by the idea. He kept washing, even when it was clear he was done.

"We have to move on, Norman."

He nodded, then saw the notebook I held. "Why did you take that?" he asked. He began to dress.

"I wanted the paper."

"He was crazed when he couldn't find it."

"Listen to this:

Nigger love a watermelon, ha! ha! ha!
Nigger love a watermelon, ha! ha! ha!
Dey comes round for it all too soon,
Ain't nuttin' like a watermelon to a hungry coon."

"Damn," Norman said. "He wrote that?"

"I imagine he did. What does that even mean?"

"Why do you want the paper?" Norman asked.

I shrugged.

"You can write?"

"Yes."

"I can read some," he said. He looked at the woods around us. "I wish we knew where we are."

"I suggest we head south," I said.

"What? Black people don't go south."

"They do when one is a cracker trying to sell a slave."

WE WALKED FOR A DAY. We dammed a stream and trapped some fish and ate pretty well. I didn't see or hear sign of other humans, and that was fine with me. The absence of dogs barking in the distance was a comfort. Clouds collected and there was no moon and the night fell hard.

"It's darker than the inside of a cow," Norman said.

I found this funny and laughed. Norman laughed and soon we were laughing like two children. It felt good. It wasn't that anything was so funny, but we needed to laugh.

WE WALKED for the better part of three days, trying to point south, but the terrain was nudging us east and we had come back to the big river, the Mississippi. Across the water was a town and I guessed, from all I'd heard, that it might be Cairo. I wished that had mattered. A fugitive slave was a slave in a free state just the same. But south of there was Kentucky, a good place to sell a slave. And we wanted the money. But there was no way to cross, so we continued on south until we came to a little town. The sign read BLUEBIRD HOLE. I removed my shirt to better look like the working slave I was and was pretending to be.

"Are we really doing this?" Norman asked.

"Yes, Massa," I said.

"Stop."

"I has ta," I said. "By the way, you need a last name. What have you been using?"

"Brown."

"Really?"

Norman nodded.

"Let's go, Massa Brown, suh."

The town looked like it might be called Bluebird. It was well populated with complacent-looking, nicely dressed white people, the scariest kind. They smiled and greeted the stranger, Norman, casting nary a glance my way. I saw a few other black faces at work cleaning and repairing. An old black woman churned butter on the porch of the general store. I could feel Norman's nervousness.

"Listen, you've got to relax," I said. "To all of them you're white. Hell, to me you're white."

"There's no need to be insulting."

An ancient white woman walked past us.

"Dat not be how I meaned it, Massa."

Norman chuckled slightly and the woman cut an edged glance at him.

"Excuse me," she said.

I looked at the dirt.

"Ma'am?" Norman said.

"Did your nigger say somethin'?"

Norman was a struck deer.

"Did he say somethin' about me?"

"Tell her I just make sounds," I mumble-whispered to him.

"He just said somethin' else," she said.

"Oh, sorry, ma'am, but my slave here that I own, he just makes noises. He likes to pretend he can talk just like us white folks. All he can do, though, is grunt and whine like a fawn. You ever hear a fawn cry out?"

"Bless his heart," she said, though it was clear she hardly wanted me blessed by God or man. She cut me a hard look. "They's like lil' monkeys, ain't they."

"Just like monkeys," Norman said.

"Did he jest look at me," she asked.

"I'm certain he didn't."

"He better not—that's all I have to say."

"He wouldn't. He's a good boy."

"Hmmmph," she said.

"And he's a good worker, if he is a little stupid, even for a nigger. He slows me down on the road. Do you know of anyone who might want to buy him? He's strong as a Missouri mule."

The old woman shook her head, turned and walked on.

"Talk about jumping right into it," I said.

"I'm scared."

I was also scared, but I was fairly drunk with the notion of seeing and freeing my Sadie and Lizzie. The old woman churning butter stared at us as if with some knowledge and I kicked myself for falling into the trap the slavers would have set for me, for me to think that there was magic in that old black woman. That moment of near-gullibility made me question my judgment about other things. For a second I wondered whether Norman was in fact black and a slave. Perhaps he was an insane white man who fancied he was black. Unlikely, of course, stranger than most things I could imagine, but not impossible. He had been able to speak slave, but it was possible a crazy white man could have learned it. Then it hit me that it didn't make any difference whether he was white or black, and what did that mean, anyway? Norman Brown might sell me once and take off for the hills, never to be seen again. But he might just as well have done that if he were a black man. Bad as whites were, they had no monopoly on duplicity, dishonesty or perfidy. All that thinking must have flashed across my face.

"What is it?" Norman asked.

"Nothing. Let's keep this show moving."

He nodded.

"Norman, you should carry this." I pulled the leather notebook from the waist of my trousers. "I shouldn't be seen with it." I hated to part with it. I had not torn out Emmett's songs—somehow they were necessary to my story. But in this notebook I would reconstruct the story I had begun, the story I kept beginning, until I had a story.

"You're right," he said.

Still, I had my pencil. I had developed a habit of periodically touching it through the fabric of my pocket, for comfort.

CHAPTER 2

I WAS PLAYING UP the slave bit, dragging my bare feet through the dust, those too-small shoes laced together and hanging over my shoulder as if I didn't know where they belonged. Norman looked to be bedraggled because he was. That I had but two lash scars across my back announced that I had not been treated too roughly as a slave, but that I had been properly supervised. I remembered those strikes of the bullwhip well. They were delivered by Judge Thatcher. I was thirteen and I made the misstep of speaking to a young white woman who said hello to me. What I said exactly was "Hello." Judge Thatcher had the reputation of being one of the *good* masters, but the sting of the leather told me what that meant. The first strike came as a surprise, not because I didn't know it was coming, but because I could feel the tinge of pleasure attached to its delivery. The relish felt through the second blow was no longer surprising, only sadly predictable.

"Hey there!" a call came from a man approaching. He was short, round and heavily bearded.

"Say hello," I whispered.

"Good day," Norman said.

"I'm the constable here in Bluebird Hole. Frank McHart." He reached to shake Norman's hand.

Norman's passing skills were well practiced and I could sense him settling in, though meeting the law must always have been nervous-making. "Norman Brown. Pleased to meet you, Sheriff."

"We say *Constable* around here. Sounds less *hard*. We like to think of ourselves as a little village."

Norman scanned the street, the couple of storefronts, the neat yards of the houses and the slaves. "Where does this road lead?" Norman asked.

"Oh, lots of places. Wyatt, Wolf Island, all the way to Memphis, if you want. Long walk to anywhere, though."

"I can well imagine," Norman said. "It will be a lot longer with my nigger slowing me down."

McHart looked at me, and I kept my eyes cast down at my feet.

"He seems able-bodied enough," the constable said.

Norman glanced at me, and I touched the shoes on my shoulder. "He is," Norman said, "but he refuses to wear his shoes."

"Dumb," McHart said. "They're all dumb. Simple. That's a better word. *Simple.* This here little hamlet is simple, but I don't mean it the same way."

Norman nodded.

"I like thinking about words like that. I'm also the schoolteacher."

"I see."

"And the postmaster."

"You're a busy man."

"A really busy man. Not too busy, but busy. Busy enough. I also run an egg business. Got thirty-seven layin' hens."

"I'd bet you could use help collecting those eggs and feeding those chickens, couldn't you. Given all your other jobs."

"Them chickens do need a lot of tendin'."

"Chickens always do—watching out for those foxes and hawks and such." Norman was a natural.

"What are you thinkin'?" McHart asked.

What I was thinking was *Don't sell me to the law, you fool.*

"You've got all these jobs and all of those chickens and I got me a slave, able-bodied, like you said, that I don't use and only slows me down, so I was thinking maybe you'd buy him from me at a good price and he could tend those chickens."

McHart looked me up and down. "I ain't never owned a slave. Are they hard to keep and care for? What's it cost to feed one?"

"Food, water. Just like a dog. Except they can sort of talk."

"What's his name?"

"His name is Jim."

My heart sunk. What if this constable had seen a flyer about the runaway Jim? For all I knew, there was a rendering of me tacked to the wall in his office.

"Much easier to keep than a dog," Norman added. "They don't leave piles everywhere to step in, don't piss in corners. They don't get into skunks and porcupines. Hell, this one can sing."

"I don't know. I'm too busy to keep a slave," McHart said.

"Well, that's why you need one." Norman had fallen into his part completely. I had that fleeting thought once again that he might be white and passing for black just for me. "He doesn't snore. He's not a picky eater. He does what you tell him, except for wearing those shoes. I have to admit the shoes are a little short on his feet. Niggers are known for their big feet."

McHart laughed. "Slave owner," he said to himself. "How much?"

"Thousand dollars."

McHart whistled. "I'd have to sell a great many eggs to see that kinda money."

"Five hundred," Norman said.

McHart shook his head. "You'd best talk to one of the farmers around here. Or maybe Old Man Henderson. He always keeps a couple of slaves. He runs a little sawmill on the other side of town."

"Henderson," Norman repeated the name. "Why, thank you, Sheriff."

"Constable."

"Oh, yeah. Constable."

McHart walked away from us as we moved away from him. "You're very good at this," I said.

"At what?"

"Being white."

"I've been practicing for a long time. It's both easier and harder than it looks." He attended to my silence, gave me a glance. "Something wrong? Something bothering you? I thought you'd be pleased I got over my nervousness."

"It's okay to be a little nervous."

CHAPTER 3

One of our stomachs complained. Perhaps both. I followed Norman across the road to the general store. On the porch there were a few potatoes and some biscuits spread out on a cloth on a table. The old woman was just feet from us, still churning away. I nodded hello to her. She didn't offer any sign of recognition, but returned her gaze to her project. A white woman, a least a head taller than Norman, stepped outside.

"A penny fer a tater. A penny fer a biscuit," the big woman said. "Don't cost nothing to look, but I don't like it."

Norman reached into his pocket and pulled out a penny.

"Take a tater or take a biscuit," she said. "Tater or biscuit. I don't care which 'un. Gimme that penny."

Norman tossed a glance my way. He was asking which one, but the giant white woman was staring at me. He moved his hand toward a biscuit, but before he touched it, the churning old woman sneezed. The giant cut the slave a hard look that bounced harmlessly off.

"I'll take a tater," Norman said.

The giant turned and stomped back into the store. The

churning woman did not look at Norman, but gave her eyes to me for the briefest second. I observed the deep wrinkles around her eyes. Then she was gone, disappeared into herself, and it was clear that she had absolutely no interest in us.

We walked to the opposite edge of Bluebird Hole, where we sat in the woods well off the road. Norman put the potato to his lips, intending to bite it. I grabbed his hand and shook my head.

"That will make you sick as a dog," I said. "We have to cook it. A potato is actually a nightshade."

"But I'm starving."

"Better to starve a little longer than to get sick. Or worse."

We built a fire, shoved a stick through the potato and set it over the flames for a good long while.

Half a potato never tasted so good, especially where it was charred.

"That woman scared me," Norman said.

"That was the biggest woman I've ever seen," I said.

"Maybe the biggest person." Norman rolled his head around and cracked his neck. "What now?"

"Henderson, the sawmill guy?"

"Who would want to buy you?" Norman said.

We laughed a bit. "You'd be surprised," I said.

WE NAPPED. Norman woke to find me writing in the notebook. I felt him watching me for a while. Finally, "What are you writing?"

"Not sure."

"Maybe you should write some songs. You know, poetry."

"Like Emmett's?"

"Yeah, just like that. About darkies trying to get back to da plantation 'cause dey miss Massa."

"I thought about tearing out his songs and burning them, but they would still exist. Those crackers would still sing them. Better to know they exist. Don't you think?"

"What if you can't escape? I mean, if I can't get you back once I've sold you?"

I didn't say anything. I closed the notebook. "That wasn't enough food," I said.

Norman pushed himself to standing. "Henderson?"

I nodded.

"What if he shackles you?"

"Can't work if I'm shackled."

Norman didn't seem convinced.

"We need the money," I said. "You can't tell them my name is Jim. They're looking for a runaway named Jim."

"What do you want me to call you?"

"Tell them I'm called February, but that I was born in June. They like thinking that we're stupid like that."

Norman nodded.

"You think you can find your way back to this spot?" I asked.

"Yes."

"This is where we'll meet. If I'm not back here in two days . . ."

Norman stopped me with a raised hand.

"Here—take this back." I gave him my notebook.

"I'll take care of it," he said.

"Let's go."

WE RETURNED TO THE ROAD and followed it south away from town. The sawmill was dirty, as sawmills always were. This one was a small, sad affair that smelled more like animal and human waste than sawdust. There were seven slaves working with axes and adzes and another two working a pit saw. A couple of the men had enough missing fingers to justify being called one-handed. There was but one building, open on one side like a foaling shed. The men were shaping and stacking good-size timber, square and round. The one white man present walked toward us. He was of medium height and slight build. As he grew closer I felt alarmed, as he looked familiar to me. I couldn't place his face.

"Kin I hep ya?" the man asked.

"My name is Brown," Norman said. "You must be Henderson."

"That's right," Henderson said. He gave me a good looking over, but showed no sign that he recognized me.

"Nice operation," Norman said. "What kind of wood you cutting up?"

Henderson glanced at Norman for only a second. "Cypress. Only cypress. Money's in cypress."

"Why's that?"

"People use that there wood for docks and such all 'long this river. Don't rot. Don't you know nothin'?"

"I don't know much about wood—that much is true," Norman said. "But I know good workers and I know slaves." Norman looked at me. "And I know hard times. That's why I'm here, looking for you."

"I don't follow ya."

"See this strapping boy I got here? Well, this is my slave,

February. But he weren't born in February. He was born in June."

"Then why for he called February?"

"Can't say. You know them darkies. Dumber than buckets of hair."

Henderson laughed hard. "Naw, dat's funny. Buckets of hair. Har har har."

"February here is strong as an ox."

Henderson stopped laughing and looked at me. "Let me see yer hands, boy."

I showed him my hands and watched him register all ten fingers. I turned my hands over to show my calluses.

"You ever cut wood?" Henderson asked.

"Yessuh," I said.

"How do you feel 'bout yo massa sellin' ya?"

Such a strange question. I was baffled and thrown off by it. I looked at him to see if he was going to break out in laughter, but he didn't. I looked at Norman to see he was as confused as I was. "Well, suh, I reckon I's his rightful propty and he kin does what he want to wif me."

Henderson nodded. He grabbed my biceps and gave it a squeeze. "I've felt stronger," he said. "How much you want fer him?"

"Five hundred," Norman said.

"You must be crazy," Henderson said. "I kin go to Memphis and buy three niggers fer that much."

Norman surprised me. "But you didn't have to go to Memphis, did you? This here slave showed up at your door."

Henderson thought. He looked at his yard and the work being done, at the two men struggling with the pit saw.

"February here can work dawn to dusk like two men," Norman said.

"Three hundred," Henderson said.

"Four."

"Three-fifty," Henderson said.

And Norman reached out to shake his hand. "Deal."

"Whew, you be a bizness man, awright," Henderson said. "Luke," he called over his shoulder.

A small man ran to us. "Suh?"

"Luke, take February over to the shed and give him some water," Henderson said. He gave me another long look.

"Food, suh?" Luke asked.

"No. He kin eat wit the resta ya'll later. Put him to work on the pit saw with Sammy. Rainbo kin hep you."

"Yessuh," Luke said. He turned to me. "C'mon."

I gave Norman a final look and saw that he appeared more afraid than I felt, and then I followed Luke.

CHAPTER 4

I TRAILED LUKE'S severe limp across the compound. He pointed to the barrel of water and watched as I splashed my face and drank.

"Don't you just hate getting sold?" Luke asked.

"As bad as getting bought," I said.

Luke laughed.

"That man beat you?"

I shook my head.

"Well, this one will. He likes the bully."

"Sorry to hear that." I stared at Luke's damaged hand.

He held it up to show me where there should have been fingers between the thumb and little finger of his right hand. "You know, dull tools are much more dangerous than sharp ones."

I paused to admire his metaphor, but he continued.

"That fool out there won't let us take the time to sharpen anything the way it ought to be."

"I see."

"All in all, he's a good master," Luke said.

"You just said he likes the whip," I said.

"He's the master. He has to keep us in our place, right?"

I studied the face of this man. He wasn't much older than me, but something was significantly different. When he turned to drink some water himself, I saw the numerous scars on his back. Had he been beaten deep into submission? I looked for compassion.

"Do the others feel like you do?" I asked. "About Henderson? Do they think he's a good master?"

"They think what they think. I think what I think."

Which was a no.

"He's fair," Luke said. "What else you expect from life? He beats us all the same, no more, no less."

I nodded.

"We better get you out there on that saw."

When we stepped back into the yard, I didn't see Norman or Henderson. I could only hope that Norman would soon be back at our rally spot. I was led to the pit saw, a large hole in the ground over which a thick log rested. A long ripsaw was held by one man above the timber and by another below it. I studied the layout of the yard, the lane that led away from the compound. When the time came, I would have to navigate my way out of here quickly and in the dark.

I was to work with Sammy, a two-handed man. He was smaller than Luke and considerably smaller than me. "You get the bottom," he yelled.

I climbed down into the pit and looked up at Sammy. He looked so far away. The gray sky was behind him. He stood on the big log we were to cut and I wondered why he so clearly preferred that position, until I felt my feet sink into the mud. I had to use my hands and arms to move my feet into a solid stance.

I grabbed the big wooden handle of the long saw. It didn't

take an expert to see that the tool suffered from neglect. Not only did it appear dull, but it held spots of rust and buckles. We started. It was some of the hardest, most miserable work I'd ever done. I was ankle-deep in mud, and possibly the waste of animals and people. It reeked something awful. Sammy was too weak, even with two hands, to pull the saw up with any power and too small to have gravity assist him on the downward stroke. The bad blade snagged frequently and would rip the big log efficiently only a few seconds at a time. Every time it pinched and caught, I flinched, fearing that the thin metal would snap and take off a finger, a hand or worse.

The day grew dark and we were still not halfway through the pile of timber. I looked up to see Henderson standing at the rim of the pit. He shook his head as he stared down at me. "You cain't do a gawdamn thin' if'n you're scared of the blade," he said. "Come on out fer your lashes."

I looked at Luke, who was standing just behind Henderson.

"Come on," Henderson said.

I had to assist my legs with my hands to pull free of the muck. I reached for the knotted rope and hauled myself out.

"Lashes?" I asked.

Henderson shook his head. "I got me a backtalker," he said.

Being a quick study and completely familiar with my world, I said nothing else. I said nothing as I followed Henderson into the big shed. I said nothing as Luke, with a hint of a grin on his now-ugly face, tied my hands with a hemp rope to a post. I said nothing as my shirt was ripped, by someone unidentified, from my body. I said nothing as the leather stung me, ripped me, burned me. Before I passed out, I was surprised by the realization that my flowing blood did not at all cool the burning of the wounds.

I CAME TO and saw the face of small Sammy. I didn't know how I was going to sit up, much less run away from that place.

"Am I alive?" I asked.

"I'm sorry to tell you, yes," he said.

I managed to sit up. It was dark, but there was some moonlight. "Likes the bully," I repeated Luke's words.

Sammy nodded. "He's going to do this for the first couple of days. He'll let up on the third day, and you'll be grateful."

I pushed myself to standing. I was in great pain, but my fear was more pronounced. "How long have I been out?" I was asking him how close we were to sunup.

"Awhile," he said.

"Where are we?" I asked. "Where's the pit?" I was trying to orient myself.

"Through the shed," he said. "Where're you going?"

It hurt me that I didn't trust this black man. Perhaps it wasn't Sammy I distrusted, but I couldn't be certain he wouldn't tell Luke, and I definitely did not trust Luke.

"I need to put that mud on my back so I can heal," I lied, but it seemed to make sense to him. "I'm going to go down into the pit to get some. Don't tell Luke, okay?"

"I don't like Luke," Sammy said.

I looked at the small man. "How old are you?" I asked.

"Don't know. Fifteen, they say. I don't know."

"Henderson beat you like he did me?"

Sammy nodded. He pulled up his shirt to show me his scars. When he did, I saw breasts.

"You're a woman," I said.

"I've never said I was anything else."

"You're a girl," I said. I looked at her face and saw the face of my daughter, imagined her back etched as this one was. "Pull down your shirt."

She did.

"Fifteen," I said. "Are you brave?"

"No."

That was a disappointing response. I had the thought of taking Sammy with me. Even then I realized how poorly thought-out that plan was, but I found it difficult to imagine leaving her behind.

"Does Henderson know you're a girl?"

She didn't answer, but I understood. Of course he knew.

"LISTEN, I'm running away from this place tonight. Do you want to run, too? Do you want to try to go north?"

Despite her admission to not having courage, she quietly considered what I was saying to her.

"I have a daughter," I said. "Somewhat younger than you, but she's my family. I wouldn't want this for her. I couldn't live knowing she felt this pain."

"How can you not want to live?" Sammy said.

"That's a longer discussion," I said. "I'm leaving here tonight. I won't be beaten again. Do you want to come with me?"

Sammy nodded.

"Let's go. Let's go, now."

I WAS PLEASED to have Sammy with me, for reasons other than saving myself and her from further flogging and from what I knew Henderson was doing to her.

We walked through the shed and there was Luke, lying in the aisle like a sleeping sentry. We froze.

"He always sleeps there," Sammy whispered.

We tiptoed past him and into the work yard. A light drizzle began to fall. I tried to figure out where I was, but everything looked different. I was fairly lost. I could not find the trail I'd followed into the place.

"Where's the road, Sammy?"

She led me out. Without her, I might have wandered either in circles or right up to the Henderson house, wherever that was.

"What are we doing?" Sammy asked. "Where are we going?"

"I need to get to the road that leads into town," I said.

"Which town?"

I didn't know. I couldn't find it in my head. I tried to recall the sign, but the voice of the constable came to me. "Blue something," I said.

"Bluebird Hole," she said.

"Yes." I was feeling stronger with each step away from that place. "We're meeting my friend and then we'll keep going."

"Your friend?"

"You'll see."

The drizzle didn't amount to anything and was gone by the time dawn broke. I saw the edge of town and then turned us away into the trees. I found the big rocks I'd noticed and led us deeper into the woods. I could see where Norman and I had broken our way through brush the previous day, and then I found the remnants of the fire that had cooked our potato. Norman was not there.

"Were you expecting your friend to be here?" Sammy asked.

I didn't answer. "How long before Henderson misses us?"

"As soon as Luke notices, he'll know. So, he already knows."

"Does he have dogs?"

"He has one."

"A hound?"

"I guess so," she said.

"Can you wait here? I mean right here and not go anywhere?"

"I wouldn't know where to go." She was terrified. I could see it.

"I promise you we're going to make it away from here." I stood and peered into the trees for Norman. Unfortunately, our rendezvous was north of Henderson's place, precisely the direction escaped slaves would run. "Sammy, just stay here. I'll be back in no time. I promise."

I stayed in the woods and worked my way up a hill so that I was looking down at the town. I could see the empty main thoroughfare. I listened for anything, especially the barking of a dog.

I waited, watched. I didn't want to leave Sammy alone for too long. I needed to see Norman walking out of that town toward me. I wondered if I had been right in my fleeting moments of distrust of him. I wondered again if he was even black at all. Maybe he was just some crazy white guy who had just sold me. But the plan to sell me had been my idea, unless of course that was such an obvious confidence scheme that he merely waited for me to come up with it. I kicked myself for being a fool as I wended my way back through the forest to young Sammy.

I found the creek that ran by the spot and so assured myself that I was not lost, but then I heard the screaming.

CHAPTER 5

I SURPRISED MYSELF as I ran through the brush. If she had been discovered by Henderson or another white man, that would be the end of her and me. However, I couldn't abandon her. I pushed ahead to find her screaming and crying, kneeling on the ground before a man. Without thinking, a method of action that was beginning to feel familiar to me, I tackled that man about the knees and brought him down. I was about to strike him a blow when I realized I was straddling Norman. He had his hand up, protecting his head.

"Norman," I said.

He pushed me off. "What's going on? Who in hell is this?" He looked at me open-mouthed.

"Sammy," I said.

"That's not an answer," he said. He looked at the girl. "That's not an answer. Why is he here?"

"She's coming with us," I said.

"She?"

I nodded.

"You not only escaped, but you stole a slave?" he said. "May I ask you a question? Why?"

"Because she's fifteen, probably younger, and that man beats her with a whip and you know," I said, flatly.

Norman heard me. He looked at Sammy, then at me, then at Sammy. "I understand. But what are we going to do?"

"Where were you?" I asked.

"I used some of our money and bought some food. Hardtack, dried meat."

I didn't complain. That sounded reasonable. "We've got to get out of here," I said. "That Henderson is bound to be closing in. Sammy, this is Norman." I let Norman get up.

Sammy was so scared she was having trouble breathing. She was hopelessly confused.

"Norman is—was—a slave," I said.

"I didn't mean to scare you, Sammy," Norman said.

None of our talking to her was getting through.

"Sammy," I said. "Look at me. Norman is the friend I was looking for. He's black just like you and me." I paused. "Well, he's black."

"That's a white man," she said.

"No, he just looks white," I said. "It happens."

Norman looked away and through the woods toward the road.

"We're together," I said.

"We need to move," Norman said.

"This creek has to lead to the river," I said.

"Or to another creek," Norman said.

"And then that will lead to the river."

"Are we going north or south now?" he asked.

"Let's not get caught. That's the first thing."

"Forget the creek. I say we go south by land. They won't expect that."

Norman was correct, of course. For some reason the river felt safe to me, but I knew it wasn't. "Okay. South."

Just then we heard more than one barking dog.

There would be no more towns for a while. Norman could not simply pretend to own both of us, not with the news of our escape spreading through the region. We'd have to stay in the dense woods. But first we needed to quickly put some distance between ourselves and Henderson.

I was the impediment to our fast movement. The beating I had received had taken a lot out of me. I might have been wiser to rest before setting out, but fear would not allow it. We ran. Much of the way it appeared that Sammy was running from Norman as much as anything else. She kept looking back at him, still not believing that he was black and certainly not convinced that he was not a threat.

Midday came and I could run no farther. We ran into a gulley with a little stream and found an outcropping of rocks, almost a cave, and there we rested. We couldn't hear the dogs anymore. I leaned against a rock and winced.

"Let me see that," Norman said. He looked at my back. His face went blank. "My God, Jim. He tore you up. What should I do?"

"Just before we stopped here, we passed by some bee balm," I said. "The plant has big red flowers."

"I saw them," Sammy said.

"I need the root and some of that clay mud from over there." I pointed.

Sammy ran off for the plants.

"Think she'll come back?" Norman asked.

I nodded.

"See if you can clean out the wounds," I said.

I removed the rag that had been my shirt and Norman used it to wipe at my back. It burned like crazy. I tried to relax my body and not bite my tongue.

"What did you do?" Norman asked.

"What did I *do*? I'm a slave, Norman. I inhaled when I should have exhaled. What did I *do*?"

Sammy came running back to us. She put down the roots and also delivered some broad leaves. "I saw this plantain," she said.

"That's good, Sammy. Thank you. Now, put the bee balm roots and the leaves on that rock and crush them good. Norman, get me some more mud from over there and make a mound."

Norman left.

"That's good, Sammy. The plantain was a good idea." I watched as she used a stone to smash the plants.

Norman returned.

"Mix it with the mud and put it on my back." Sammy and Norman applied the mud together. "This is a safe place, I think." I was guessing, hoping, saying it mainly because I knew I would only slow them down if we ran. "We'll wait here and move at night. Does that sound right?"

"I guess so," Norman said.

Sammy nodded.

"We should sleep now. I should sleep now." I think I passed out.

CHAPTER 6

I AWOKE TO FIND Sammy and Norman staring at me while they gnawed on hardtack. "Biscuit?" Sammy asked.

"Thank you," I said and took it from her.

"Here's some meat." Norman pushed the paper holding the dried meat toward me.

"No, thanks. Just the biscuit."

"It tastes like sawdust," Norman said.

I looked around. It was just getting dark. "Any sounds out there?"

"No," Sammy said. "No dogs. No voices."

"What about birds?" I asked.

"Birds?" Norman cocked his head.

"Birds get quiet when people move through the forest."

"I think I've been hearing birds," Sammy said. "I guess so."

"We'd better move on then, get far away from here." I pushed myself to my feet and was momentarily unsteady.

"Are you well enough?" Norman asked.

"I'm just well enough," I said. "Let's go. I think we've got to get to the river and cross it somehow."

"We don't even know where we are," Norman said. "Bound to be a slave state on the other side of the river."

"Probably," I said. "We're slaves, Norman. Where we are is where we are."

"What's that mean?"

"I don't know. Sounded better in my head."

"I know what it means," Sammy said. "We're slaves. We're not anywhere. Free person, he can be where he wants to be. The only place we can ever be is in slavery." She looked at Norman. "Are you really a slave?" she asked.

"I am."

"And you're colored," she said.

Norman nodded.

"Who can tell?"

"Nobody," Norman said.

"Then why do you stay colored?"

"Because of my mother. Because of my wife. Because I don't want to be white. I don't want to be one of them."

Sammy looked at me. "That's a pretty good answer."

"I thought so," I said.

"Can we go now?" Norman asked.

"Let's go," I said.

It was a moonlit, cloudless night that dropped rings of shadow at the bases of trees. We moved easily, at times swiftly. Our notion was to follow the water, follow small water to bigger water. When people run, they forget terrain, they forget nature. I wondered how many snakes simply had just been startled by our rushing feet, too surprised to lash out, how many missteps had not led to plummets because the next step had come so quickly that we flew past the danger. And yet, with all that running, no place appeared like a new place. Perhaps that was the nature of escape.

THE ROAR OF THE RIVER announced its presence, but right up on it the Big Muddy felt peaceful and quiet. Except for the muted, rhythmic churning and a steamboat's paddle out in midstream.

"Look at all that water," Sammy said.

"You've never seen the river?" I asked.

"I was never twenty yards from that pit saw."

We were all quiet for a bit while that sank in.

"Well, you're seeing it now," I said. "The mighty Mississippi. Goes south to New Orleans and north to . . ." I stalled.

"Freedom," Norman said.

"Supposedly," I said.

"Are we going to cross that?" Sammy said.

"Yes," I said.

"How?" Sammy asked.

"How?" from Norman.

"Can you swim?" I asked them both.

"No," Norman said.

"I don't know," said Sammy.

"If we stay on this side, they'll find us." I looked around. We were still some yards from the water. Between us and the flow was an expanse of muck. "Too thick to navigate and too thin to plow. I heard someone say that once."

"Appears true," Sammy said.

I looked at all the driftwood sticking up from the mud. "We'll have to make a raft. There's plenty of timber, but we'll need rope or something to tie it all together."

"I'll go find some," Norman said. "I'll even buy it if I have to."

Sammy and I watched Norman disappear into the brush.

"He's really a slave?" Sammy said.

"So he says. I reckon I believe him."

Collecting the wood turned out to be extremely difficult. The muck not only held fast the sticks but also sucked us in. The more we pulled, the more we sank. On more than one occasion we needed the other to get free.

"This is harder work than at Henderson's place," Sammy said.

I nodded. "The pay is better."

"Why did you bring me with you?" she asked.

"I couldn't leave you."

"You left the others."

"Maybe I shouldn't have. But I did. I can't undo that now. That Luke wouldn't have come with us, anyway."

We dragged the wood we'd gathered down the shore to a gravel beach. We tried to wedge and lock the timbers together as much as we could without twine or rope.

"So, you were born at the mill?" I asked.

"I was told so."

"Your mother?"

"I don't recall her. Father, neither."

"I'm sorry."

"You remember your mother?" she asked.

"I'm not certain," I said.

"I'm glad I ran away," Sammy said.

"Why is that?"

"Seems like the right thing to do."

I nodded.

"He's raped me since I was little," Sammy said.

I nodded. "You're still little."

"Almost every night at first."

I wanted to say something, but I didn't know what. I imagined my daughter again and I felt rage. "He's not going to rape you again."

MUCH OF THE DAY passed while we waited for Norman to return. Clouds formed in the south and moved up the river toward us.

"Storm?" Sammy asked.

"They're not so dark," I said. "Maybe only a shower." I looked into the woods. "I hope Norman gets back before it's too dark. I'd like to get this wood tied together while we can still see a little bit."

WE SAT, and I must have fallen into a nap, because I was startled awake by shouting. It was Norman. I looked to see Norman emerge from the brush at the edge of the muck. I called to him. He saw us and ran as hard as he could toward us.

"Henderson!" he shouted. "It's Henderson!"

I have to admit that I was too scared to immediately move. He was pretty much in my face when he yelled again, "That slaver's coming."

I looked at the ball of twine in his fist and I took it from him. I began to assess the situation. It was dusk. I started to ask Norman how far away our pursuers were when Henderson popped out of the brush.

"Push," I said. "Push what we have into the water."

We tried to push the loosely connected logs into the river, but they fell apart.

"There they are!" Henderson shouted. Two more white men emerged. They carried pistols.

Sammy, Norman and I pushed three good-size logs into the river. "Hang on and kick your feet," I told them. "I'll try to tie us together in the water." The air was disturbed by the report of a pistol. "Hug the timber," I shouted.

Another report.

"I'm slipping," Sammy said.

Some yards separated the three of us and we drifted farther apart. The river always looked slow and lazy from the bank, but it wasn't. We were lucky that there was no traffic at that moment, but we had control of nothing.

Another pistol report.

"Norman," I yelled. I thought I could see the top of his head. He didn't respond. I looked back at the bank to see the angry Henderson pointing at us. I could see his mouth working, but I couldn't hear him. It was then I realized that the men were still shooting, but I couldn't hear that, either. I somehow was able to kick my way to Sammy's log. I grabbed her and pushed her up onto the wood. I then used the twine and lashed our logs together. It was rough going and I was terrified I would drop the twine. I was terrified about everything.

Sammy gulped air, but said nothing. I saw her eyes for a flash and then they were closed again.

"Kick," I said. "Try to get to Norman."

Norman was at the mercy of the current. I could see that he was not kicking. I chose an angle and tried to cross his path. It was hard to see anything now. Rain had begun to fall, but not hard. The wind kicked up some waves.

Our logs slammed into Norman's back. I grabbed him, pulled him to our logs. He said nothing. Then he snapped to and almost lost his grip.

"I've got you," I said.

"They were shooting at us?" Norman said incredulously. "Where's the girl?" he added.

"Hanging on," I said. I looked at the top of Sammy's head. Her arms were thrown over the log. "Sammy," I said. She didn't answer.

"They were shooting at us," Norman repeated. "You can't work a dead slave. Why would they shoot?"

"They hate us, Norman."

The river churned us about.

"We'll never make it across like this," I said.

"What?"

"We're going to float downriver and end up on the same side," I told him. "It's dark, though, so they can't know exactly where we land. They probably think we're swimming to the far side. At any rate, we're going to be miles from them."

"Okay," Norman said. He tried to collect himself.

"Sammy," I said. "Sammy?"

"Is she all right?" Norman asked.

I moved behind her and lifted her head. She was limp.

"Did she drown?" Norman asked. "Is she dead?"

I put my hand against her back.

I MANAGED TO HOLD us together. The river did her job, pushing us into an undercut bank covered with thorny bushes that might have been blackberry. The branches snagged clothes and skin as we worked our way onto a small beach. The thorns dug into the wounds on my back and I wanted to cry out, but I was more concerned with Sammy. I shielded her with my body. Norman was clear first and pulled us from the water. I turned Sammy over and looked at her face. Her eyes were closed and I could feel no breath in her.

"Is she dead?" Norman asked.

I rolled her onto her stomach to try to force the water out of her. I pushed on her chest and her shirt came up to reveal a hole.

"Is that . . ." Norman stopped.

I touched the blackened indentation. "She's been shot," I said.

"Good Lord," Norman said.

"She's dead."

"We should have left her where she was," Norman said. "At least she'd be a live slave. Not just another dead runaway."

I studied the lifeless body on the ground before me. "She was dead when I found her," I said. "She's just now died again, but this time she died free."

"That's bullshit," Norman said.

"Is it, Norman?"

He looked down at Sammy. "I don't know. She's dead."

I stood and looked with him.

"She's so small," he said. "Do we bury her?"

"Do you believe in God?" I asked.

"I suppose I do," he said.

"I don't. But maybe Sammy did. So, yes, we'll bury her. Isn't that what people who believe in God want?"

"I don't know."

"Would you want to be buried?" I asked.

"Wouldn't matter to me," he said.

"In case it matters to Sammy."

I found a couple of thick, forked sticks and started digging into the beach. The night was so dark I could barely see the hole we were making. Norman dug with an energy that I didn't have. He dug like he wanted the job done. We stood back to back and tore into the ground like we hated it.

WE SCRATCHED and clawed open a hole in the world and placed little Sammy inside it. As we began to cover her, Norman said, "I suppose we should pray."

"Okay. Say it."

"Lord, meet Sammy." Norman opened an eye, looking at me as if to ask if that was enough.

"What more is there to say?" I asked.

"I suppose we should cover the grave with stones," Norman said.

"Don't bother. The river's not going to let her stay here," I said. "The river is going to dig her up and claim her. River's going to claim us all in due time."

Norman turned to regard the Mississippi. "That sure is a lot of water."

"That's the least of what it is," I said.

"Couple of hours and it'll be light," Norman said.

"I'll tell you this: I'll never be a slave again."

CHAPTER 7

SAMMY WAS BURIED in the night, in the darkness, in the rain. Our hands patted the mound that represented her life right as the rain stopped and the clouds parted to reveal a fingernail of a moon. I hadn't realized until that moment that I was freezing.

"We have to get out of these wet clothes," I said. Though I had managed to retain the glass I used to start fires, it was, of course, useless with no sun. We moved farther back into the brush, out of the wind, and huddled together. It helped.

I awoke to find Daniel Emmett's leather notebook on my chest. It was soaked but had held its shape.

"It was in my sack," Norman said.

"Thank you." I was afraid to open it for fear it would fall apart. "I should let it dry, I suppose."

"What now?" Norman asked.

I looked at the river in the morning light, flat and still-seeming. Last night played over and over like a horrible dream. Yards away from us the girl's grave looked quite obviously like a grave.

Norman sat beside me.

"We work our way south until we find an unattended canoe or boat and we steal it," I said.

"Steal it? And if we get caught?"

"I'll steal it," I said. "If we find one. Maybe we can stow away on a northbound paddleboat. Maybe you can sell me again."

"Yeah, that went really well last time."

I nodded. "Now that everybody and his dog is looking for us moving south, I say we just get north."

"What makes you think we'll find a boat?"

"People just leave them around," I said. "Folks can't lug a boat home every time they come off the river. We just have to be certain the owner isn't anywhere near. Takes a while to get out of sight in a boat."

"Hmmm."

We left that spot without another glance at Sammy's grave. We walked south through the woods, keeping the river in sight as much as we could. I was certain we were clear of Henderson and his men, but not so confident that word of our escape had not reached so far south.

Around midday we wandered cautiously closer to the river and I spied a trotline stretched across a branch. There was also a skiff tied nearby. I waded out while Norman stood watch. I took four good-size catfish from the rig and we hiked well into the woods to eat. We finished two and I cut the remainder into strips and hung them over the smoking embers of our fire.

"Do we take the boat?" Norman asked.

"No. They'll come check their line before it's too dark, then head home. We'll take the boat when it's dark."

We lay back and looked at the sky.

"You seem very comfortable with all of this," Norman said.

"I know this river. I know the white people on it." I opened the notebook now and peeled some pages apart so they would dry.

JUST BEFORE DUSK Norman woke me. There was splashing down at the river. Closer, we could see a man and a boy rowing out to check their trotline. There was plenty of catch so they had no suspicion that we had robbed them. They collected the fish and left their boat again, tied and unguarded. They took the oars.

"They won't be back until morning," I said. "We'll need to make some paddles."

We spent an hour using what was left of our twine, lashing smaller sticks to a stiff, forked branch. We had only enough to make one. It was good and dark when we untied the skiff and set out. We also took the couple of fish that had been hooked in that hour. The opposite bank was dark and distant and invisible to us. I wasn't certain we would have been able to see all the way to it in daylight. The boat rocked.

"Is this thing safe?" Norman asked.

"We'll find out," I said. Then I remembered that Norman couldn't swim and considered how terrified he was. "It's safe. Just sit calmly and the river will take care of us."

"That's what I'm worried about."

"We'll be okay."

I was exhausted by the time we were mid-river. We were pretty much at the mercy of the current. I didn't know how far south we would travel before we could manage the eastern shore, but I kept trying to move us that way.

"Look," Norman said. "Lights."

I looked to see the lamps of a riverboat. It was far away and headed upriver toward us. We could not yet hear it, but I got an idea. "Norman, come back here," I said.

He crawled to me.

"I need you to paddle as hard as you can."

"Okay. What are we doing?"

"I want to get us right in front of that boat."

"Are you crazy?"

"If it's a stern-wheeler, then I can try to tie us to a bumper or rope and we can climb aboard."

"But?" he asked. "There's always a but."

"If it's a side paddleboat it will be more difficult," I said. I didn't tell him that we could be chopped to bits.

We heard the thumping of the wheel as it drew toward us. We had managed to get directly in front of the vessel. It didn't matter to me whether we found the port or starboard side, but we had to be ready for the turbulence and the undertow.

Norman was screaming and doing everything but jumping out of the skiff as the steamship became huge and loud. We nearly capsized as we folded into the wake on the starboard side. We were spun around so that our bow was facing upriver. Norman clutched the seat. We were up against the hull and then pushed to the side. I felt I might be pitched out of the boat at any second while I tried to find anything I could to tie us on to.

"Oh, my God!" Norman shouted.

I looked to see that this vessel was a side-wheeler and that the paddle was churning the water behind us. I could feel the wheel pulling us. The sight of the paddle tearing up the water was terrifying. The skin of my hand was scraped badly as I tried to grab the huge rope draped on the side of the ship. I got the tie rope under the riverboat's huge line and held us there, but I wouldn't be able to hang on for long. I almost lost the sack that was slung around my neck.

"Grab on to me!" I shouted to Norman. I stood at the bow of our little boat. The big paddle was pulling at us harder now, sucking us toward it. "Grab on!" I felt Norman's weight land on me. I pulled myself up onto the fat line of the ship just as I couldn't hold the tie rope any longer. Norman screamed. "Get on the rope!" I shouted. His weight lessened and so I knew he was at least partially on the rope. I didn't have to tell him to climb. His fear pushed him away from the water and up toward the deck, stepping on my shoulder and head on his way. It was a short, sheer climb, but the row of ropes provided footholds for us. I followed, pushed him as much as I could. I looked back and saw the little skiff chopped to splinters by the paddlewheel. Norman must have seen it, too, because he launched away from me and onto the planks of the deck. I struggled up and lay beside him.

"Oh, Jesus. Oh, Jesus," he kept muttering.

"Jesus had nothing to do with any of this," I said. "Good or bad."

"Are we alive?"

I didn't answer. I sat up and looked around. I could hear many footfalls on the level above us. The ceiling was a low one, such that we could not stand fully erect. The feet of the people above felt as if they were on us. We could hear them yelling, some weirdly cheering, as they spied the wrecked skiff.

"Lawdy!" a woman screamed.

"They must surely be dead!" a man shouted.

THERE WAS NO RAIL at the edge, not even a lip. The sounds of the river sloshing and the paddle churning made scary music.

"We'd better hide," I said.

We could hear someone approaching. We opened a wooden hatch and entered a noisy room that was so dimly lit by lamps that nothing was discernible. We slid into the deeper shadows and waited. The engine noise was deafening. If anyone approached us we would never know. Tar had gotten pushed under my nails and they ached terribly.

CHAPTER 8

"WHO DAT?" the voice screamed through the roar of the engine. There was so much clanking and hissing. "Who dat be?" A wiry black man stepped through the pipes and looked down at me. "Whatchu doin' in here, boy?" He carried a candle in a holder.

I didn't know if there were any white people nearby, so I answered, "I's hidin' out." Norman was behind me, behind a post.

"You ain't s'posed to be in heah."

"I knows."

He moved the lamp a bit and suddenly was able to see Norman. "Suh, I's sorry. I din't see you dere."

Norman was about to put the man at ease, but I stopped him with a subtle shake of my head.

"My massa brought me down heah to tie me up," I said.

He thought it was strange that I was talking at all and he said as much. "Why you talkin'?"

Norman caught on and stepped in. "Don't you talk to my slave like that."

"Suh, I's so sorry." He dropped his eyes to the floor. "I

jest din't know why anybuddy be down heah. Ain't nobuddy allowed to be down here. Black er white."

"What did you say, boy?"

"Nuffin, suh."

"Now, go away and let me talk to my slave."

The man sulked away. We watched him disappear behind the crankshaft.

"He can't hear us from over there," I said.

"Why? Why am I passing for him?"

"We don't know if we can trust him," I said.

"He's a slave."

"So?" I said. "There are some slaves who don't mind being slaves. I found that out just recently. What if he's one of them?"

Norman looked in the direction of the man. "I can't see him."

"What if he tells? He doesn't need to know I'm a runaway. That we're runaways. What's that going to do for us?"

"You're right. Do we just wait down here?"

"Do you think you can go up there and get us some food?"

"Look at me." Even in the dim light I could see how disheveled he was. Aside from being soaked, his clothes were filthy from the hull's tar. Looking at him like that gave me a renewed appreciation of the power of his skin color. That alone had been enough to faze and control the slave in the engine room. Even though Norman looked like the poorest and worst-off white man, he still commanded fear and respect. But he would not be able to pass through the throng of white people on the decks above us—though they could never identify him as black, they would see him as something worse, a very poor white person.

The slave who had approached us came back into view. "I

sho am sorry, suh, but ya'll cain't be down heah. I gonna git in a worl' o' trouble," he said.

I whispered to Norman, "Ask him where they keep the steamer trunks."

"Where do you keep the baggage, boy?"

"What?"

"Don't 'what' me, nigger. You heard me," Norman said.

The man looked at Norman, at his clothes. He was confused.

"The trunks, boy."

"Dey's in da hold up front." He paused. "Suh, I gots two jobs. I's s'posed to stoke da fire and keep dat boiler boilin' 'n' I's s'posed to keep foks outta heah."

"Go shovel more coal, then," Norman barked with an authority that surprised and impressed me.

"If'n Mistuh Corey come down heah and sees you, he gonna put me in dat fire. And prolly you, too." He looked me quickly up and down. "And especially you gone get put in da fire."

"Then don't tell him. Now, go!"

The man scurried away.

"That was good," I said to Norman. "Believable."

"I hate it," he said.

"I know." I pushed him forward. "Let's find you some clothes. Anything will be better than what you've got on."

The forward hold turned out to be an open area at the bow of the vessel. The trunks were more piled than they were stacked and had accumulated a layer of soot from the coal-burning fire. We could just see and reach the edge of the pile near us, as the only light came from the lamps well behind us.

"So, we just open them up?" Norman said.

"You open them. If he sees me doing it, he'll run to tell for sure," I said.

Norman opened trunk after trunk. Some he pried open with my knife. "Everything is women's clothes," he said.

I kept a lookout for the engine room slave or for anyone else. "Just keep looking," I said. "You'll find something."

In a few minutes, Norman issued a sigh of relief. "I found some."

"Get dressed."

I took a few steps away and watched the black man shovel coal into the furnace. The orange-and-red glow made him appear strange—if not a demon, then a demon's helper. He smiled as he worked.

When I stepped back to Norman, he looked stranger than the engine man. Norman had found the garments of a shorter, fatter man. A fat man with bizarrely long arms. The britches fell only to his middle calves. The cuffs of the jacket sleeves covered his hands. He rolled the sleeves up while he mumbled.

"What?" I asked.

"What if the man up there recognizes these clothes?"

"God?"

"Not that 'man up there,' the man whose clothes these are." Norman shook his head, almost laughed.

"He won't," I said. "White people are vain. Those clothes look awful on you. He believes his clothes are beautiful."

"I hope to the-man-up-there that you're right. If I have to leap off this boat, I'm dead." Nerves and the extreme heat of the room had him sweating profusely.

I nodded.

We walked to the furnace and the man stared at Norman.

"How do I get up to the next deck?" Norman asked.

"Ya don't knows?"

Norman gave him a stern look.

The man pointed.

Norman turned to me. "You wait right here. You hear me, boy? Don't let this nigger here tell you no different."

"Yessuh," I said.

Norman climbed up the short stairway and disappeared through a short door. I noticed how light his steps were. He moved like a large cat. I also regarded how the engine man watched, with hatred perhaps, certainly fear, but finally what I saw was awe.

"So, that's your massa," the man said.

"Yes."

"Something funny about him."

"What's your name?" I asked.

"Brock. What's yours?"

"Jim."

"Well, Jim, come over here and shovel coal."

"What?"

"If you're down here, you're working. That's my rule. Or I can go up and tell Massa Corey you're down here. And then he'll come down with his braided bullwhip and tan your hide."

I admit that he had me scared near to death, but I was more confused than anything else. I took the shovel and served coal to the fire. The noise of it was as intense as the heat. The wooden shovel handle was hot and hard to hold. I kept shifting my grip to better control the tool.

"Keep it going," Brock said. "Keep it up. You do it long enough and you'll get used to it. You'll start to like it."

"Do you like it?" I asked.

"I like it," he said. "It's for my massa."

"Why do you say *master* like that when you're talking to me?"

"That's how you're supposed to say it." He stared at me. "Don't think I don't know that something's going on."

"What do you think is going on?" I asked.

"Something." He grabbed a filthy towel that was hanging on a pipe overhead and wiped his face and neck. "Something's going on. When Massa Corey comes down here, I'm going to say something."

"I wish you wouldn't," I said.

"Why was your massa down here in the first place? How come you talk to him like you do? Something's going on."

I heaved more shovelfuls into the furnace. "How much more do I have to put in?" I asked.

"You can't put too much in. The engine eats all the time. Hotter the fire, faster the boat goes."

"You never rest?" I asked.

"I rest between shovels."

"What about sleep?"

"I take little naps." He paused. "Between shovels."

The furnace felt hotter than ever. "You don't have any help down here."

"You're here."

"No one else?"

"It's my engine. I keep it going."

"Fo massa," I said.

He took offense. "This is my engine."

"Do you ever leave this room? Do you go outside to piss or shit?"

"Got a hole in the floor. In the stern."

"There are no windows down here," I said. "How do you know when it's daytime or nighttime?"

"Doesn't matter. The fire is hot and the wheel turns. One bell, I open one valve. Two bells, two valves. Four bells, I close these and open this and I put all the steam to the wheel. That's what makes us go."

"What about when the boat makes port?"

He stared at me.

"When it stops," I said.

"That's when they dump more coal down the chute and I wipe off the gauges and the fittings. That's when they put more water in the tanks."

"That's when Corey comes down."

"Massa Corey," he said.

"Massa Corey. He comes down then?"

He didn't answer the question. "The coal comes down and I get the fire hot again and the wheel turns and we go."

"When's the last time Massa Corey was down here?"

"Sometimes the boiler makes a noise, a bang-like. I don't know why. It's a new noise. She shakes some."

I looked at the giant boiler, dark gray and black with soot and red with rust. I rubbed the sweat off my face and observed the soot on my hand.

"You breathe this in all the time?" I asked.

"There's nothing wrong down here. I breathe just fine. But there's something funny about you and that man you say is your massa."

The bell rang four times.

"Got to open her all the way up," Brock said, seeming excited. He turned some wheels and pulled some levers.

"More coal," he said.

I shoveled.

The pipes hissed and the boiler shook and made almost human noises. I didn't know enough to know whether the sounds were strange or not.

"Hear that?" he said. "Listen. It's like a woman crying."

"Have you told Corey about the sound?"

"Massa Corey."

"Have you told him?"

"I don't need to tell him," Brock said.

"Listen, I'm tired. I'm taking a break."

Brock took the shovel from me and tossed in a load.

"It's so hot in here." I sat on the floor with my back against the wall. "Do you have any food?"

"No food."

"When do you eat?" I asked.

"When it's time to eat. I go up and grab my tray from outside the door and I eat it. Every day."

"You don't leave this room at all?"

"This is what makes us go," he said. "Massa Corey sees to that." He raked at his forehead with his wrist. "Sometimes I have corn bread."

I closed my eyes and tried to not feel the heat. I couldn't sleep, but I became mesmerized by the rhythmic tossing of the coal. Then Brock started singing. His voice was deep and not so pleasant, raspy and uneven.

I'se a slave in dis boat,
Hoo Ya Hoo Ya!
I'se a slave in dis boat,
I makes da boat go.

Da rain fill up da river,
Hoo Ya Hoo Ya!
Da rain fill up da river,
I makes da boat go.

Da boat pushes da river,
Hoo Ya Hoo Ya!
Da boat pushes da river,
I makes da boat go.

Massa Corey bring me cone bread,
Hoo Ya Hoo Ya!
Massa Corey bring me cone bread,
He makes da boat go.

I opened an eye and watched him awhile, then shut it again because I did not like the sight. Unfortunately, neither I nor the engine's roar could block out the sound of his dreadful singing.

Hours went by. I may have slept, though when I was awake I was convinced I hadn't. Time stood still, but it stood still for an exceedingly long time. I imagined Norman upstairs, nervous, but perhaps physically comfortable, not hot and covered with soot, but no doubt more frightened than I was, more lost. I wondered if he was angry. I wondered if I had ever not been angry.

I suddenly realized that the singing and shoveling had stopped. I opened my eyes and saw that Brock was eating with his dirty fingers from a tin plate.

"What's that?" I asked.

"Corn bread," he said.

I looked up the stairs at the door. "Do you have any left?"

"No," he said and popped what I took to be the last morsel into his mouth.

"You didn't think to share?" I asked.

"You ain't supposed to be down here in the first place."

"Did you tell Corey about me?"

"Massa Corey."

"Did you tell him?"

"You ain't supposed to be here."

"You didn't see him. He just leaves you food by the door like you're a dog. What does *Massa* Corey look like?"

"He's the massa, that's all."

My stomach complained. I had a mind to lick the crumbs off his plate, but I didn't. Instead I closed my eyes again.

THE DOOR OPENED above us. I ducked into the shadows. What if it was Corey? I didn't believe I could survive another flogging. By *survive,* I meant that I might not have stood for it. I felt more fully the anger I had cultivated for twenty-seven years or so.

But it wasn't Corey, it was Norman. "What did you find?" I asked him without thinking. Brock's head whipped around to look at me. I had addressed a white man without employing slave speech.

"Lawdy," Brock said. "I knowed somethin' was gwine on. I still don't knows what, but it gwine on, awright."

Norman was startled by the man's animation. "Come over here," he said to me. "We need to talk."

"Lawdy, Lawdy. This be jest awful!" Brock said.

I followed Norman and left Brock shoveling. He was shoveling hard, fast.

"What is it?" I asked, once out of earshot.

"Emmett is up there."

I looked into the furnace.

"He didn't see me, but the trombonist might have. I never liked that man." He reached into his pocket. "Here's some bread."

"Thank you."

"There's something else," Norman said. "The boat is packed with people. Stuffed. People are trying to get home to the north because there's a war."

"War?"

"The slave states are trying to leave the union. That's what I heard. I'm not certain what it all means. Anyway, they're scared."

"War," I said.

"What's been going on down here?" Norman asked.

"First of all, this slave loves being a slave," I said. "He appears to love his 'massa,' as he calls him."

"I guess it happens."

"Here's the thing, I don't think there is a *massa*."

"What?"

"I don't think there is a master. Massa Corey. He's just down here keeping this boat afloat and moving along this river. Massa Corey's probably dead. Maybe he's in that furnace."

Norman peered past me at Brock. "Look at him go."

I turned to see him. Brock was moving crazily, shoveling like mad, and the fire seemed to be trying to reach out and grab him. The big boiler screamed again, only louder this time, higher-pitched. Higher-pitched and sustained. The whole engine shook once hard, and then rattled. The rhythm of the engine thumped out of time with the pounding of the paddle outside.

"Something's wrong," Norman said.

CHAPTER 9

THE WHOLE ROOM began to shake and rattle. Aside from the boiler noise, there was a hum that was more felt than heard. The bell rang not four, but six or seven times. I walked back to Brock. Norman followed me. Brock still shoveled furiously.

"What does seven bells mean?" I asked.

"I's dunno," he said. "It ain't never rang but four times fo'. I ain't know what seven bells be meanin'."

"Why is he going so fast?" Norman asked.

"He's crazy," I said.

Brock stopped his work. "Why fo you be talkin' lak dat to dat white man? I knewed sumptin' was off. You ain't his slave."

"I'm not a white man," Norman said.

Brock's face went blank. "What say?"

I was sorry Norman had said that. "Settle down, Brock. Everything is all right."

"You's still doin' it."

"I'm not white," Norman repeated.

It was then that the rattling of the room got exponentially worse. The boiler screamed even higher, the pipes hissed, the shaft looked like it was buckling. A rivet popped from somewhere and hit the wall just behind Norman, could have killed him.

"Jesus," Norman said, ducking and looking for the next one.

Brock turned and looked at the engine. The drive shaft seized and stopped moving altogether. Brock turned and looked at us with a fear I had never seen on any man, white, black, free or slave. "Shit," he said.

THE NEXT THING I KNEW, I was coming to in the freezing water. Drowning was a terrible but effective way to come to my senses. The sky told me it was dawn, but that hardly mattered. I was surrounded by planks and trunks and chairs and screaming, crying men and women. Heads bobbed everywhere. A man floated into me. I pushed him away. A woman's lifeless face bumped into my shoulder. She looked like she was smiling. "Norman!" I called out. I studied the eyes, the mouths, dead and alive, trying to find my friend. People disappeared under the water and never came back up. The shore was about one hundred yards away, perhaps more. "Norman!" I felt what might have been a hand grab my foot and then the pressure was gone.

"Jim," a voice called out to me.

I searched the floating planks and furniture, realizing that my shoulder was badly burned. The scars on my back felt as if they'd opened wide again. Then I saw him. Norman was perhaps thirty yards from me, bobbing in and out of view. He clung to a small section of plank. He struggled to keep his head above the surface. He called to me again, trying to wave to me. He was trying to find something big enough to cling to. He could see me seeing him and I saw relief flash across his terrified face.

"Jim!" another voice called to me, a higher voice.

The voice was familiar. I found Huck's face. He was treading water. His forehead was red with blood. He was also perhaps thirty yards from me.

They both called to me, one, and then the other. They were equidistant from me but not near each other. I felt I was in some poor philosopher's example. Huck slipped under and came back up, slapping the water. Norman struggled with his plank. I was frozen there, moving in neither direction, but needing to choose one.

The air was filled with screams, shouts, cries, but I could hear only two sounds clearly, two voices calling my name.

PART THREE

CHAPTER 1

I DRAGGED HIS BODY onto the beach by the seat of his britches. I was exhausted, spent, and he was barely conscious. But he was alive. He coughed up some water, but remained facedown in the sand.

"You's be awright?" I asked.

"I ain't dead?"

I patted his leg and fell onto my back, looked at the bright-blue sky.

"Jim?"

"Yeah, Huck?"

"Where'd you come from?" the boy asked. "How you come to be in the water jest then?"

"Hannibal, jest lak you. That's where I comes from." I looked up and down the shore and saw people and wreckage strewn about. I didn't see Norman. "We gots to get into dem woods." I pulled and pushed the boy into standing and we staggered together into a dense thicket.

"I'm confused."

"It be okay."

We sat on the stiff grass, peered through the branches and

listened to the people moaning, crying and swearing down on the shore. Some of them could possibly have been dying.

"Should we go help them folks?" Huck asked.

I shook my head.

"But they're hurt."

"We ain't no doctors," I said.

"You know there's a war comin'."

"What kinda war?"

"North agin the south," Huck said. "Folks on the boat said the north wants to free you slaves."

"Is dat what dey say? Tell me, Huck, how you come to be on dat boat?"

"The King and that Bridgewater fella took me on there. I tried a couple of times to run from them, but they caught me. They heard about the war coming and I guess they's from the north. Anyway, they got scared and wanted to go to Ohio. I reckon they might be dead now. Maybe they're down there on that beach."

"Mo' reason not to go down dere," I said.

"There was a man callin' to you when we was in the river," Huck said. "Who was that callin' to you?"

"A friend," I said.

"A friend? What kinda friend?"

"Jest a friend."

"What was his name?"

"His name be Norman."

"He was in trouble," Huck said. "He went down. I'm sure he's dead. I don't know about the King and Bridgewater."

I nodded.

"He was callin' to you."

"I know, Huck."

"But you saved me."

"I reckon so, Huck."

"What was his name again?" Huck asked.

"Norman."

"You were friends with a white man?"

"He weren't no white man, Huckleberry," I said.

"Why did you save me and not him?" Huck asked.

"I jest did, s'all. I couldn' save you boff."

"Why me, Jim?"

Maybe because I was tired of the slave voice. Maybe because I hated myself for having lost my friend. Maybe because the lie was burning through me. Because of all of those reasons, I said, "Because, Huck, and I hope you hear this without thinking I'm crazy or joking, you are my son."

Huck shot out a short laugh. "What?"

"You are my son. And I am your father."

"Why are you talking like that?"

"Are you referring to my diction or my content?"

"What? What's content?"

"Never mind that. Your mother and I were little children together. We were friends. And we grew up. And. And you're my son."

Huck was more confused than ever and I couldn't help him. So, I closed my eyes and let exhaustion push me into sleep.

WHEN I AWOKE I found Huck staring at me. It was still daylight, but the sun was a few hours from setting behind us. I was again on the Missouri side of the river, the side where the runaway slave Jim was known and recognizable and hotly wanted by several bad-intentioned parties.

"Did Pap know?" Huck asked.

"I'm not sure."

"He sho' hated you. You think that's why he hated you so much? Causin' he knew about it?"

"He could have hated me just because I'm a black man."

"I reckon that's true," Huck said. "But I always thought he hated you somethin' special."

"I thought so, too."

"Jim?"

"Yes, Huck?"

"So, I am a nigger?"

"You can be what you want to be," I told him.

"Am I a slave?"

"Who cares what the law says you are? Nobody else knows who your father is and so you're not a slave. Even if Pap knew, he's dead now. Remember that house in the flood?"

Huck nodded.

"Remember that body? The one I wouldn't let you look at?"

"Pap?"

"Yes."

"You been keepin' a mess of secrets."

"I'm sorry."

Huck looked at his naked feet. "I always hated Pap. He beat me."

"I know," I said.

"Tom always said my hair was like a duck's back, that it wouldn't get wet and stay wet," Huck said. "Is that why?"

I shrugged.

"So, you always been my daddy?"

"That's how it works."

"So, Lizzie, she's my sister."

"Sort of."

"What is Sadie to me?" he asked.

"Nothing."

"And you always talked like this?"

"Yes."

"You've been lying to me this whole time? You been lying to me my whole life?"

"I suppose I have."

Huck fell silent. He closed his eyes, curled up into a ball and found something like sleep.

IT WAS DARK when we woke up. The beach was quiet, but a few torches burned up the beach. I couldn't stop seeing Norman's eyes, his bobbing face, his waving hand as he went under. He had trusted me. Now he was dead. All of those dead white faces, and none of them mattered a note to me, but Norman's, with skin just like theirs, was the world.

"WE'S BEST BE GETTIN' out of here," Huck said.

I looked at him in the moonlight.

"Where fo we be headin'?" Huck went on.

"Why are you talking like that?"

"I be yo son, so by law I be a slave."

"Like I said, I don't know what the law says about you. But stop talking like that. You sound ridiculous. Besides, you don't know the language."

"Then you gotta teach it to me."

"You don't need to know it."

"I'm a nigger like you, like my daddy."

"I'm not a nigger," I told him. "You can be what you want to be. You, especially. You can be white or black. Nobody will question you."

"What should I be?"

"Just keep living," I said. "Just remember, once they see you, or see me in you, you've been seen. I know you don't understand. But you will one day."

He said nothing, but stared at me or into me or through me.

"Just keep living," I repeated. "You can be free, if you choose. You can be white, if you choose. Me, I have to go north, find some money and send somebody back to buy Sadie and Lizzie."

"If the north wins the war, they'll be free," Huck said.

"I don't know about this war you're talking about. I just know I have to get my family. I have to get them out of slavery."

"I'm your family."

"You're no slave. Be the white boy you can be, Huck. You go back to Hannibal and keep your secret. I'm going north."

"But the war . . ." the boy said.

"The war won't do anything for me, Huckleberry."

"I want to go with you."

"You can't."

"You don't even know where you are," he said.

"I know north is that way." I pointed with my nose.

"I want to go with you."

"No."

"Why did you save me if I can't go with you? You gonna need my help. I can get us food."

"I saved you because you're my son."

Huck stared at his hands.

"They're not going to get darker."

"You're a liar, Jim. You're nothing but a liar. I don't believe a word of it. If you been lying to me this whole time, then you're probably lying now. You've been lying to me my whole life. About everything. Why should I believe anything you tell me?"

"Belief has nothing to do with truth. Believe what you like. Believe I'm lying and move through the world as a white boy. Believe I'm telling the truth and move through the world as a white boy anyway. Either way, no difference." I looked at the boy's face and I could see that he had feelings for me and that was the root of his anger. He had always felt affection for me, if not actual love. He had always looked to me for protection, even when he thought he was trying to protect me.

"Liar," he cried.

I took it.

"I ain't your son. I ain't no nigger."

CHAPTER 2

I HAD HEARD of an underground railroad. I wanted it to be real, even if I could have no truck with it. Some people were finding a way north—that was what I, so many of us, needed to believe. It pained me to think that without a white person with me, without a white-looking face, I could not travel safely through the light of the world, but was relegated to the dense woods. Without someone white to claim me as property, there was no justification for my presence, perhaps for my existence.

I looked down at the beach from our hiding place. The living had staggered to a common spot downriver. The dead remained were they lay. I looked for a long body with short, ill-fitting clothes. I don't know why. I didn't want or need to see a dead Norman. But next to a lifeless fat woman was a small brown square. Without realizing what I was doing, I walked from our cover on the hill and through the patches of grass and onto the beach. The closer I got, the more certain I was that I was approaching my notebook. It was just that. I should have looked about, tried to employ some stealth, but I didn't. It was an absent-minded, foolish misstep.

Someone shouted out, "Hey! Look over there! That nigger's robbing a dead white woman!"

"Did he touch her? Did he touch her?" another one yelled. "Lawd amercy, I believe he touched her body."

"Hey, I know him!" Like an idiot, I turned to see them all pointing at me.

One of them was Daniel Emmett. I watched as Emmett put together the scene in front of him. "That slave's got my notebook! He's not robbing her, he's robbing me!"

Luckily, the people on the beach were too physically spent to do anything but point fingers and rail loudly. With fear as my inspiration, I broke into a sprint. I ran north along the beach and then dashed back into the woods.

I fell, exhausted, against a sycamore and tried to catch my breath. I was too busy breathing to notice, until I was startled, that Huck was with me. He'd been right on my heels the whole time.

"They're not coming after us," the boy said.

"Yet." I looked at him. "What do you think you're doing?"

"You saved my life," he said. "Your friend was drowning and you chose me. You saved me."

"Yeah, well."

"We have to stick together."

"That's not what we have to do at all," I said. "I have to go north and get free. I have to work for money and send someone back to buy my family."

"I'll help you."

"Even though I'm a liar?" I studied his face. "Listen, you go on down there, and when the sheriff shows up, you tell him you're from Hannibal and they'll get you home." I stood and walked away. Huck followed.

"What is that?" He pointed at my notebook.

"It's a book," I said.

"And you can read? I knew it. Ain't we been friends forever? And you never trusted me enough to tell me that. What kind of book?"

"It's blank. I write in it."

"It's soaked."

"It will dry."

"You can write? I cain't hardly write. What else can you do? Can you fly? What else you ain't told me, Jim?"

"I've told you everything now."

Huck just stared at me.

"I suppose we'll just go our separate ways now," I said.

"No, I'm going with you."

"Why? I've been lying to you. I don't trust you."

He ignored those words and said, "Jest like before, I can say I own you in case somebody white sees you. I can say to 'em that you're my slave and we're on our way home, that we was trying to find a cow what went lost or stolen."

"And like before, you're just a boy. Nobody will believe you own me. It was and is a dumb idea." I walked away again.

He stayed in my footsteps. "You need me."

I hated that what he said was true. His story would make sense to any white person we encountered just as long as I played the devoted slave. There was also a part of me that didn't want to leave him alone there. So, I walked and he followed. We walked for hours, the river constantly at our side, flowing against us.

CHAPTER 3

WE COULDN'T FIND any trotlines to pilfer and we didn't have any line of our own, so Huck and I decided we'd dog for a catfish. It was a scary business, dogging, not just because a catfish had teeth, which it did, but because some were bigger than one could imagine. Grown men had drowned wrestling with the wrong fish. So, I was the fisherman and Huck was there to help me if I got into trouble. We waded up to an undercut bank and I got down and felt around. I wiggled my fingers like so many worms and groped around the wall of mud, looking for a hole in which a catfish might hide. I understood the principle, but I had never done it. I understood that when the fish tried to eat my hand I was to shove it down his throat and pull him free of the water. Just thinking that gave me a chill. *Eat my hand.*

"Don't try to grab it," Huck said. "If'n you get caught by a spine, you're cooked."

"Spine?"

"Them spiky things on their sides got poison. So, just make 'em want to come get you."

Only my head was out of the water now. My fingers wiggled. Minutes went by and then a lot of minutes. "This isn't going to work," I said.

"It'll work."

"What are the chances I'll find a snapping turtle?"

"I cain't get used to the way you talk," Huck said.

"That's your problem. I'm afraid the turtle thing is quite likely. There could be a beaver in there, for all I know. There could be a cottonmouth in there. What am I doing?" I looked at Huck. "I'm not doing this."

"Give 'er some time," he said.

I felt a nip at the middle finger of my right hand. "I feel something. I mean, I felt something. Something felt me." I wiggled my fingers faster and another digit was bumped. Suddenly, I was being held by the wrist. It was a terrible feeling, made worse by the fact that when I pulled back I was also sucked forward, the mouth now surrounding my forearm. It was large enough to erase my fear of turtles and snakes.

"You got one?" Huck asked.

"It's got me," I said.

"Pull."

"I am pulling."

"Let me help," Huck said, and he waded toward me, only to find the water over his head. He came to the surface somewhat panicked.

"Stay there," I said. The fish felt enormous. I couldn't find any purchase with my feet at all—they kept sliding in the mud—so I had only my arm strength to work with, and that was somewhat diminished, what with the flogging and near-drowning. The fish twisted. I imagined it twisting because I, in fact, was twisting. The world went wet and black. I was submerged in the muddy Mississippi. I could see absolutely nothing. I couldn't right myself. I couldn't hear anything, even though I knew Huck was screaming. I might have felt pressure in my chest, but I could not pinpoint it. I fought hard. I imagined Norman's face. I recalled his expression as he went down the last time I saw him, a mixture of complaint, fear, confusion and anger. In other words, in that moment, he looked like a slave. I saw young Sammy's lifeless face, and in her face I saw my beautiful Lizzie. I had to push free and breathe if I was going to see Lizzie and Sadie again. And then there was John Locke again, appearing to me, if for no other reason than to show me that my life was in jeopardy.

"You, again," I said. "Have you come to continue your defense of condoning slavery?"

"Imagine it all as a state of war," Locke said. "You have been conquered, and so as long as the war continues, you shall be a slave."

"When does the war end?" I asked.

"Does it end? That's the question. Who gets to say that it's over? A war continues until the victor says it's over."

"If I am in a war, then I have the right to fight back. That follows, doesn't it? I have a right, perhaps a duty, to kill my enemy."

"Well, now."

"My enemy is those who would kill me. Am I correct, John?"

"Well, now."

I pulled and pushed and my head popped out of the water. I sucked in the world and saw the cloud-filled sky. I mustered my strength and pulled back with all I had. The animal popped free of its muddy home and came shooting forth, head, gills and tail, clean out of the water.

"Jesus, Jim!" Huck cried out.

I fell away into shallower water, my arm still lodged in the fish.

"He must weigh fifty pounds," Huck said.

I saw the whiskers first and the animal, momentarily, looked nothing like a fish. Then I saw it clearly and it truly scared me, the way it stared at me with black and deep eyes, the way it insisted on living. I heaved the fish over the water and onto the shore. Only then did my arm slide free of its wide mouth. The animal flopped on the bank. Huck crawled up, grabbed it by the gills and pulled it into the grass.

"Jesus, Jim," he said again.

I washed the slime off my arm with the Mississippi's muddy water. Huck was correct—the fish might have weighed fifty or more pounds—and I had fought it out of its cave and onto land, but I felt no sense of accomplishment, no joy, no relief. Huck struck the fish's head with a big stick until it struggled no more.

"Dinner," Huck said, standing straight.

I lay back on the bank, shrub roots digging into my back, and closed my eyes tight, as if locking them.

Huck showed the excitement of a boy at the sight of our catch. I was reminded that he was just that, a boy. He could have gone through life without the knowledge I had given him and he would have been no worse off for it. But I understood at that moment that I had shared the truth with him for myself. I needed for him to have a choice.

CHAPTER 4

FIFTY POUNDS OF CATFISH is far too much for any two people to eat. I overate, as I saw myself owing it to the fish. So much of the creature would be wasted, as we had no time to dry any of it for later. Huck rolled up some chunks of flesh in leaves, saying that he would use them as bait along the trek. There were a few hours of light left and we chose to rest before walking along the river at night. It was clear that the people we had escaped on the beach were not following us; they were too concerned with being survivors. White people often spent time admiring their survival of one thing or another. I imagined it was because so often they had no need to survive, but only to live. No, they were not chasing me now, but there was no doubt that pursuit would come, with the theft of the notebook added to my continually lengthening list of crimes.

We walked through the dark, the river at least in earshot, if not right beside us. I didn't know if Huck was still angry with me, but he didn't speak. I didn't mind that, as I was too tired for conversation, too angry to entertain anyone else's thoughts. My anger fascinated me, still. It was certainly not a new emotion, but the range, the scope, the direction of it, was entirely novel and unfamiliar.

I decided that sticking to the river was not the wisest course. We would be too easy to track in the soft ground and too easy to spot. "We need to move inland," I said.

"It's too dark," Huck said.

He was right about that and he got no argument from me, but I was also correct. "Then we'll have to rest and move on at first light," I said.

The boy appeared to understand my concern. And so we did rest. I found deep sleep quickly and I believe he did also, because he was difficult to rouse when the sun came up too soon.

"I'm hungry," Huck said.

"So am I, but we have to keep moving," I told him.

We hiked about a mile west, where we found a north-south trail. It had seen so much recent activity that I was wary of following it. I wondered if we had stumbled onto the path of the underground railroad. Just moments after this thought, I pulled Huck into the bushes because I heard the approach of a large party.

Huck was wide-eyed as we watched seven men, dressed alike in blue, stomping south. They carried rifles and packs on their backs with shovels and rolled-up blankets. They were young and white.

"Them's soldiers," Huck said. "Jest like the folks on the riverboat said. They said the slavers had attacked South Carolina. Said it happened months ago and that's how the whole thing started."

"I don't like all of those guns," I said.

"Some other folks got mad when they said 'slavers.' A couple of men got into a fight. One feller knocked a tooth right out of the other feller's head. That was when the boat shook and broke up."

The soldiers were out of sight now.

"What side you suppose they was on?" Huck asked.

We both froze at the sound of someone approaching. We were unable to hide before a boy-faced white soldier appeared. He must have fallen behind the rest. He confronted us on the trail. He stared wild-eyed at me, then settled his eyes on Huck for a longer few seconds. He said nothing, just collected himself and marched on quickly to catch up to his party. I could almost smell the fear on him.

"A war. Can you believe it?" Huck said. "He weren't much older than me."

The thought of war didn't mean much to me. I didn't know what war meant. I didn't know who would be fighting whom or why it should matter to me. Considering it—rather trying to consider it—left me feeling naïve and childlike. Even Huck's boyish and romantic fascination with the idea of a war revealed that he understood more than me. The only thing I could think was that I had to keep moving north.

"I want to follow them," Huck said. "I bet they's going to a battle or somethin'."

"North," I said.

"You don't own me," Huck said.

I studied his face, his set jaw. "No, Huck, I don't own you. I hope no one ever does. You wouldn't like it. Will you, please, just walk north with me?"

"Why?"

"Because I would like to know you're safe. You'll be safe with Miss Watson and Judge Thatcher."

"What about you? You gonna turn yerself in?"

"No, son. I'm going to keep running. Since I can't buy them, I'm going to find Sadie and Lizzie and we're going to run to a free state."

"What state is that?" he asked.

"I don't know. Illinois, maybe. Maybe we'll go all the way to Canada."

"And you weren't considerin' takin' me," he said. "Why wouldn't you take your son with you?"

"You're already free," I told him.

"Maybe I'll join up and fight in the war," he said. "I'm free to do that, right? I can do whatever I want."

"I suppose that's true. Tell me, which side would you fight for?"

"I don't hardly reckon. Them fellas looked sharp in their blue coats. I wonder what side they be on?"

"One side is the same as the other to me. One side is against slavers, is what you've told me. I don't know what precisely that means. People who sell slaves or people who own slaves."

"What difference does that make?" Huck asked.

"I don't know that it does."

"To fight in a war," he said. "Can you imagine?"

"Would that mean facing death every day and doing what other people tell you to do?" I asked.

"I reckon."

"Yes, Huck, I can imagine."

Huck studied the tracks of the soldiers who had just passed, as if they held some meaning.

"I think we need to find our way back to the river so we can see where we are," I said. "These creeks just confuse me.

Lord knows where this trail leads—could be a circle, for all we know."

"What will you do when we get back to Hannibal?" Huck asked.

"If you don't tell anybody I'm there, I'll try to leave with Sadie and Lizzie. I'll hide out and wait for the right time. I can't get any money, and even if I did, a slave can't buy slaves. I heard of slaves buying themselves. But I'm a runaway."

"And you'll leave me?" he asked.

"You'll be okay."

"What does that mean?"

"Like I said, you'll be safe. Miss Watson loves you. They all love you. Even Judge Thatcher wants to take care of you."

Huck fell quiet and stared off.

"What do you want? Do you want to be on the run with us? Do you want to pass as a slave? I can tell you that you don't want that. Nobody wants that. There's no adventure in it, Huck."

"But if what you say is true, that you're my father, then shouldn't I be with you?"

"When you believed Pap Finn was your father, did you think you had to be with him? Think about that."

"I musta known deep down that he wasn't," the boy said. "I can't believe you didn't tell me this a long time ago."

"A father's job is make sure his children are safe, right?" I felt bad offering such platitudes. I, in fact, had no idea what I or anyone else was supposed to do.

Huck didn't answer.

"Let's find the river. We'll sort this out later." I led the way due east through dense brush.

The problem with being lost on the river was that things appeared different facing south from the way they did looking north. It was as if there were two different bodies of water. The Mississippi, in fact, seemed like many different rivers. The level was always rising or falling. Sediment got pushed around, changing the locations of bars and shelves. Islands changed shape, sometimes becoming completely submerged, and old outcroppings disappeared while new ones materialized overnight. The upshot was that we had no idea where we were. There was no reason to look for a boat to steal, as fighting upriver with oars would be slower than walking, with far more effort. So, again we hiked, the river on our right, not always in sight.

CHAPTER 5

IF ONE KNOWS hell as home, then is returning to hell a homecoming? Even in hell, were there such a place, one would know where the fires were just a little cooler, where the rocks were just a little less jagged. And so it was in my hell. There was my family and there were the bad things, the cesspit, the patrolling overseer. Huck and I arrived at night, having slept on the beach facing Jackson Island. It felt like so long ago that we had stationed ourselves there in that cave. With Huck's pap dead, it felt as if we had less to fear in these woods, but of course that wasn't true. I was wanted as a runaway and perhaps also for kidnapping, theft and murder. We came to the edge of the slave quarters well after sundown. The fire burned where it had always burned, but hardly anyone stood around it.

"Run on to Miss Watson's house," I told Huck.

"Ima stayin' with you," he said.

The boy followed me across the yard toward my house. The world there felt changed, different from how it had the last time I was there. There was a stillness, and I began to fret. I stepped faster.

"Jim?" It was Doris. He looked at me as he closed the distance between us. "Jim? My goodness. Where on earth have you been?" He looked past me to see Huck and so repeated his question. "Lawd a'mercy. Where ya'll bin all dis time?"

"My God, you, too, Doris?" Huck said.

"What's going on?" I asked. I could feel the world crushing down on me, like all the water in the Mississippi.

Doris's eyes darted to the door of my shack and then back to me.

I pushed through the doorway. A woman stood over the fire, her back to me. A man lay on a pallet in the far corner. I fell a surge of anger. Could Sadie have been assigned a new husband? Could it work that way?

The woman turned to me. She was not Sadie. This fact both relieved and alarmed me. The man was standing now. He was tall and wide.

"Who are you?" I asked the woman.

She regarded Huck, stared at him for a long beat. "I's Katie. This heah be Cotton." She pointed back at the man.

"I been tryin' to tells ya, Jim," Doris said.

"Relax," I said. "The boy knows."

"Da boy know what?" Doris said.

"About our language," I said.

Doris sighed. "This is a fine mess."

"Tell me what, Doris? What were you about to tell me?"

"Sadie and Lizzie," he said.

"Where are they?" I scanned the tiny shack again.

The woman looked at Doris and then dropped her eyes to the dirt floor.

"Doris?"

"Jim, they were sold."

I had heard his words clearly, but I said, "What?"

"They were sold."

Just what happened next is blurry in my memory, but I remember being on my knees. I cried, really cried. I realized that Huck was hugging me. I could feel his concern through his hands. I looked up to see the confused faces of Doris, Katie and Cotton. I had never felt such grief.

"Who bought them?" I asked.

Of course they wouldn't know and could tell me nothing.

"Which way, Doris? In what direction did they take them?"

Doris shook his head. "But they went together," he said. "That's a good thing, Jim. They didn't split them up. That's a good thing, isn't it? The overseer, Hopkins, came and got them and then they were gone."

I looked at Huck's face. I think for the very first time in his life he was actually seeing me.

"Huck, you've got to help me," I said. "Someone has to help me." I had never sobbed so. "Huck?"

"What kin I do?" he asked. His eyes were as red and wet as I imagined my own were. "I'm just a boy."

"After what you've been through?" I said. "You're a man, Huck. You can find out who bought them and where they went."

"How am I supposed to do that?"

"You're smart. Figure it out. Just ask. Ask any of them, all of them. Go through papers in Judge Thatcher's desk and find a bill of sale. He handles all of Miss Watson's business. Whatever you can think of. Think of it as an adventure."

This appealed to the boy, as he was suddenly just that again, a boy. "Maybe Tom'll help me."

I nodded.

"You can't stay here, Jim," Doris said. "You're a wanted man. If they find you, they'll string you up for certain."

"That's true," Cotton said. "They want you real bad. For all sorts of crimes. I heard them talking." The big man seemed a bit afraid of me. My fearsome reputation had apparently been established.

"Huck," I said, "run on to Miss Watson's and tell her you found your way back from the dead. And tell her you saw me drown when that riverboat blew apart. Tell her a good story."

"You want me to lie?" Huck asked.

"Yes, I want you to lie. You can't very well tell her I'm dead and have it be true. Yes, I want you to lie. Lie hard. Now go."

Cotton cocked his head as he watched Huck scurry out of the shanty. "You must be a real bad man, giving orders to a white cracker like that. Even if he is a boy."

"I'm sorry to have barged into your home," I said to Katie and Cotton. "I've had a rough go of it."

They nodded.

"Would you mind if I slept for a while near your fire?" I could tell he was scared, if not for himself, then for Katie. "It's okay. I can find a place to sleep in the woods."

"Are you hungry?" Katie asked. She took Cotton's hand.

"No, just tired."

"We'll try to keep your secret," Doris said. "You've got to stay out of sight. If the overseer sees you, you're a dead man."

"And us, too," Cotton said.

"I know," I said.

Doris sighed and took a peek out the door.

"Okay, Doris. Thank you." I looked at Katie and Cotton. "They won't find me. I promise."

Cotton nodded.

I lay down on the dirt floor by the flames. The warmth was numbing, just what I needed. The smell of burning green wood was the familiarity I needed. I felt my eyes shutting. Someone draped a quilt over me.

CHAPTER 6

NOUS DEVONS CULTIVER notre jardin." This was spoken to me by a lean boy I didn't recognize. He was squinty-eyed and looked white.

"I'm sorry—I don't speak French," I said.

"And yet I have spoken it in your dream."

"And yet you have," I said, dismissively. "I suppose it's possible also, in a dream, to recognize someone I've never met." On second glance, I could see that the speaker was neither a boy nor white-looking. I pushed up to see just where this dream had put me. I sat back against a wide tree, maybe a live oak, overlooking a verdant valley. There was a meadow dotted with cattle. Birds flew lower than I sat. "Pretty," I said.

"Do you believe your family is down there somewhere?"

I stared. "I do."

"And you think you'll find them?"

"I do."

She laughed.

"What's so funny?"

"I don't know. Hope? Hope is funny. Hope is not a plan. Actually, it's just a trick. A ruse." She stretched the *se* of that word, as if enjoying the sound of it. "You're looking at this hand while the other is shoving a stick up your ass. A pointy stick. You think they want you because you can carry a load. You think they want you because you can hammer a nail. They want you because you're money."

"What?"

"You're mortgaged, Jim. Like a farm, like a house. Really, the bank owns you. Miss Watson gets a bond, a piece of paper that say what you're worth, and you just keep living in this condition. Living. You're a part of the bank's assets and so people all over the world are making money off your scarred black hide. Make sense? Nobody wants you free."

"Somebody does. There's a war."

She nodded. "Maybe you won't be a slave, but you won't be free."

"Who are you?"

"My name is Cunégonde."

I looked at the valley below, the cliché of a stream that split it. "And yet you come back at the end of the story."

"Your point?"

"HIDE!"

I awoke to find Katie whisper-shouting at me. "Hide!" She looked at the door. "The overseer is coming. Get in the corner behind that barrel. Hurry." I crawled as quickly as I could across the packed dirt into the shadows. Katie grabbed a straw broom and erased my track.

Katie was scared and recoiling even before the door opened.

The overseer, Hopkins, walked through the door. He raked his hand through his stringy hair.

"Cotton ain't here, Mistuh Hopkins." Katie trembled.

"Naw, you know I ain't come here to see no Cotton. I know jest where Cotton is." He unfastened a button on his sweaty shirt, kept his eyes on the woman. "Pull up them skirts, girl."

I imagined that Katie looked in my direction, but she was merely looking everywhere but at him.

"Bend on over, girl,"

"Please, Mistuh Hopkins."

The slapping of their flesh was terrible, sickening, bad music for any ear at any time. Katie begged him to stop. "Not again. Not again." She cried, her face pressed against the rough wood of the table.

In my mind I was rushing to her aid, grabbing the monster by his head and twisting it until I heard a snap. In my mind. In the world I stayed in the shadows. If I killed that man, if I attacked that man, if I was discovered by that man, then all of the slaves would be punished, some perhaps killed. And the white men would return again anyway to do this to Katie. I saw my Sadie in young Katie's face. I saw my child. I did not look away. I wanted to feel the anger. I was befriending my anger, learning not only how to feel it, but perhaps how to use it.

"There naw, girl," Hopkins said. The white animal covered himself and walked out of the shack.

I came out of hiding and sat by the fire while Katie adjusted her clothes. I put a stick from the pile into the flames.

I wanted to tell her I was sorry, but that really didn't make any sense. We both knew where we were and we knew that we didn't know anything else. We knew that she, I, all of us, were forever naked in the world.

COTTON WALKED INTO the shack and I stood up. I can't say that he smelled anything in the air or that he spotted any obvious cue from Katie, but his shoulders sank. He and I shared a glance and I walked past him to the door. I didn't turn to see their interaction, didn't listen for their words or sounds. I peeked outside at the coming dusk, saw no one and left.

I sneaked between huts and found my way to the edge of the thick woods and realized that the best place for me was Jackson Island. I knew the cave there, could fish there, could wait there for Huck to return with information about my family. I didn't tell Doris or anyone where I was going. Them knowing was courting disaster, for me and for them. There were probably even a couple of slaves that couldn't be trusted, who liked their condition, as I had learned. I felt ashamed that I had hid out even one night in Katie and Cotton's home. I had given them new cause to fear for their lives.

When Huck came but failed to find me in the slave quarters, he would know to check our cave on the island. That was if Miss Watson, Judge Thatcher and the rest would give him a minute to himself after his extraordinary return from the dead.

I waded into the river and swam across the channel at dusk. Instead of risking a crawl through the thick brush at night, on terrain that might have been altered by weather and memory, I slept on the sandy beach. At first light I found someone's trotline and stole a single catfish.

With some difficulty, several missteps and a detour because of a cottonmouth, I found the cave. It took me the better part of two hours to get a fire going with two stones and dry moss. I'd lost my glass along the trail someplace. I cooked the fish and set to the business of waiting. I felt the weight of my pencil. It had survived.

CHAPTER 7

TO SAY THAT the following four days crawled by would be a gross understatement. Days of forced labor always seemed to last weeks. Twenty-minute floggings took months. The waiting for some tear in the invisible curtain that bound us felt like centuries. In fact, was centuries. But this waiting for some news of my family's whereabouts was endless, dead spaces separated by dead spaces. No one had troubled the island. There was nothing there for anyone. Only the occasional deer. Raccoons were no more numerous than they were on the mainland, and why risk an encounter with the riot of snakes? White men came now and again to burn fires and get drunk on one beach or another and watch the riverboats roll by. I fished, ate, slept, thought and wrote. I wrote to extend my thought, I wrote to catch up with my own story, wondering all the while if that was even possible. My sleep was bothered by the scene of Katie's rape. I hated that man. I hated myself for not intervening. I hated the world that wouldn't let me apply justice without the certain retaliation of injustice. I hated that such violence had been served to my wife and would be served to my daughter. I hated that the overseer would return to Katie. Again and again.

And then one morning, I watched a skiff of white men leave the beach they favored. A canoe remained behind and, with it, the overseer, Hopkins. He stoked the fire they had made and continued to pull from the bottle the group of them had begun. No one knew I was there. He had been left drunk on the island. He muttered a song to himself. They had been laughing together, maybe talking about their rapes and other crimes. I found my anger and stoked it. I used the quiet of the woods around me as a buffer as I entertained the notion of opportunity. No one knew I was there. I recalled a young slave who had chanced a look at a white woman. The end of the rope that had named him had been left in the tree as a warning to all others for years. I remembered his face as death had frozen it. He didn't look any less like a boy for having been murdered. I recalled Hopkins chastising his friends for being poor shots when bullets from their pistols failed to find the boy's body.

My anger found full flower as I approached him. He was half sleeping, still drunk-humming his song. I took the pistol from the ground beside him and put it in my trousers, as I had seen white men do. I put a log on his fire, and another, until the flames were tall. The wall of heat made him uncomfortable and he woke to see me through the flames.

"Who that?"

"It be jest a nigger, Mistuh Overseer, suh."

"What nigger that be? I know you?"

"You knows me, suh," I said.

"I do, do I?" His hand fell to the ground, searched for his pistol.

"I gots yo gun raght heah, suh."

"Give it to me," he said.

"You be scared, suh?"

"Give me my gun, nigger."

"Why you needs a gun, Overseer Hopkins, suh? You 'fraid I gonna shoot ya?"

"Nigger, is you crazy?"

"Which answer would frighten you more?"

"What?"

"It's actually a simple question, Hopkins. Which would frighten you more? A slave who is crazy or a slave who is sane and sees you clearly?"

"You ain't no slave, talkin' like that. Who are you?"

I leaned my face toward the fire.

"Nigger Jim?"

"In the flesh," I said. "Let me translate that. Yessuh, it be's me, Overseer Hopkins." I paused. "Suh."

"Hey, what's this all 'bout?"

"I'm going to walk around to you now. If you move, I will shoot you. If you believe anything, you believe that. Now, just sit still."

Hopkins was trembling. He wanted to believe he was drunk-dreaming. I walked around the fire toward him. He followed me with his eyes. I hadn't touched his weapon, the handle of it showing at my waist. I came up behind him, behind the rock that supported his back. I slowly put my arm around his neck, his chin resting on the crook at my elbow, and applied pressure.

"So that these minutes aren't wasted, Overseer Hopkins, I'll ask you to think about the women you have raped. Think about Katie. Think about her fear, her voice, her begging you to stop." I tightened my grip on his neck. It was more than my physical strength that held him there. It was more than merely me. He kicked his legs. "Can you see those women, Mistuh Hopkins, suh. Can you see them right now."

He tried to speak.

I released him slightly. "What was that?"

"Nigger, are you crazy?"

"Possibly. Tell me, what part of raping Katie did you enjoy? Her soft brown skin? Her sweet smell?" I tightened my grip. "Her palpable fear? Yes, that was it. Her fear. You liked her crying like that, didn't you? You can tell me."

He kicked more. I squeezed. I twisted. My breathing was measured and deep. His feet went wild as he kicked the fire, embers flying. And then all was silent. No kicking. No words. I looked down to see that he had pissed. Or maybe it wasn't piss.

"That must be embarrassing," I said.

Spittle flew from his mouth.

"You're going to die, Hopkins. And you know what part of this I'm enjoying? Do you know? Guess."

Hopkins flailed his arms and kicked crazily again. I smelled the sourness of his hair and didn't like it. His kicking slowed.

"It's not your fear. I know that's what you were thinking. It's the fact that I don't really care. That's the best part of this—that I don't care." And I didn't care that he was dead and unable to hear those final words. He didn't matter.

I dragged Hopkins to the canoe. With a jagged rock I smashed a hole into the hull of it. I dumped the man into the boat. I considered putting his pistol beside him in the boat. I felt the weight of it and recalled what such a thing had done to young Sammy. I set the boat adrift. I watched it fold into the current and go under.

CHAPTER 8

MORE DAYS PASSED. I looked for voices in my dreams, trying to find some comprehension of what I had done. Of course, on one level it was all too simple. I had exacted revenge. But for whom? For one act, or many? Against one man, many men or the world? I wondered if I should feel guilty. Should I have felt some pride in my action? Had I done a brave thing? Had I done an evil thing? Was it evil to kill evil? The truth was that I didn't care. It was this apathy that left me wondering about myself—not wondering why I didn't feel anything or whether I was incapable of feeling, but wondering what else I was capable of doing. It was not an altogether bad feeling.

I WAS LYING on the same bed of leaves I had lain on when recovering from that rattlesnake bite. I could hear the church bell in Hannibal so far away and I knew that it was Sunday. I hadn't known for so long what day it was. I went to the mouth of the cave and listened to the bluebirds. I heard footfalls on the dry leaves. I ducked into the thick brush and crouched down.

"Jim?" It was Huck.

"Huck. I knew you'd find me."

"I swear they been watchin' me like hawks. I couldn't even pee by my lonesome. I only got away now because I sneaked outta church."

"Let's sit down. Did anybody see you paddle across?"

"I don't think so," the boy said. "I din't tell nobody anything. They asked me fifty times, if they asked me once, if'n I seen you and I said no every time."

"I thought you were going to say I was dead," I said.

"I just couldn't kill you off," the boy said.

"Thank you, Huck."

"They asked me where I been and I told them. I told them about the King and Bilgewater. I told them about how the riverboat blew up. They'd heard about that. They already heard tell of a slave what stole another slave. Was that you, Jim?"

"What else?" I asked. "Did you ask about Sadie and Lizzie?"

"I tried, but they looked at me funny when I did. That overseer, the one named Hopkins, he knew. Said something about a Graham farm, but I don't know where it is. Now he done disappeared."

"Disappeared?"

"Up and vanished, they say. Somebody found his boat. Maybe the river got him." Huck studied my face.

"I remember him," I said. "He was always ready with the whip."

"Judge Thatcher thinks he was drunk and did what drunk folks do on the river. Fell in and drowned."

I was upset with myself for not thinking to question Hopkins when I had him. I had let my emotions, specifically my anger, my need for vengeance, get the better of me. I vowed to never let that happen again. From then on, I would never lose control.

"I hope they never find you," Huck said. "You'll be wishin' you was drowned in the Mississippi."

"Yes?"

"They want to hang you twice."

I nodded. I realized I couldn't be made more afraid than I was, than I had been my entire life.

We sat quietly for a long spell.

"How's the fishin'?" Huck asked.

I shrugged.

"They won't even let me go out to fish by myself."

"How's the war going?" I asked.

"Still goin'. Judge Thatcher says I'm too young to go join up."

I considered the northern white stance against slavery. How much of the desire to end the institution was fueled by a need to quell and subdue white guilt and pain? Was it just too much to watch? Did it offend Christian sensibilities to live in a society that allowed that practice? I knew that whatever the cause of their war, freeing slaves was an incidental premise and would be an incidental result. "Have you picked a side yet?" I asked.

"The Union," he said.

"Are they for or against slavery?"

"They're agin it."

I nodded. "Thank you, Huck. Now, you had better get back before they miss you. I don't need a search party prowling around out here."

I walked the boy back to the beach and watched from the trees as he paddled across. The Graham farm. I needed to find out where that was.

CHAPTER 9

THAT NIGHT, under a gibbous moon, I waded and swam across the muddy channel, rations, notebook and pistol wrapped in a bundle and held over my head. I would not be returning to Jackson Island. Night felt like a different animal, its own season. My voice, even in my head, had found its root in my diaphragm, had become sonorous and round. My pencil had more firmly grasped the pages of my newly dried notebook. I saw more clearly, farther, further. My name became my own.

HANNIBAL WAS DEAD QUIET as soon as the sun was gone. Mosquitoes bothered me. I made my way to Judge Thatcher's house by staying in the shadows. Dogs barked at my sounds, but dogs were always barking. I knew the judge's dog and he knew me, so he did nothing but raise his large and lazy head, give me a glance and put it back down. The back door, the only one a slave would ever use, was unlocked, as all doors in Hannibal were unlocked. The pistol in my bundle felt incredibly heavy and the weight scared me. I crept inside and through the kitchen. The planks of the floor spoke, but sounded enough like the settling of the house that no one would take note. I eased into the judge's library room. I paused, breathed in the musty smell of the books, his pipe tobacco, felt the dust of paper in the air. I had sneaked into this room many times before, had hidden in one corner or another and read. But not tonight. Tonight I sat at the desk and felt the books as if served up as a meal there was no time to eat. I found matches by the lamp and lit it. I pocketed the matches. I found a satchel and decided I would take what I needed. Books, matches, several pencils. I found a map, but I didn't know how to read it. I packed it anyway. I opened drawers. I was looking for the bill of sale, the document that would tell me where the Graham farm was and, therefore, where I would find my family. I found no such paper.

A shadow and then a figure filled the doorway. It was Judge Thatcher. "Who is that there?" he asked.

I said nothing, but sat straight in his chair.

He stepped forward. "A nigger?" he said.

Still, I remained quiet.

"Boy, you best have an excellent, an extraordinary reason for sittin' in that chair," he said.

My hand had slipped into my bundle and found the pistol. As I grabbed it I was reminded of my ignorance of such things. I knew only which end was dangerous. However, the pointy end of such a thing speaks loudly, and when I leveled the barrel at the judge, he stopped in his tracks.

"Jim?"

"James," I said.

"Boy, they're gonna lynch you every day but Tuesday," he said.

I was so confused by his expression of white-hot anger that

I let the barrel of the pistol drop. He approached slowly. Without threatening him with the gun again, I said, "Please, don't do that."

He stopped. He studied me and then looked out the window behind me, as if for help. "What are you doing here?"

"Where are my wife and daughter? I know you handled the sale of them. I need to know where they've been taken."

"Why are you talking like that?"

"Confusing, isn't it?" I said.

"Slaves get sold. It happens," he said.

"Who bought them?" I cocked my head. I pointed the pistol at him again. "Have a seat." I nodded to the chair in front of the desk.

He sat. "Why are you talking like that?"

"I'm pointing a pistol at you and asking about the whereabouts of my family and you're concerned with my speech? What is wrong with you? Where is the Graham farm? That's where they are, correct?"

"Yes," he said. "The farm is in Edina."

My head swam. I heard the word, but it meant nothing. "Where is that? Another state?"

"Edina, Missouri," he said.

I threw the map down, spread it across the face of the desk. "Show me on here where it is."

He pointed.

I scanned the colors of the paper, the lines. MISSISSIPPI RIVER was clearly written. "I see the river," I said. "Show me where we are now."

"We're right here," he said, putting his finger down.

I had a sense of things. "Mark it."

He grabbed a pen, dipped it in the well and circled Hannibal and Edina. Hannibal was labeled on the paper, but Edina was not.

"Why isn't Edina written here?" I said.

"You can read?" he asked.

"Why isn't it written here?"

"It's a new settlement."

"How far is that?"

"Nigger, you are in more trouble than you can imagine," he said.

"Why on earth would you think that I can't imagine the trouble I'm in? After you've tortured me and eviscerated me and emasculated me and left me to burn slowly to death, is there something else you'll do to me? Tell me, Judge Thatcher, what is there that I can't imagine?"

He squirmed in the chair.

"Could you have imagined a black man, a slave, a nigger, talking to you like this? Who's lacking in imagination?"

"Are you going to kill me?"

"The thought crossed my mind. I haven't decided. Oh, sorry, let me translate that for you. I ain't 'cided, Massa."

I had never seen a white man filled with such fear. The remarkable truth, however, was that it was not the pistol, but my language, the fact that I didn't conform to his expectations, that I could read, that had so disturbed and frightened him.

"What now?" he asked.

"Let's walk out of here. Quietly. I'm not familiar with the workings of this pistol and it might go off at any second, so let's go slowly and quietly, please. I need rope and twine from the shed and then we'll go for a walk."

On our pass through the kitchen to the back door, I grabbed biscuits and some apples and a knife.

I herded Thatcher out of town, through the woods and to the river. There were several skiffs and canoes there at the floating dock. I chose a skiff and had Thatcher sit center, facing me. He rowed while I watched. He rowed against the current near the shore and we made slow but steady progress.

"Jim, I'm disappointed," Thatcher said.

"Excuse me?"

"After all I've done for you. I fed you all those years. I put a roof over your head. Gave you clothes."

"I'm a slave." I looked at him, rowing there, struggling, realized that now he was working for me. "Look at the way you're working, Judge. Looks like you're my slave for a little while."

This offended him. "I'm no slave."

"Do you want to be rowing?" I asked. "No," I supplied his answer. "Are you getting paid for rowing? No. Are you rowing because you're afraid of me and what I might do to you? Yes, Judge Thatcher."

"I'm no slave."

I pointed the barrel of the pistol at his face. "Row faster," I said.

He did.

"Oh, yes, you're a slave." The old man was getting tired. "Slow down. You can't row if you're dead."

"Where did you get that gun?" he asked.

"From a man," I said, without hesitation.

"It's a Colt Paterson," he said.

"If you say so."

"Tom Hopkins has a pistol like that."

"Had," I said.

"Did you kill him?"

"Yes." I looked at Thatcher's eyes. "I didn't shoot him, though. I strangled him. Watched his feet twitch as he died, just like he was dangling from a rope. It was quite ugly. I actually felt a little bad for him. I guess that's the difference between you and me."

It was no longer my diction that scared him. It was not the fact that I had premeditatedly killed. He was frightened now by the knowledge that I didn't care that he knew of my crime.

"I watched Hopkins rape a slave woman," I said. "I watched and I did nothing. Have you ever raped a slave? When you were young and strapping, before you became the slave you are right now? Did you ever rape a woman?"

His silence was profound.

I nodded. "Judge, I have no interest in killing you, though it wouldn't make my lot any worse, would it? I can't feed your fantasy that you're a good, kind master. No matter how gentle you were when you applied the whip, no matter how much compassion you showed when you raped. So, you dispensed fewer lashes when you punished. You often let us rest when temperatures soared."

"I'm going to see you dead, nigger."

"No doubt."

WE MADE OUR WAY a few miles upriver. The sun was just rising now, and we had to get out of sight. A white man rowing a black man was bound to attract attention. The judge was soaked with perspiration. He had not labored at anything since his youth. I watched him start to drag the boat onto a pebbly beach. I instructed him to cast it adrift. "Just push it out there," I said.

He did.

"Drag yourself over here," I said. I looked at the trees. "This spot should stay shady most of the day."

"What are you going to do?" he asked.

"I'm going to tie you to this tree."

"I don't think so."

"The alternative is loud and, in my estimation, a bit extreme. I don't think you would like it."

"Why are you talking like that?" he asked again.

"Just sit down before I shoot you."

He sat, and I tied him securely, but not too tightly, to the sycamore. He might eventually work himself free, if he really wanted it. I left him ungagged. I left him with his voice and he was free to scream and shout as his energy allowed.

Someone would come by on the river eventually. There was always traffic. Barring the appearance of a bear or some ambitious raccoon or his heart failing him, he would probably survive.

"What's in the satchel?" he asked.

"A few books. I don't think you'll miss them."

"What books?"

"That's an interesting question," I said. "You've surprised me. A narrative of some slave. That's one of them. It's never been opened, so I know you won't miss it. I don't know why you have it. *Candide*. Something else by Voltaire. John Stuart Mill."

"My God, what in the world is going on?"

"Call it progress," I said.

He squirmed against his ropes. "You can't leave me here like this," he said.

"Like what? Alive?"

He spat and looked away from me at the water.

Looking at the map, I could see that Edina was well west of the Mississippi and still north of me.

"You'll never make it," he said.

"Maybe not."

CHAPTER 10

THE WALKING WAS DIFFICULT. I dared not confine my movement to the nighttime now. I didn't know when Thatcher might get loose or be discovered and tell everyone what had happened. And he knew where I was headed. So I pushed forward. I covered a lot of ground and, though I understood myself to be closer to my family, I was still nowhere near them. I walked for the better part of three days. I was out of biscuits and hungry.

AT THE EDGE of a spent cornfield, a black man and I surprised each other. He started to run and I called out to him.

"Friend," I said.

He stopped and turned to me. "Where did you come from?" he asked.

"The woods. I'm a runaway."

"You don't say. From where?"

"Hannibal. I'm looking for the Graham farm."

"The breeder?" he asked.

"What do you mean?"

"Graham's a breeder. He breeds slaves and sells them."

"My wife and daughter were taken there."

The man was silent.

"Do you know where it is?"

"Sort of. I've never been there. It's near a town on the other side of the valley."

"Edina?"

"I think so."

"That way?" I pointed. He nodded and I thanked him.

"Are you hungry?"

"I am."

"Wait here."

I did wait there. I was pleased it was a cornfield, as the tall plants offered good cover. I went into my satchel and came out with the narrative by William Brown. I read and was struck with pangs of guilt and sadness, as "Brown" had also been the last name chosen by Norman. I read the first pages of the narrative, and it might as well have been my story. It was, in fact, my story. I read even though I wanted to sleep. I read of how he had boarded a boat headed toward free states, toward cities he had imagined as real, toward Canada. Oh, to be in Canada with my wife and child.

Apparently, I did fall asleep. I awoke to find the slave who had left me. He and a woman squatted near me. I sat up. "I'm James."

"I'm April," the man said. "This here is Holly."

I nodded hello.

"We brought you some food. Chicken necks and some gizzards," Holly said. "Some rice."

"Thank you." The food was greasy and amazing.

"How long have you been running?" April asked.

"Awhile. I'm trying to find my family, my wife and daughter. I was told they were taken to the Graham farm."

Holly shook her head, as if to free herself from a bad thought.

"Have you ever been there?" I asked.

"No. It's an awful place; I know that."

I finished the food and stood. It was nighttime now, a good time to move through farmland.

"What are you doing?" April asked.

"I'm going to find my family," I said.

"Just like that. You're going to walk into a plantation and ask for them?" April stared at me with disbelief.

I understood all too well his question. I had entertained it myself, but not enough to have formed an answer. "I'll know what I'm doing when I get there."

"You're crazy," he said.

"You have no idea," I said. "I'm wanted for being a runaway, kidnapping, theft and murder."

"Are you guilty?" Holly asked.

"Does it matter?" I asked.

"I suppose it doesn't."

"And yes, I am."

I WALKED THROUGH THE DARKNESS, across a wide valley, muddy in its trough. I saw fires dotting the far side and imagined, hoped, that it was Edina. I could hear more human sounds. There was nothing scarier than human sounds. Voices, laughter, whimpering. I saw a ring of shacks that I guessed were slave quarters. I smelled the waste from an open latrine and moved away from it. There was a group of four slave men shackled to a common post, a bowl of mush in the center of them.

They were frightened by my sudden appearance, but I shushed them. I sat with them and looked at their chains.

"Is this the Graham place?" I asked.

"It is," said a large man. They were all larger than me.

"I'm looking for my wife and daughter."

"Women in the other camp," another man said.

"Why do they have you chained up?" I asked.

"They're afraid of us," the first man said, and then they all laughed. "We don't know. I think they think it makes us feel more like animals. So we can mate like animals."

I looked at the rusty shackle locks. They were like the lock on the chain that used to hang from Miss Watson's root cellar door, and I knew that a knife could open them.

"Do you men want to run?" I called them "men" quite deliberately. First, because they were men, and second, because they needed to hear it. "I'm going to get my family and I'm running north." I took out the knife I had taken from Thatcher's kitchen and unlocked a shackle. "I want to find my wife and daughter."

"Damn," said one of the men. He rubbed his freed ankle.

I released them all. We stood. They towered over me.

"What is your wife's name?" the first man asked.

"Sadie. And my daughter is Lizzie. She's nine."

"I saw a woman come in with a little girl," he said. "Maybe two weeks ago."

"Do you know where they are?" I asked.

"With the other women, I suppose."

I reached into my satchel and pulled out the pistol. The men stepped back. "Any of you know how to use one of these?"

"My last owner used to shoot at everything," said the one who had not spoken yet. "I watched him. You have to pull back that thing with your thumb." He pointed. "That's the hammer."

"Does it have bullets in it?" I handed it to him.

He took it, looked at it and handed it back to me like it was hot. "Yes."

There was a half-moon in the western sky. I knew that the best thing would be to wait and to watch and to be patient, to strike when everything was right. However, I was not patient. And I knew that things would never be right. I also knew that the longer I waited, the more likely I was to be discovered, by chance or by warning from a rescued Thatcher.

"Let's go," I said.

"That's your plan? 'Let's go'?" the largest one said.

"I'm afraid so," I said.

"Who are you?"

"My name is James. I'm going to get my family. You can come with me or you can stay here. You can come and try freedom or you can stay here. You can die with me trying to find freedom or you can stay here and be dead anyway. My name is James."

"Morris."

"Harvey."

"Llewelyn."

"Buck." This from the smallest of them. "Let's go."

CHAPTER 11

A PLAN OF ACTION came to me as we approached the women's quarters. It was hardly a plan. A white man prowled the camp, a bully lashed to his belt. He swaggered like white men did after rape.

"Don't we need to know where your family is?" Buck asked.

"They're in there. I know that. I can feel it. Anyway, we're taking everyone with us," I said.

"Everyone?" said Morris.

"Everyone. Is there a path north?"

"There's a road," Buck said.

"And a path," added Morris.

I looked at the giant white house to the west of us. Breeding must have been a good business. South of it was a field of spent corn like the one where I'd hidden. "Do you believe you can subdue the overseer?" I asked Morris.

"I know I can. I want to. When?"

"When he starts running toward the cornfield."

"Why would he do that?" Llewelyn asked.

"He will," I said. "Once we start this, there is no turning back."

I ran, crouched low, to the cornfield. I grabbed a plant and crunched it in my fist, satisfied myself as to the field's dryness. I judged that the wind was blowing southwest. I pulled a match from my pocket, struck it and set the corner where I stood ablaze. It caught and spread quickly. Thick smoke filled the night. Someone near the house screamed. I ran back to the quarters. Women in sleeping gowns were out of the house quickly, looking and pointing toward the flames. I turned and observed again. It looked like hell. I ran back to the others to find the overseer out cold on the ground. Morris held the man's whip.

Across the compound of shacks, standing at the low, open door of the smallest structure, was a woman I could not look away from. I took one step, another. It was my Sadie. I could not believe it was her. I stumbled, then ran across the yard toward her. I stopped in front of her while we inspected each other.

"Jim?" she asked. "Is it you?"

I put my hands on her shoulders. She threw her arms around me.

Lizzie came out of the hut. My child. She paused in disbelief just as we had. I reached out and pulled her to me.

The men were near us. "Get everyone running north," I said. "Grab all the food you can and run!"

The fire was wild and lapping at the sky. I was certain it was visible for miles. The wind shifted, and now the embers were flying toward the house. An old white man in a nightshirt came out and joined the women. He carried a shotgun. He stared, horrified, at the fire and then looked at us slaves. He marched our way, shouting for us to hurry and put out the fire.

"Nigger! The fire!" When he saw that all of his chattel

were running away from the fire, away from him, into the trees, he raised his weapon. "Niggers, where do ya'll think you're goin'?!"

I stepped in front of him.

"Who the hell are you?" he asked. He pointed his gun at me.

I pointed my pistol at him. "I am the angel of death, come to offer sweet justice in the night," I said. "I am a sign. I am your future. I am James." I pulled back the hammer on my pistol.

"What in tarnation?" He cocked his weapon.

The shot I fired rang through that valley like a cannon blast. It echoed, seemingly forever. All of those with me stopped and watched the man receive the lead. His chest exploded red on his nightclothes. He did not fall like a tree. Nothing about him was that big. He merely fell, face-first, into a darkness none of us could see. The women behind him screamed, but their sounds were lost in the roar of the flames and the night. The wind became wild and stirred the fire.

"Let's go," Sadie said, at my arm.

We ran. We all ran north, some up the road, some up the path. I carried Lizzie in my arms. She kept whispering, "Papa, Papa, Papa."

CHAPTER 12

As HAPPENS with the frightened and unprepared, we scattered. Some of us would be caught. Some of us would be killed. Probably some of us would go crawling back.

Sadie, Lizzie and I made it north to a town we were told was in Iowa. Morris and Buck remained with us. The white people didn't seem happy to see us, but there was a war on. It had something to do with us. The local sheriff met us in the street and regarded us suspiciously.

"Runaways?" he asked.

"We are," I said.

"Any of you named Nigger Jim?"

I pointed to each of us. "Sadie, Lizzie, Morris, Buck."

"And who are you?"

"I am James."

"James what?"

"Just James."

ACKNOWLEDGMENTS

I would like to thank my editor, Lee Boudreaux. Working with her on this book has been a highlight of my literary career. For twenty-nine years, I had the honor, the pleasure, the joy, of working with Fiona McCrae at Graywolf Press. The artistic freedom and support offered by her and all the folks at Graywolf have been a gift. My agent, Melanie Jackson, is my guide, keeper and first reader. She and Fiona are family to me. None of this work would exist without my best friend and wife, Danzy Senna. She and my sons, Henry and Miles, remind me that I am part of the world. Finally, a nod to Mark Twain. His humor and humanity affected me long before I became a writer. Heaven for the climate; hell for my long-awaited lunch with Mark Twain.

ABOUT THE AUTHOR

Percival Everett is a Distinguished Professor of English at USC. His most recent books include *Dr. No* (finalist for the NBCC Award for Fiction and winner of the PEN/Jean Stein Book Award), *The Trees* (finalist for the Booker Prize and the PEN/Faulkner Award for Fiction), *Telephone* (finalist for the Pulitzer Prize), *So Much Blue*, *Erasure*, and *I Am Not Sidney Poitier*. He has received the NBCC Ivan Sandrof Life Achievement Award and The Windham Campbell Prize from Yale University. *American Fiction*, the feature film based on his novel *Erasure*, was released in 2023. He lives in Los Angeles with his wife, the writer Danzy Senna, and their children.